n't let China get away with its blatant lies

China 'build

ased on st...esigns'

US anger at over Star Wai deal with Chin

hina's spies
nd it easy
steal secr

Bush was acting
ke a bully
ver spy plane

ton "playing with fire" in his

of Chin

Were ou
Trident
secrets
stole

CHINA'S ARMY
OF SPIES IN U.S

G000123280

Wu's Revenge

 a story of
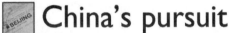 China's pursuit
 for nuclear
  supremacy

Hector Hill

MurGo Publishers

Published by MurGo Publishers
20 Portsmouth Avenue
Thames Ditton
Surrey KT7 0RT

Text set in Baskerville.

Cover design by
DP&D Design, Four Marks, England & Florida, USA.

Printed and bound in Great Britain by
Biddles Ltd., Surrey. www.biddles.co.uk.

ISBN 0 9540767 0 2

'Political power grows out of the barrel of a gun.'
Mao Tse-tung

This book is dedicated to
my wife with love and thanks.

Main Characters

Jerry Flood	a Special Branch police officer
Yong	Wu's father
Fu-fang	Wu's mother and Yong's wife
Chin-yee	Wu's sister
Wu	a Chinese Secret Service official
Algernon Stanhope	a British weapons company executive
Fluer	an immigrant from mainland China
John Poon	a half Chinese scientist
Vincent Yates	a half Chinese university lecturer
Wong	a Triad connection

Acknowledgements

Hardly a week goes by without some reference to China in the world's media, making one sit up and wonder what power-seeking aims are likely to emerge and to what extent those aims will be contrary to the interests of the West.

We've seen the hand-over of the territories of Hong Kong and Macao, but how long will it be before pressure will be brought on Taiwan to surrender to the mainland too? How interesting it is that Yugoslavia, even under new leadership since the NATO bombing offensive, is being reconstructed with China's assistance.

We see the West bending over backwards to secure valuable trade advantages with China, even offering membership of the World Trade Organisation. But is the West being misguided in their pursuit of money-making, being blinded to the more dangerous spectre of Chinese military strength with its Army the largest in the world? Is it likely in the future that the President of Russia, Vladimir Putin, will 'cosy up' to China and form a much dreamed of strategic partnership to oppose the forces of America and NATO? Does the US Star Wars project signify an underlying insecurity about the unpredictable use of nuclear weapons by the Soviets, the Chinese or their satellite countries? Is there a new distrust emerging after the Cold War period?

At the end of the 1990s the news reported the alleged theft by China of highly sensitive Western nuclear and military secrets from America's Los Alamos Laboratory, as well as from Britain's Holy Loch. This reinforced a suspicion that while the West was loosening its guard, the cunning Chinese stealthily moved in to acquire our secrets.

I discussed this with two brave and fascinating Chinese sources, both very special people, who related to me the story of their own secret lives. I am indebted to them for their help. It has provided me with the vital springboard, enabling my story to connect with the espionage and sexual entrapment techniques which the Chinese Secret Service perfected in the 1920s and 1930s with its more recent skills in acquiring the West's secrets. A family's history of service to the Communist cause goes right back to the 1920s. The ability to deceive to further the Communist Party cause required a committed life, dedicated to constant risk and danger in acquiring and discarding different identities in order to achieve their aims. By the time their stories ended, I have to admit to a respect and admiration for the sources. Some names have been changed to protect identities.

The other day I met a distinguished businessman at a drinks party in London and we discussed my concerns at the apparent laxity of security by the West. He reinforced my fears by telling me the story of a brilliant mathematician who went to Los Alamos, the USA's major nuclear research laboratory, and was able, without being given the necessary code, to break the combination of a top secret safe there within forty minutes!

There are several individuals who have given me immense support and encouragement, without whose advice and inspiration I would never have continued on my faltering steps as an author. It is not possible to reveal them but they know who they are.

Hector Hill

Prologue

In the colonial days of the 1920s and 1930s, Shanghai was divided into neighbourhoods: the International Settlement, which occupied the northern half of the city was where the British, most Europeans and Americans lived; and the French Concession, which was contained in an area known for its fine old houses, occupied hardly at all by French people but by White Russians. Then there were the narrow alleyways of the Old Chinese City.

In the French Concession today the elegant Avenue Joffre is renamed Huaihai Road and is lined with Japanese department stores and designer-label fashion shops, but little else has changed. Here, as in the past, at night Shanghai comes to life in another form: brightly coloured neon strips light up the garish signs, and hoardings beckon punters into the famous night clubs and bars where the fashionable and wealthy Chinese are entertained by almost-naked dancers. In the old days it was the foreigners who were blamed for the prostitution and corruption, but now it is bred from within.

Walking from the Huaihai Road towards the Bund on the waterfront is the Old Chinese City. It is a maze of narrow greasy streets, permanently crowded with pyjama-suited Chinese with pungent smells of Eastern food, herbs and incense mixing together to form that special aroma that is essentially recognisable as Far Eastern. The People's Square in the centre of the city later became the symbol of the Chinese Communist Party.

No story about China can ignore the impact that Mao Tse-tung had during his lifetime on such a vast country and population. Even now aspects of his legacy live on. Coming from a peasant family, he founded the Chinese Communist Party back in 1921. From the early years of the formation of the Chinese Secret Service, in which he held high office during the 1930s and 1940s when the Communist Party was gaining its reputation as an effective guerrilla force, he unhesitatingly ordered his critics to be beheaded, shot, buried alive or drowned. So brutal was his grip that even his Moscow-trained chief executioner, armed with a ferocious dog, searched out counter-revolutionaries. In the 1950s Mao ordered the execution of landlords and some estimate that they could have amounted to over 750,000 people. Another group, the intellectuals and writers – always the target of insecure dictatorships – amounted to over 500,000. Despite being invited to criticise Mao, when they actually did so between 1957 and 1958, they too were brutally purged. He had acquired an appetite for achieving his aims through murder, and yet he had not fully come to power then.

The forerunner to the Chinese Communist Party was the Soviet Communist Party under Stalin, who had been Mao's mentor. The long planned Communist victory led by Mao against the weakened Chinese Nationalist Kuomintang forces in 1949 signalled the beginning of one of the world's most brutal regimes. For some time enthusiastic and idealistic student activists on their university campuses around the world in the 1950s and 1960s gave fashionable support for the sayings in Mao's famous *Little Red Book*. The theme of his sayings encouraged the people to rise up in revolt to join in the class struggle by overpowering one class and replacing it with another. It was not surprising that it appealed to rebellious young people who firmly believed that they had discovered an ideology which promised to change their world for the better.

The dark years of Mao's Cultural Revolution in China are still remembered by the many who suffered years of unrestrained terror and an obsession to control. There was suspicion of anyone being anti-Mao. Children were forced to tell tales against their own parents who, having been betrayed by their own offspring, were tortured and imprisoned under appalling conditions. Some children unable to bear the guilt of betraying their own families committed suicide.

The three-year period covering 1959-61 saw the most serious crop failures in China's history. Thirty-million Chinese died in the worst famine ever known, all because Mao, surprisingly ill-informed for a man who came from the soil, ordered farmers to plant their seeds on top of each other, which he judged would neutralise weeds and produce a greatly enhanced yield.

Mao's obsession with control could only be effective by maintaining an efficient and ruthless spy system and creating a climate of fear and suspicion. Spies were even inside their own families. In desperation the living ate the dead and children were exchanged for food. The years 1966 and 1967 signified the start of Mao's Cultural Revolution. But at no time was Mao prepared to change his ways. Children continued to be brainwashed into reading whole passages from the *Little Red Book*, dressing up as Red Guards, killing their teachers and betraying their parents.

Chou En-lai played a key role in the formation of the Chinese Secret Service right from the start and rose up the hierarchy of the Chinese Communist Party with Mao and ended up as the first Prime Minister of Communist China under Mao as its Chairman. In the story, Yong worked under Chou and during the early years of the Chinese Secret Service their fortunes were linked.

The difference in the backgrounds between the two titanic men could not have been more marked: Mao, of peasant stock, championed the cause of the peasants and the workers; Chou, on the other hand, had been educated at Nankai University and in Paris where he became a key figure in the Communist group there. He had also been an instructor at the Wampoa Military Academy. For a long time Chou was senior to Mao. From 1927 he was building up the Communist Party Secret Service organisation successfully using aliases and developing clandestine operational techniques, ruthlessly penetrating the Kuomintang intelligence and security organisations. During the early years – the late 1920s and early 1930s – Chou engaged in urban revolution in Shanghai while Mao established a guerrilla base in the remote mountainous border regions of Hunan and Jiangxi. Although elected to the Communist Party Central Committee in 1928, Mao was still junior. But as the urban revolution collapsed, Mao won support for guerrilla warfare. In late 1931 Mao emerged as the Chairman of the Chinese Soviet Central republic and guiding Red Army strategy, but he was criticised by the Chinese Communist Party leadership in late 1932 for extremism and replaced as political commissar of the Red Army by Chou.

The Long March, which started in October 1934, signalled the Chinese Communist Party leaders, their dependants and the troops of the Red Army to break out of the Central Soviet and ended one year later when after 6,000 miles survivors entered the safe territory in Northern Shaanxi. About 86,000 men and women began the march but at the end there were only 4,000 survivors. It left Mao Tse-tung as the Party's supreme strategist and well placed to begin his climb to the eventual unchallenged political authority in the Chinese Communist Party and the Communist victory over the Chinese Nationalist Kuomintang in 1949. By then Mao's ruthless quest for domination had been asserted and despite internal disagreements with Chou, Mao ended up as Chairman and Chou as the Prime Minister.

But internal plots and character blackening didn't stop then. At the height of the Cultural Revolution in 1968, when Mao was Chairman, evidence was gathered against

Chou, passed to Madam Mao and to members of the Chinese Communist Party leadership, which required Chou to explain himself at the leadership conference in 1972. Chou had a nagging fear that anyone should suggest that he was a traitor and that weighed heavily with him until the end of his life in 1976.

Such was the background in which Yong's Secret Service career was lived out, and succeeded by his son Wu.

1

'When the waters sink, the stones show.'

A naked, bloated corpse with a half-missing skull lay inert at the edge of the river near Blackfriars Bridge, tossed up on the jetsam. It was low tide and the bank on the south side was stony, about five metres wide when the tide is at its lowest ebb. Gulls normally gathered there but they had moved off downriver.

Gumbooted police and medics in white overalls were preparing to heave the body shore. Blue and white tape was being placed across one side of the street. Several police cars and ambulances had formed up already and the bridge was blocked off to traffic at both ends.

Looking over the heads of the gathering but silent commuters and standing on tiptoe, a newly-arrived spectator, despite being late for the office, looked on speechless. Someone near to the bank spoke quietly, 'It looks like the body of an Oriental!'

Muffled, respectful whisperings quickly passed the message through the crowd. For the moment it satisfied their curiosity and confirmed their witness to unusual events.

There was no need to hang around any longer. The crowd broke up and rushed off, making up for the lost time and eager to tell colleagues in their offices. No doubt it would be on the television and radio news later in the day.

There was only one problem. No news ever did come of the death. The incident was soon forgotten. A body had been found washed up on the riverbank. Only a few people knew the truth.

Chief Inspector Jerry Flood, Metropolitan Police Special

Branch, had seen it all before. He had been trained to be impersonal, and dead bodies of all shapes, sizes, colour and creed were commonplace to him. He took the call at home: it was the Incident Room ordering him to report to the riverbank. He called out to his wife but wasn't sure that she had heard him through the din of the washing machine on its final spin: he hadn't kissed her goodbye for at least five years. Slamming the white-painted front door with its brass knocker and letterbox, he climbed onto his powerful motor bike, gave it a handful and zoomed away from his modest three-bedroomed semi in Bromley, swerving and threading the BMW 1100 through the busy morning traffic. So close to clipping car bonnets, he charged towards what seemed certain disaster. Protecting himself from the elements and danger, he wore intimidating black leathers, a hefty crash helmet, a suit underneath but no uniform. It was hard for him to get excited; he had been in the Force too long.

'Another bloody Chinese! Christ Almighty!' he mouthed, meaning it to be under his breath but it was heard by a couple of young constables standing nearby. Jerry's cynicism was well known in the Force and was respected and feared by some.

2

'Without determination, man is an untempered sword.'

'I want to tell you how pleased I am with you,' said the senior Communist Party official. He had ordered the young man to come to his office on the third floor of the Party's block in Central Shanghai.

The room was shabby and bare, and smelt musty of old leather-bound books, except there were none. It was larger than most, reflecting the interviewer's superior status. In the Communist Party, paradoxically, status was important and the pot-bellied, gone-to-seed official had been particular in arranging his room to make sure the feng shui was just right. He had about him a polite but nevertheless offensive indifference. The large plain wood desk, upon which lay mounds of papers, had been placed in a dominant position across the far end of the room. Since his back faced neither a window nor a door, the official could observe all entry and exit points, giving him control over his own safety and covering anyone who entered the room. Ashtrays brimmed, and he gripped a cigarette between nicotined finger and thumb.

'Thank you, sir,' replied Yong formally. Age is respected in China and he was kowtowing to his senior in the appropriate manner. Before entering the room he had knocked on the door, not too forcefully, more in deference, before the booming voice of this superior shouted back at him: 'Come in, come in!' Impatience cut into his words.

'It's dangerous work you're involved in.' said the senior official.

'I don't see it that way,' replied Yong modestly, clasping his hands behind his long back. He was still standing and glad he'd had a good breakfast of boiled rice with egg before coming in to the office. It was midday and he hadn't eaten since the early morning.

'Give yourself more credit! Although you speak like a dedicated comrade, we don't want anything to happen to you. You're far too valuable to us, do you understand? You have the use of a safe house in the city's foreign concession areas, but if the Kuomintang ever found out about your activities and your growing status in our Party, you could end up with a long jail sentence or even worse. How old are you now?' asked the official, screwing up his cheerful face, but an unusually beaked nose and close-set eyes gave him the appearance of an eagle.

'Twenty-five, sir,' replied Yong, puzzled as to the reason for the interview.

The long windows opened out to the sounds of the street below where shiny black motor cars, imported by prosperous Western expatriates, forced their way noisily through the throng of trams and trucks, mule carts and rickshaws. Like everyone in Shanghai, everyone was on their way to somewhere. The strong summer sun had been beating into the office all morning without let up. Now that it was early afternoon, the rays had moved round to behind another block, plunging the office into shadow. Despite the shade it was still hot and the coolness of the evening would come shortly but the humidity would remain.

'How's everything going?' asked the senior man, beginning to relax. His bald, shiny head, set off with a pair of utility steel-framed spectacles hiding tiny black eyes, dominated a fat hairless face. The cigarette was now smouldering on the pile of old ends. He jabbed impatiently at the nearest mound of papers. Yong had heard that the senior official was a skilled tactician but not so good at handling people: to him a staff interview was an awkward inconvenience that he could well do without. Looking around him, Yong noticed how the office was devoid of personal possessions.

'We've managed somehow to survive a most intense period of terror the Kuomintang has inflicted on us. Now I'm looking at a new angle, working much more closely with left-wing writers,' replied the young man.

'So I hear. I can't stress enough how much we appreciate what you're doing for the Party.' The senior official was continuing to flatter him as graciously as he could.

He was testing Yong to see if he had a weakness for boasting. But the way he reported on his progress showed that he had just the right qualities. The senior official continued a little awkwardly, 'It hasn't taken you long to acquire the skills needed for survival in this business. My colleagues and I believe you have the ability to conduct the Party's underground activities. From now on we want you to be involved in more highly sensitive work, and I have been ordered by the highest authority to invite you to join the Chinese Communist Party's Secret Service. What do you say to that?'

'Thank you, sir. I will be pleased to dedicate my life to the Party in whatever way you suggest,' replied the new recruit, feeling greatly honoured.

'Good. I warn you, the work will be dangerous. You'll be required to lead the urban intelligence battle in Shanghai. For this you'll need a quick brain as well as being a good shot with the Mauser! There'll be much bloodshed. Many operations will involve espionage and assassinations, but the rewards will be high if you're ambitious enough to rise to the highest office in the Service. You'll mix with some of our up-and-coming leaders too, like Mao Tse-tung and Chou En-lai, all destined for great things.'

The senior official had sat at his desk, hands together and fingers interlocked. He noisily sipped the cup of light brown tea he had let cool down, and then became distracted. Yong, still standing, hadn't been offered any refreshment and didn't expect any.

'You can go now. I know you'll do your best. You have a

promising future ahead of you. Report to your new chief, Gu Shunxang, tomorrow morning at eight.'

'Thank you, sir,' he replied respectfully, retreating backwards out of the office. His impression of the senior official was that although he spoke smoothly there was hardness in his heart.

That night Yong, feeling in good spirits, told his future wife Fu-fang that he was being promoted in the Party and could look forward to an exciting and challenging future. More than that he couldn't say. He had already acquired the spy's distrust of talking too much, even to those closest to him. He loved Fu-fang; her handsome face with her glorious black hair swept back from the temples had a look of maternal kindness. If she infuriated him sometimes with her vagueness, he thought highly of her judgement and grew to regard her as a wise woman. Some who didn't know him well thought Yong to be a rather cold and unromantic man, but he appreciated Fu-fang's intelligence and her usefulness about the home, believing he had chosen her well to be a good wife and mother.

'Why do you look at those big Western women so longingly?' she asked whenever they went out together to join the mixed Chinese and rich fashionable foreign crowds that sauntered round the bright lights and high-spending shopping areas.

'These people represent the decadent capitalist West, but they look so sophisticated. There's something about them that fascinates me. Perhaps it's an air of sensuous opulence. A glittering society out of reach to people like us!' replied Yong.

He liked women and they responded to him. He had chosen his future wife right from the word go and nothing would change that; in some ways this was evidence of a calculating streak in his make-up. In all other respects he was unscrupulous in furthering his career and the

Communist Party cause, early indications of a potential conflict.

Yong was welcomed into Fu-fang's home, a one-bedroomed flat she shared with her mother and brother. The familiar smell of home cooking greeted him; Fu-fang's mother had cooked up rice, vegetables and chunks of fish on a rudimentary stove in a single pan, stirring it all up together. They ate frugally, keeping strictly to the staple ingredients that had served the Chinese well for generations.

'Do you ever think what it might be like to eat at one of those smart Western hotels on the Bund?' asked Fu-fang during one mealtime.

'Very rarely, it's another world there,' replied Yong.

'I hear there are rich pickings to be had from the dustbins!'

'It must be good for the scavengers!' chipped in her mother.

'It shows how we must redress the imbalance of the poor and the rich. The powerful Kuomintang warlords are very much in league with the Western expatriates, but time will change all that if I have anything to do with it!' exclaimed Yong with passion.

'That's quite enough of a party political broadcast for tonight! Let's have some rice wine,' said her mother.

'Just a drop. Thanks.'

Fu-fang's father hadn't been well and had died of painful, lung-wracking consumption three years earlier, leaving her mother to bring up their two children single-handedly. Despite the poverty, her mother had managed to cope with life pretty well. But she was still reliant on Fu-fang, whose commitment to her wouldn't end with her marriage.

Yong was aching to have Fu-fang to himself, to talk to her, to be warmed and wanted, but he knew there was no way they could have any privacy in her mother's flat. In the past, her mother and brother had discreetly arranged to be out for a few hours to give the couple an opportunity to be alone together. He felt strong and passionate; a way had to be found.

'Come for a walk with me?' he whispered to Fu-fang after the meal. She recognised the pleading tone.

'Can I go, mother? Is there anything I can do to help to clear up?'

'No, I'll do it. You two go out, but don't be late!' she said, quite forgetting that her daughter was old enough to look after herself.

'Don't worry, and don't wait up,' replied Fu-fang, looking forward to having Yong to herself and sensing his need for her.

The dusk was closing in as the couple set off down the street and to avoid the oncoming headlights of traffic they turned the corner into a small garden planted with shrubs. At five feet eight inches Yong was tall for a Chinese man, but his thin body suggested a degree of nervous energy. The thinness masked strength and stamina, both mental and physical, which he concealed cleverly from his enemies. His full head of jet-black hair swept back from his forehead was kept sleek with the cheap grease he applied each morning. Fu-fang, though slender too, was much shorter, making them a somewhat incongruous couple. After a few treasured moments of privacy the couple continued their night walk together.

'Look Fu-fang! Can you see those coffins being launched from the funeral piers at Nantao?' exclaimed Yong. 'See how simple and undecorated they are.'

'They must belong to the families too poor to pay for a burial. Look at the flimsy paper flowers on the coffins, being borne away out of control by the strong tide,' replied Fu-fang.

'But they'll return on the flow the next morning, ending up on the Shanghai waterfront with garbage discarded by the great city stuck to them.'

'It's so depressing. The islands of paper flowers seem to gather like magnets forming floating gardens to cushion the swollen bodies of those old men not in coffins. I've heard that mothers and small children too are transported through the night borne by the mighty Yangtze river,' pondered Fu-fang, cuddling up closer to him as he put his arm around her protectively.

'Let's get away from here and go to the fish market. It should still be open. We can see the fresh catch lying out between the tramlines,' suggested Fu-fang.

'If it is open, I want to haggle for some rice and pieces of fish. It would be a nice present for your mother.'

As darkness fell, the salty smell of fish enveloped them. Nearby the black mud beaches, creeks and waste tips were littered with fragments of old opium-running ships and a stench from some fly-ridden dog carcasses. All the time the coffins were drifting shoreward on the tide.

Finally the couple crossed Soochow Creek towards the International Settlements and the culturally Western suburbs of Shanghai. With aching feet they passed several fine houses that stood back from the road majestically, with individually manicured gardens, outwardly serene.

'They must be rich people living there. I've heard that the houses have billiard tables and there is plenty of fine wine and alcohol.'

'It looks like another world doesn't it?' commented Yong, leaning across to help Fu-fang put on her thin jacket to protect her against the evening chill. As he did so he took her in his arms and held her tightly to him. The window of one of the houses further along was open and they heard the unrestrained sound of laughter and clinking glasses.

3

'One rat dropping spoils a pot of rice.'

The following morning Yong reported to his new chief, Gu Shunxang. He entered an anonymous building bearing a spurious government departmental sign, which meant little but it hid the true purpose of the goings-on inside. A young guard stood beside a strong wooden door. The bolt on the door had already been released. Yong was escorted up to the first floor of the two-storey building by a young different fresh-faced guard. He wondered if the young man had started to shave yet, and if so how many times a week. There were a few adolescent spots on his neck.

Having heard so much about the charismatic figure that was to be his boss, Yong was intrigued to meet him. The interview was very different from the one he had had with the senior official the day before. Gu received him in his small office, wearing a simple khaki-coloured cotton tunic with short sleeves and long trousers, very much in the military style. He was a tall well-built man, with a full mop of jet-black hair, his face scarred, possibly from smallpox, with deep folds and lines. He offered his sweaty hand and Yong noticed the damp and smelly patches under his armpits and wondered how fit he was. He was known to be addicted to the pleasures of life; no doubt that accounted for his premature ageing. His beady eyes, scarcely visible above swollen pouches, regarded Yong with an arrogant stare from across the room where he stood, head tilted back slightly, feet apart and arms crossed firmly over his chest. Positioned with his back to the light coming from the closed and grimy window, Gu watched his new recruit closely from the very moment he walked through the door.

On the walls of this insignificant room hung military style

maps and detailed photographs of wanted targets in the Kuomintang. Otherwise the room was bare and uncluttered as if Gu was just passing through, like a waiting-room at a railway station.

'Welcome, Yong! You've come to me with a first-class reputation. You must help us crush these bastards in the Kuomintang. We need raw intelligence and aggressive tactics. That's all I'm going to say for now! I expect you'll pick things up as we go along. Come back here at lunchtime, say noon, and then we'll get to know each other better, OK?'

Yong knew that the invitation was an outright order and it made him apprehensive. 'Yes, sir,' he replied obediently. At first sight he didn't like Gu particularly, but he didn't want to upset him either. He considered it to be a test of his self-control, a challenge to get on with his new boss.

'No need to be so formal, you may call me by my name,' barked Gu irritably.

'Yes, Gu.'

'That's better! Until noon then.'

Yong left the office escorted by a minor official who accompanied him down the permanently dusty and wide concrete stairs, white enamel spittoons filled with a little water placed at each landing, and along drab corridors with unpainted and unwashed walls. Entering the large open-plan room, he was formally introduced to his new colleagues who sat hunched in concentration, heads bent diligently and noiselessly over their metal desks, rising only to politely but impassively meet their new staff member. At noon, after an introductory briefing, he reported to Gu.

'Come on in, Yong! I won't keep you a moment. Sit over there on that chair, if it's not too rickety for you!' said Gu. Luckily for Yong his mood had changed quite unexpectedly to one of jollity.

Gu slipped away into another room, a washroom of sorts, with a basin and a lavatory. He had left the door open so that Yong couldn't help hearing the sound of him urinating. Then he heard running water as he splashed his face. Through a space in the door Yong saw him comb his hair and check himself in the small cracked mirror hanging above the basin. He adjusted his clothing and returned to the room. Yong thought the time Gu spent in sprucing himself up was bordering on vanity.

'Let's go and see what life's like outside this hole! I've got clean underpants on and a shirt especially for this lot!' he said heartily, slapping Yong on the back. Gu smelt fresh, of soap, no damp patches under his armpits – yet.

Gu led the way down a dreary side road, stopping on the pavement and turning back, checking for a tail, then left into a tree-lined avenue leading to a smarter area of Shanghai. Here, small terraced town houses stood neatly in line without being too conspicuously expensive. He paused outside one of them, strode purposefully towards the front door and knocked three times using the heavy brass knocker made in the shape of a lion's head. They had to wait only a short time. The door opened slowly and a young woman's face peered round it. Straightaway she recognised Gu and gingerly opened the door just sufficiently to let both men in. Yong noticed that she was agitated, looking nervously outside the front door and glancing furtively behind them.

'Are the usual lot here?' Gu asked the woman roughly, as she led them down a narrow passage and into a warm smoke-filled room. Through the haze he saw the contorted figures of partly naked men and women sprawled on the floor and draped over the furniture. A sweet smell lingered in the air, a compound of strong female scent, cigarettes and opium. Dark-coloured curtains were drawn tightly across the windows, shielding the room from the strong sunlight outside. Around the room were seven divan beds, each covered with plain cotton material to create the style of a sofa.

'Hello, Gu!' welcomed a scantily-clad pretty Eurasian girl who could have been no more than eighteen years old.

'Hello, Lucy Koo – you look as beautiful as ever!' replied Gu. He drew her closer, put his hand round her firm buttocks and squeezed. 'I've a good friend here who needs fixing up. See what you can do, it's his first time!'

'What's your name?' Lucy Koo purred at Yong.

'I am Tiger!' he replied nervously, not wanting to give away his true identity.

'OK, Tiger, come and meet my Su-su. She will look after you. Su-su, come here!' Another young girl who had been sitting on the bed filing her nails came forward in the dim light.

'Tiger here is a friend of our favourite customer, Gu, so mind you treat him well, understand?'

'Hello,' Su-su said cheerfully and bowed before him, signalling her obedience. His eyes were beginning now to adjust to the semi-dark room. Yes, he thought, Su-su was certainly pretty; her long black hair hung over her narrow shoulders not quite reaching the top of her silky red dress. When she had bowed towards him, her dress had fallen away allowing him a brief preview of her pert nubile breasts. As his eyes became fully adjusted, he saw naked couples sprawled on divans caressing each other and in various stages of arousal. They were oblivious to others around them, for their eyes appeared to be unseeing, as if in a trance. As he peered around him he saw Gu disappear into a private room, arm in arm and giggling with a girl he seemed to know well.

'You like me a little, Tiger?' asked Su-su seductively, her eyes looking up to his, appealing to him.

'Yes, but you must excuse me, I have to get back to my office soon,' replied Yong evasively. He was no prude as it was common practice for Chinese men to pay for women.

She led him towards an unoccupied divan in the far corner partially obscured by a screen. 'OK, Tiger! Are you a man or a mouse? You stay with me for a long time and I'll make you a happy man, OK? We'll play and have nice time together. You feel my body and I feel yours, yes?'

Suddenly the girl's obsequious manner changed to reveal the hard edge formed by the experience of her profession. She took control of events and beckoned him to sit down, pulled the screen across to provide some privacy then sat down next to him. The atmosphere in the room and her personal scent were clearly beginning to have an effect on the innocent young man. Su-su loosened his clothing, and started by running a finger around his lips, then slowly moved her hand down his chest, running circles around his nipples, then navel. She was wise enough to know that she could not do this for too long for he was already in a high state of excitement. She stood for a moment facing him and let her dress fall to the floor. Su-su pulled his hand so that he moved to lie along the divan and then she straddled Yong's lap, putting her knees either side of him. She knew the closeness of her naked body would have the desired effect. To Yong, the next few minutes passed in a flash. His eyes never left her breasts and before he knew what was happening, he briefly felt himself in her warm body. All too soon it was over. Su-su rose and knelt in front of him. She stooped to pick up a fresh cloth from under the divan and gently cleaned him, then stood up and slipped her dress back on.

'You stay a little longer with me, Tiger? Next time it will be better. You're a very handsome man.' He sat up and dressed himself.

'Thanks, but I must go now,' he told her, determined not to give in to her charms any longer and walked towards the front door.

'Will I see you again?'

'Possibly,' he replied evasively and paused. 'Will you tell Gu that I have had to get back to my office to attend to some urgent business?'

'Of course.'

The front door closed behind him and he was back out on the tree-lined avenue. As he walked away he reflected that his experience had been short and not particularly enjoyable, for he had gone along with Gu just to ingratiate himself.

Unknown to Yong, Gu's arrogance and reluctance to accept the strict disciplines of the Secret Service, together with his unstable private life, had brought his dubious habits to the attention of his superiors. Chou En-lai, his immediate boss, ordered specially selected senior colleagues to keep a close eye on him. As 'minders' they reported back to him secretly on a regular basis. On more than one occasion Gu had been discovered by the 'minders' on a bed, stark naked, highly aroused and cavorting with naked prostitutes.

The following morning Gu summoned Yong to his office to ask him if he had enjoyed himself, unable to resist for a moment longer, going into intimate details about the woman he had been with. In return he asked for exchange information about the girl Yong had been with. Gu listened in rapt silence, though disappointed that he wouldn't go into more graphic detail. Later Yong backed the original impression he had of his new boss: the man was an arsehole.

'I must remember your girl for next time! I'd like her for myself. Now that we've had a good time together, you must come with me to a drinking den where there are strippers, musicians and magicians.'

'I do need to see my fiancé sometime,' Yong replied evasively.

'Don't worry about that. You can see her tonight, and tomorrow we'll go out on the town together. All in the cause of duty, you understand!' urged Gu, knowing well that the junior man could hardly refuse.

The bar was in a seedy residential house in the International Settlement, especially set up to lure thirsty expatriates to call in on their way back home after a day's work. Gu was well known there, too, and was immediately shown to a table close to the raised platform stage with a prime view of the non-stop cabaret with musicians, conjurers and strippers taking it in turns to keep the customers entertained. Yong was to accompany Gu on several occasions to similar dives around the city, on each occasion somewhere new yet always Gu was well known.

'Do you know something, Yong?' he asked one night after rather a lot of drink.

'What is it, Gu?'

'All my life I've really wanted to be a magician! I can do all sorts of tricks with cards and make things disappear and reappear again. I taught myself when I was a boy. I get a tremendous kick out of seeing an audience mesmerised and expectant, watching every move I make. It's quite a contrast to our work in the Secret Service!'

Yong had no idea that a plan was being hatched for Gu to be demoted and assigned to a less sensitive department, this despite having distinguished himself by leading a group of senior Party officials from Shanghai right through the Kuomintang-held area and into the safety of the Communist Party base area. His undisciplined ways were so unrestrained and eccentric that it was hardly a surprise when he was arrested in Hankou's new market on a rather paltry charge of performing magic in public.

'You know that Gu has been arrested?' asked a colleague in Yong's department, 'it happened last night. It'll be a major coup for the Kuomintang.'

'Bastards! This is very bad news,' replied Yong, 'I know Chou En-lai has been worried Gu might blow his cover. There's so much information he could pass on about our operations against the Kuomintang. He knows the addresses of Party officials, our methods of espionage, the identities and locations of many Secret Service agents, including those working under deep cover inside the Kuomintang itself,' Yong realised at once the demoralising effect Gu's arrest would have amongst the network of Secret Service operatives.

Chou En-lai took immediate action, calling a conference a few days later when he addressed key Secret Service staff. Looking drawn and stooping slightly, he was clearly feeling the heavy responsibilities in risking people's lives in secret work. It had weighed heavily upon him, and brought on him a succession of sleepless nights. Yong had hardly been home since Gu's arrest, and not for the first time he had to tell Fu-fang he was out on important secret Party business.

Yong had noticed that Chou En-lai possessed that rare, natural but distinguished presence about him. Whenever he entered a room, he brought with him an aura of calm and dignity, earning him respect from his subordinates and unswerving loyalty too. His high-necked plain grey tunic reinforced the air of military authority he deliberately wanted to project. There was something old-fashioned in his manner too, a little formal.

'Comrades, thank you all for your unstinting hard work and dedication to the Party's cause over these last few days. I can't pretend that Gu's arrest won't weaken us for a short time, but we'll be strong again if we take the right measures now. Gu was taken to Nanjing for interrogation and we've been told by our top secret sources inside the Kuomintang that it wasn't long before he was offering his services to his captors. He has, to put it quite simply, defected to the enemy. You'll understand, comrades, that I have no sympathy for him and I certainly don't expect you to have any either.'

The audience looked attentive and a faint hum could be heard followed by a shuffling in their seats. Chou En-lai paused to sip from the glass of water that had been put before him on the bare unpainted table. Then with the loose-fitting sleeve of his tunic he wiped the small beads of sweat from his forehead. His face had a certain maturity, lines engraved around the mouth and chin, his eyes old beyond his years and watching out attentively.

'We'll put our damage limitation plan into immediate effect. All units that might have been exposed by Gu are to be moved out of Shanghai with immediate effect and to new safe houses. We're getting reports that many hundreds of Communists are being arrested already as a result of the information he has given away under interrogation. I can't impress upon you all enough how strongly I regard Gu as the most shameful traitor in the history of our Party, and he is to be expelled for life. Our colleagues' lives are at stake here. Morale and co-operation from our brave agents and field operatives must be restored as quickly as possible. That is our task: go to it, comrades!'

The staff stood up out of deep respect; heads bowed as Chou En-lai left the room. They shuffled and whispered quietly to one another before dispersing to attend to their duties and to carry out Chou's instructions. For a few minutes groups of grey-suited Secret Servicemen spilled from the auditorium in an orderly fashion, much like a retreating army.

As he was leaving, Chou En-lai's second-in-command came up to Yong and asked to see him straightaway. 'You know that Gu has a family, don't you? I understand his wife, her parents, her sister, his niece, his cousin, his brother's wife, her brother and his wife, all hold positions in the Secret Service. Together they know an awful lot about our operations. Up until the time of Gu's arrest they've been exemplary members of staff, but we're uncertain how they'll react now. If they decide to stay loyal to Gu, they might well follow him and defect to the enemy, taking our secrets with them. On the other hand, the Kuomintang could blackmail them into becoming agents-in-place, hoping they'll stay inside our organisation while covertly working against us in return for sparing Gu's life. We must search his house and rescue any of our Party documents kept there. Goodness knows what material he's left lying around. As a rising star in this organisation, Yong, tell me what you think of this situation?' he said.

'Gu's relatives could be removed from their homes and held in custody but this would call for our best underground connections in Shanghai to provide a guard for the whole of his family. Another option might be for the entire family to be exterminated without delay? But that might be regarded as rather too extreme. I confess I don't have many other ideas at the moment. I need to think about it more,' Yong replied.

'I see. Since there is little you can add, I've already decided on a plan. I want you to take a small, select team with you to Gu's home. You have total discretion as to the action you take on the spot, according to the situation and in the best interests of the Party and our Secret Service. Is that clear?'

'Yes. I'll do my best.'

'I'm sure you will. Report back to me when you've finished.'

4

'To move a tree, dig under the root.'

Yong knocked on the door of the shabby but elegant three-storey house that the Secret Service had acquired for Gu and his family. He and his colleagues wore light inconspicuous clothing for the job. There was silence in the house, the front door locked and bolted, rooms unlit for sleep.

'Is there anyone in?' he called through the door when no reply came from his knocking. A few moments later he heard the sound of water running down a drainpipe and flowing over a leaf-blocked drain cover.

'Hello! Can I help you?' A woman whom he took to be Gu's wife, dressed in a silk dressing gown done up tightly to the neck, opened the door. She looked younger and prettier than Yong had expected.

'Good morning, madam, I'm from the Kuomintang. We've come to give you some news,' announced Yong, showing her a form of identity that the forgery department had rustled up at the last moment. 'I have to inform you that your husband has defected to the Kuomintang. I wonder what you think of this? For us it's excellent news.'

'I'll follow my husband, whatever happens,' she replied defiantly, her dark eyes blazing.

The team of six men armed with knives, pistols and ropes, carrying hoods to disguise their faces, had waited at the side of the house expecting at any moment to be given the code word by Yong to move in. They had rehearsed the sequence of events over the previous few days and now they were trained up and ready to do the business.

On the code word 'Two' the team barged roughly past Gu's wife, carelessly pushing her out of the doorway where

35

she was standing obstructing the way.

'Hey! Just a minute – what's going on here? You can't just charge in like that. You're nothing but a bunch of thugs. Get out!' she screamed, hands on her hips, defiant.

'Please be quiet. If you don't co-operate we'll have to gag and bind you. The choice is yours!' She stood silent, menacingly, powerless against a superior force.

The team divided up. Some stayed downstairs; others leapt to the floor above. They searched everywhere, under beds, inside cupboards, up in the attic and loft space, under loose floorboards. Two went into the garden to head off any escapees at the back of the property. By degrees the team winkled out seven members of Gu's family, dragging screaming and kicking by the scruff of the neck or by their hair. Many were surprised while they slept, slow to react to the unexpected onslaught.

All the time Yong stayed close to Gu's wife. He wondered how she could have been blamed for Gu's self-indulgence in prostitutes and his constant search for hedonistic gratification. He couldn't understand how Gu could have left the handsome and loyal woman he saw before him for a life of reckless debauchery. But Yong was a young man, an idealist and close to the day of his own marriage. To become a successful spy he would soon have to learn that he lived in a world that was far from perfect. Gu had already led him astray, and without realising it had played a crucial part in Yong's formative years in the Service.

'We have the victims lined up now,' reported the leader of the team gruffly. He was a hefty, slanting-shouldered man built like a weight-lifter and not to be messed with. Yong had no idea where the Service got these men from, but he didn't dwell on that thought for long. The operation had gone well. The team had kept up their cover as Kuomintang supporters to enable Yong to get to the bottom of where Gu's true loyalty lay, but the time had come to reveal their true colours.

'There's one more, right here,' Yong said to the henchman, pointing to Gu's wife.

'Come with me – no fighting – nice and quiet now!' The henchman led her to join the others in the back room. Yong followed behind and entered the room.

He saw the trussed up bodies, clothes torn, arms tied behind their backs and joined together by one single long piece of rope, which cut into flesh leaving only their legs sufficient freedom to hobble. He had never seen such a look of terror in anyone's eyes: cowering figures, some defiant, others resigned. Gu's wife was thrown roughly to the floor with the rest of the family, bruising her knees as she hit the bare wooden floor with a dull thud. Then she was bound up with the others and attached to the end of the single piece of rope.

'Please, please! Don't,' she pleaded, tears flowing down her cheeks desperate to save her family.

Yong's emotions were so completely detached that he carried on with the operation, ignoring her protests. 'Take these people to the back of the house!' he ordered, 'you know what to do next.'

All eight captives were led out by the rope and ordered to face a high brick wall. From behind them a member of the team slipped simple garrottes round the neck of each as they screamed, kicked and squirmed, using up every bit of energy left in them.

'Put something in their mouths, for goodness sake! Stop this bloody noise!' ordered Yong. The rough rope of the garrottes was uncomfortable against soft flesh, but they could do nothing about it with arms tied down to their sides. In their eyes there was only fear and hatred. They mumbled through mouths stuffed with bits of old rag. Some shit themselves and a foul odour surrounded them. Urine had trickled down their legs.

The executioners went down the line, one by one, pulling the nooses tight, at the same time snapping back the neck of each sharply. Horror struck eyes, bodies grotesquely shook and shivered. Some clung to life longer than others. In the throes of death the bodies jerked. When the nerve-twitching had finished, the bodies were laid on the ground for burial in hurriedly dug shallow graves in the garden of the terraced house. Around the garden birds sang eerily in the trees, and as the early morning sun got stronger it beat down on the fresh topsoil shovelled over the bodies. Certain that the operation had been completed, Yong and his team left the scene quickly and undetected.

Yong didn't dwell too long on the operation; although he found it unsavoury and shocking, he was nonetheless proud to be involved with such an important task. When he got home that night, he went round to Fu-fang and after a supper of fried rice and pork they played mahjong together. He told her nothing about his experiences earlier in the day, somehow having turned his heart to stone, thereby separating his work and his personal life. Then he said goodnight and walked back to his apartment alone, expecting at any moment to be pounced on. But he made it through the dark streets to his rooms without incident and a long night's sleep overcame him before another early start.

It didn't take many days before the District Police were involved, despite having received no immediate report of the murders. There had been a suspicion from the people next door, who heard some unusual sounds but thought it was a family row. Police went to the house, and finding nothing inside went out to the garden. The foul stench of defecation and newly-turned earth drew them towards the makeshift graves, already disturbed by scavenging dogs.

'Over here, sir!' exclaimed a young policeman to his superior.

'What is it?'

'See for yourself!'

'Phew, what a smell! Put a handkerchief over your face. Have you got one on you?'

'Yes.'

'What's under those earth mounds? Use your foot to dig it up.'

'Right.' The young man kicked the topsoil away from a piece of red cloth, breathing heavily through the tightly tied handkerchief, eyes smarting from the acrid atmosphere around him. He found what he was looking for. First it was a leg, then the torso facing downwards, neck broken in a rope necklace. The soil was sodden with excreta. The policeman stood back.

'How's it going?'

'I'll need some help.'

'Right.'

After fifteen minutes the shallow nature of the burial revealed all the bodies, in a similar state. The District Commissioner had his own ideas about the culprits, aided by informers among the contract-killing fraternity used by the Communists.

A few days later a man was arrested and interrogated for the murder of Gu's wife. The suspect, a Lim Shan, sat in the cheerless basement room of the District Police Headquarters in Shanghai. There was no ventilation or natural light, and because the basement was so deeply subterranean it was permanently chilly. Two electric light bulbs were suspended from the ceiling on long cords, which accentuated the starkness of the high-ceilinged room. No effort had been made to shield or deflect the light with simple shades.

Grave faced, Lim Shan had been strapped tightly into a large high-backed wooden chair with webbing belts. For two days interrogators, their breath smelling of their last meal, had fired questions at him, but it had taken time to break him. He became a man in constant fear. He hadn't eaten for days, his body weakened and dehydrated to such an extent that the interrogators undid the webbing straps believing his confession was imminent. Food deprivation, hooded isolation, the steady sound of dripping water, stripping him naked and making fun of his puny genitals were techniques the police used.

'You're a foul little man! Confess, you smelly pig! Have you shit yourself? It's only a matter of time before you confess,' persisted one interrogator, a sadist who took pleasure in humiliating his victim, kicking him in the crutch, pouring cold water over his head and punching him repeatedly on his already swollen lips. The blood drained from his face, feeling the vomit rise.

'You must be hungry and concerned what your family think about you? We can make your life more comfortable if you confess.' The other interrogator had taken a deliberately softer and contrasting approach and spoke more soothingly. The technique of alternating between the 'hard' and 'soft' methods of interrogation was a well-established method of breaking down resistance.

By this time, Lim Shan's frail body was like an empty sack. He was cold, hungry and in pain, his unwashed hair unruly. His unshaven face, disfigured by blows, had tufts of thin black hair sprouting out from a series of birthmarks. His eyes had a hollow, sunken look, terrified as he faced his tormentors who sat on the edge of a table opposite him. They swung their legs through impatience, deliberately blew cigarette smoke into his face, flicked ash on his arm and stubbed embers onto his exposed skin. The sickly smell of burning flesh filled the air and high-pitched screams of pain were his only response. He closed his eyes and the sound of voices became muffled.

'You're tired now. I expect you're looking forward to some sleep but you'll be disappointed. You will be kept awake until you confess, you little shit. Do you like this sound?' The interrogator had switched on a wireless and upturned a glass to fill it with water from a jug. Chinese music screeched out from it at a deafeningly high volume, monotonous, without rhythm.

'Did you commit the murder? Come on now. We'll wait no longer.'

Lim Shan raised his head and with a voice that was barely audible whispered 'Y... Y... Yes... I confess.' He was utterly exhausted but he didn't weep or show any emotion. The interrogators had won.

When Lim Shan had recovered sufficiently he led the police to the graves of thirty-nine other murder victims of Yong's Secret Service operation. Shanghai's Chinese, French and International Settlement police joined together in the gruesome task of digging up the bodies. As a result of this incident and the adverse publicity attached to it, the Communist Party in Shanghai went into a low ebb. The atmosphere was tense a few days later in the aftermath of the operation when Yong debriefed those involved.

'Well done everyone. You did a difficult job well. The publicity, although not in our favour, should deter anyone from ever thinking of defecting to the Kuomintang again! We're concerned that the International Settlement, French and Chinese police will soon combine to mount joint operations against us, preventing our members seeking sanctuary in those particular parts of Shanghai. I fear the anti-Communist press will have a field day now,' said Chou.

'I agree. There are many implications,' replied Yong passively.

'We want you to continue to plan other operations. Keep up the momentum, starting with the extermination of the Secret Service man who gave away the whereabouts of Gu's wife's body to the police. Any questions?'

'No, not at the moment, chief.'

When the police rounded-up known Communists, those arrested had few choices: either they defected to the

Kuomintang to divulge Party secrets or, if they resisted, they were tortured and often left to die. Some revealed such trivial, possibly bogus information about their colleagues that the authorities felt there was little value in continuing the exercise.

Chou En-lai reported 'the Gu affair' to the Chinese Communist Party Politburo. Reluctantly he had to admit his responsibility for the debacle, acknowledging the need to put right the lapse in basic security and to constantly monitor colleagues' behaviour. Political loyalties and standards of training had been neglected, but he would rectify that immediately. Having got that out of the way, Chou then went on to talk his way back into the upper strata of the Secret Service, determined to avoid ever making the same mistakes again. Chou was consoled by his informants inside the Kuomintang who reported that once Gu had exhausted the information he gave up and was shot by guards.

Many secret agents had avoided arrest after Gu's defection, but there were those that did not. Those who survived fled Shanghai and turned their backs on the Communist Party forever. What Yong and his colleagues in the Secret Service needed urgently was a morale booster in the form of a dramatic face-saving assassination, to surprise the Kuomintang and make them sit up and take notice. At a meeting with his department, Yong set about making a plan and preparing for a spectacular operation.

'We desperately need a target, someone who is a prominent Kuomintang official or a military officer, preferably one who's been a former, now defected, Communist Party member and Secret Service employee. When I thought hard about it, it suddenly came to me. Wang Bin is the man! He is a really good example for what I have in mind. My assistant just happened to spot his photograph in Kuomintang uniform the other day in the window of a photographer's studio near the Bund. Since his defection to the Kuomintang, he's risen rather surprisingly to the rank of Detective Superintendent. He liaises over extradition matters between the Kuomintang military in Shanghai and the Special Branch of the British-led police of the International Settlement. What isn't generally known, our researchers tell me, is that he is also directly responsible for the deaths of many Communists. I've got approval to go ahead with this operation, so find out all you can about our target. Then we'll meet again to plan how best to approach him,' announced Yong.

For two intense weeks the team worked on the project and formulated plans late into the night. The initial problem had been that many of the Secret Service's sources in the Kuomintang military had dried up and gone to ground. After Gu's defection no one knew Wang Bin's full name and address, despite researchers painstakingly looking through the Shanghai telephone directory with several pages of entries under the name of Wang. The team had to report back that they were having difficulty. It was a slow business. But in the nick of time, just when all avenues had been exhausted, Yong found out from an agent in the literary world, one of his old contacts, where Wang was hanging out. The agent told him that Wang Bin regularly visited a brothel in the French Concession area after work.

'Do we know the routes he takes each day? What is his daily routine?' asked one of the team.

'I think you'll find we've put together all the information you need,' replied the agent.

'Good. Have you any idea where the assassination should take place?'

'We know from our surveillance teams about Wang's daily routine and we have the photographs to prove it. I think we're ready,' ordered Yong in a down to earth and decisive manner.

A team of two, as the assassination squad, was briefed.

Having studied the photographs and the information available to them they decided to take their target one lunchtime, the time when he was known to smoke a cigar in a favourite rickshaw.

At the appointed hour, the assassins got close up to Wang, standing behind a pillar talking to each other casually about the weather, all the time keeping an eye on the target and weighing up their next move. There was no way they would stand out in the crowd. They edged closer still, the only giveaway to a keen observer being the bulge in one of their jacket pockets, but no one suspected anything. People's thoughts were concentrated more on the weekend, food, sex and other pleasures.

The hustle and bustle going on around the static rickshaw provided the best diversion from the first assassin detailed to distract the rickshaw driver who hadn't yet taken up the strain of the worn wooden handles. As soon as the driver had finished off the butt-end of his roll-your-own cigarette, he looked out for his next fare. As his attention was diverted, the second assassin siddled up beside the target. With a gloved hand he deftly thrust the sharp blade of his steel knife into the man's chest, just below the ribs, leaving it there. Blood seeped through the shirt. The man slumped back into his seat, neck lolling, eyes open but glazed, lungs punctured; murdered. The two assailants had only a few vital seconds in which to escape into the womb of the busy crowds unharmed, undetected and without traces of blood on their hands.

'Let's get out of here!' whispered one.

'Come on, let's go then.' They had agreed to walk, not run, to avoid drawing attention to themselves and escaped easily into the constantly moving ocean of bodies.

'I feel like a plate of noodles!'

'Good idea.'

The next day's newspapers were full of the assassination, forcefully bringing home to the people of Shanghai that the arrest and defection of Gu wouldn't diminish the Communist effort. Instead, the murder made the enemies of the Chinese Secret Service look to their own personal safety in the dark alleyways and back streets of the city.

As soon as Chou En-lai had returned from the Politburo meeting, he sought out Yong.

'Yong, thank you for coming. Congratulations, you are to be promoted to Third Deputy! For your first task, I want you to find new premises for you and your colleagues to meet securely. Report back to me when you've found somewhere suitable. I want to be kept fully informed.'

'Yes, sir,' Yong replied, but feared that he had been taken away from front-line operations and assigned to an administrative desk job.

At first it wasn't easy. He called on contacts he had made earlier in his career in the Service. Painstakingly, he visited sites whose location or structure weren't at all suitable for what he had in mind. What he needed was good cover; an ordinary office in a block was no good. A factory or manufacturing type of environment, with trucks and goods constantly moving around to mask the comings and goings of himself and his own people would have been ideal. After several weeks of searching, Yong finally came up with his proposal for suitable premises and reported back to his leader. But it took him a whole week to get an appointment with Chou.

'Sir, I'd like to put our new headquarters in the offices of a coal briquette company. To everyone outside, the other three deputies and I will be the bosses of the company. We'll meet in the mornings to review the day's operations. Occasionally we'll visit a real company production site to help establish the location as an ideal front for our secret work.'

'What about security in the office from outside callers, for instance?' asked Chou.

'I've devised a rather complicated system of safety signals at the office, the factory and at the homes of all our staff. If the signals don't match, it will indicate that an enemy or foreign police trap has been set to ensnare us. I've also established a separate office in a lane off Beijing Lu where I plan to spend the afternoons in peace and quiet, thinking out strategy. If anyone needs to contact me there by telephone, they can easily do so but only by using known aliases and cryptic language. I intend that only a few people will know of this location.'

'Are you sure that's wise?'

'I believe so,' Yong replied.

'Already too many people know of your plan. You're showing signs of security breaches and slackness. You must tighten up.'

'I don't understand what you mean. I've taken every precaution.'

'Don't argue with me. Do as I say. You still want the job, do you?'

'Yes, of course.'

'Well then, watch your step. Idleness about security will finish us off. My impression is that you're getting over-confident, so take heed from my warning.'

'Yes, sir.'

Chou's mood could change very quickly. Sometimes his subordinates didn't know where they were with him. Some thought he was sick, taking strong painkillers which made him erratic. From then on Yong tried hard to keep out of his way and not aggravate him further, but it called for restraint on his part.

'Go ahead with the plan, Yong. I can't waste any more time discussing it,' said Chou with sullen irritation. He fidgeted nervously with a small notebook, flicking the pages for no apparent reason, then stomped off in a foul mood.

5

'The peony is beautiful yet it is supported by a stalk.'

As a newly married man, the Secret Service had allowed Yong to find his own quarters and he was anxious even in those early days to provide a suitable home for his wife and young daughter, Chin-yee. Through his many contacts, he had the opportunity to rent a small terraced town house in an insignificant suburb on the western edge of the city.

One block down from their new home, a small square surrounded by unexciting shrubs and narrow concrete pathways gave Fu-fang the chance to walk with her baby. Every day she stopped at a wooden bench to meet up and gossip with other young mothers with their babies. She was careful not to become too friendly. Her husband had warned her against the dangers of becoming too friendly with strangers in Shanghai.

Yong's success in planning the operation to assassinate Wang Bin had helped to raise morale within both the Communist Party and Secret Service. But it was generally agreed that the Secret Service would not be able to eliminate all their Kuomintang targets by this method alone. Yong wanted to introduce an imaginative and unconventional strategy; at the next weekly staff meeting with his select and chosen lieutenants he allowed discussions to run free. It was also a way of implementing, without wasting time, those practices that Chou En-lai had especially ordered for guarding against internal subversion, by encouraging the continuous motivation and training of talented junior staff.

'Today, comrades, I have an interesting problem for us to discuss,' announced Yong to his three most talented assistants. He had been up half the night, kept awake by

47

Chin-yee's crying; breastfeeding on demand meant that he had little to do with the baby, but his sleep was still disturbed. He had been warned that lack of sleep would sap his strength, but he had become used to it.

'We need to think up new ways to destroy the Kuomintang. Please let your fertile minds run free for a few minutes, then I want to discuss the ideas you come up with. Don't be embarrassed, comrades, say whatever comes into your head!'

Strolling over to the office window, he opened it to allow the stale tobacco smoke out and fresh air in to revive his subordinates' stuffy heads. He had studied his colleagues' faces while their eyes were closed in deep thought and passed the next few minutes trying to assess the potential of these inscrutable people. Which one would get to the top? Which one was the brightest? Which one was loyal? Would they all be totally loyal? Where might they all be in thirty or forty years' time? He snapped back to reality when he noticed the time, but it was well spent: he firmly believed that success came from consulting with wise people.

'Right, comrades, you've had enough time. Let's start with the possibilities. Who's going to be first?'

A small twenty-three-year-old from Shanghai with close-cropped hair and spectacles, a recent graduate of St John's University, spoke up. 'May I suggest that we plant one of our own officers inside the Investigation Section of the Kuomintang or some other Kuomintang department?'

'A good idea. We've had some success with this method before, but it has a major drawback. It needs a long lead time before we get results. Unfortunately time isn't on our side. We would need to find from our own staff someone who wouldn't have been compromised by Gu and other defectors. He would have to be specially trained and floated right under the Kuomintang's noses. Let's assume that if we manage to get someone in, it could take months for them to have sufficient confidence to allow him access to valuable secrets. In the meantime, comrades, the Kuomintang is still able to act against us using Gu's information. Any other ideas?' He was pleased that suggestions were coming forward quite easily.

'I have one,' announced a rather burly young man in his mid-twenties. In addition to his powerful physique, his mean-looking face dominated by a high forehead and tiny dark eyes sunk deep in his skull, coupled with the thickness of his bull-neck gave him a thoroughly menacing appearance. 'Why can't we recruit a serving Kuomintang intelligence or counter-espionage team?'

'I can't see it being any more practical than the last suggestion. Despite Wang Bin's successful assassination, we, the Communist Party, are generally seen to be of minor influence in the so-called White Areas, but our rural bases are under remorseless military attack by the Kuomintang. I doubt we could succeed in subverting an existing Kuomintang unit with a view to them working for an organisation that appears to be on the decline. Any other thoughts, comrades?'

The third member of the inner circle to speak up was older, in his early thirties and recently recruited direct from business. He brought with him experience of the outside world and many contacts. This was a remarkable but unconventional man who had sat nervously scratching his small, slightly ridiculous black pencil moustache.

'Perhaps I'm on the wrong track here. Why don't we persuade a Kuomintang official that he's dealing not with the Communist Party nor one of our Secret Service officials, but with someone neutral and non-threatening, with no axe to grind as far as the war against Communism is concerned? It would be as if the contact was on the same side, a sort of false flag.'

'Hmm. Let me think. Yes, I like it. That's very original. You have a gift, my friend, and you mustn't be afraid of expressing your ideas. I'll think very hard about your idea.

Now, comrades, we've had enough discussion for today.'

The meeting closed, members began filing out of the room. One of the men paused in front of Yong.

'Excuse me?' asked the third member, 'could I have a private word with you before you go?'

'Certainly. What is it? We can talk now,' said Yong, drawing the man towards the corner of the room to make sure they wouldn't be overheard.

'I'm rather embarrassed. I've got my girlfriend pregnant, and we haven't married yet. I want you to know, in case you notice that my work might be suffering.'

'Thanks for confiding in me. I'll make allowances for you, but you must learn that your duties to the Service come first. Are you going to marry her? Think of the implications if you don't, especially with your promising career in the Service. There could be a time in the future when she could blackmail you or threaten you in some other way. If you are really fond of the girl you have no problem, but if you feel forced to marry her against your instincts, that's a different matter. I don't want to know the answers now, but keep me informed of your situation. Don't forget, I'm always here to talk to but I may not always give the advice you want to hear!'

'You've have been a great help,' the subordinate replied, feeling as though a weight had been lifted from his shoulders.

'You have a promising future ahead of you but I cannot repeat this too often: the Service and the interests of the Party come first. As a member of the Service you are someone special, and each one of us has obligations quite different to those in other professions.'

It was typical of Yong, intensely loyal to the Service. He couldn't tolerate complacency; he liked to get on with things, make plans work and keep a full programme of operations going, regardless of personal feelings. He disliked leaning back and resting after a success. He believed the momentum had to be maintained. As he pushed himself, so he pushed his colleagues. Everyone knew he was a man in a hurry, and the Service respected him for firmly sticking to their strategy.

The target for the false flag operation was identified: a certain Hanqi, a former political officer who worked as an intelligence analyst, specialising in Communist and left-wing politics for the Shanghai Kuomintang Municipal Social Bureau. Ouyang, Yong's secretary, was appointed as the contact and reported back to him about the meetings.

The Empire Restaurant, close to the Bund in Shanghai's smart district, was the chosen venue for Ouyang to meet Hanqi. The restaurant was Western in style with wide banquettes covered in deep red velvet. Framed oil and watercolour paintings hung on the walls, lit at night by brass wall and picture lamps and a huge chandelier suspended from the ceiling. In the corner of this lush establishment a piano player entertained with gentle tunes, providing relaxing but unobtrusive background music which appealed to the mixed taste of Western and rich Chinese customers. Many Western men regularly took their European, Oriental or Eurasian mistresses there; it was well regarded, too, as a top venue for business entertaining. For someone to be invited to the Empire was the treat of a lifetime, and so it was for Hanqi.

Ouyang recognised Hanqi as he rushed through the entrance to the restaurant, having sprinted the last few yards through heavy rain. The bottom of his sopping trousers stuck to his calves and his feet squelched inside his shoes. Beads of sweat and rain ran from his forehead, down his eyebrows and settled uncomfortably behind thick spectacle frames. His lenses started to fog up as soon as he entered the warm dry atmosphere, adding to his nervous confusion and embarrassment: he was not used to being entertained in such an opulent establishment and wondered what the importance of the occasion was.

'Hello,' he said breathlessly, 'I'm so sorry I'm late but it's been difficult getting a taxi in the rain. Everyone wants one at this time of night in Shanghai.'

'Don't worry. Come and sit down and relax over here. I've booked a quiet corner for us. Can I take your coat? The waiter will hang it somewhere to dry. Will you sit on my right, here? Let's have a drink.'

Hanqi sat down and began to regain his composure.

'Congratulations on getting to such a prestigious position in the Kuomintang Social Bureau. I think you've been promoted since we last met!' announced Ouyang, once they had settled at the table. The Secret Service had plenty of information on him, which Ouyang had looked up with Yong's help just before the meeting.

'Thanks. Has life been good to you too? Other than our brief business contact I really don't know much about our situation,' commented Hanqi.

'I'm secretary to a British-educated lawyer who once served Sun Yat-sen. I run the foreign affairs programme of the left wing of the Kuomintang, arranging meetings between delegations from foreign social-democratic parties, labour groups and left-wing Kuomintang politicians,' Ouyang replied, noting that Hanqi was most attentive.

'That's interesting. Perhaps we can do each other a favour,' replied Hanqi always on the lookout for new contacts, but still wondering what the objective of the meeting was.

The treat of roast Chinese duck accompanied by chilled white Burgundy, imported into Shanghai at considerable cost, was much enjoyed by the pair. As expected, the impressive and luxurious atmosphere lulled Hanqi into a sleepy reverie.

'One of my duties is to monitor left-wing political activity. Your job gives you access to just the sort of information that my Kuomintang masters want me to collect,' said Ouyang, knowing that Hanqi was anti-

Communist. This fact had prevented Yong having closer contact; his final words at the briefing had stuck in Ouyang's mind: 'Don't forget, you're to cultivate Hanqi using false, non-Communist cover.'

'More wine, Hanqi?' asked Ouyang, becoming more confident as he realised his plan was working. Hanqi nodded as Ouyang leant across to the right side of the table to retrieve the bottle that rested at an angle, chilling in the ice bucket. Ouyang continued, 'I have to write reports on the activities of the Chinese Communist Party and the trade unions they influence. I have a sizeable budget, but so far I haven't found any productive source.'

'It's such a stroke of luck we've met!' announced Hanqi impetuously, then he became subdued. 'Look, this is just between you and me: I maintain a young and beautiful concubine. She's demanding and expensive. I'm permanently short of money. It's a real problem for me. Surely we can work something out to our mutual benefit?' whispered Hanqi, looking directly into Ouyang's eyes, leaning forward to deliver the information in a conspiratorial manner which heightened Hanqi's sense of intrigue. His disdainful eyes suddenly became mild.

When the meal came to an end the two men made their way outside to the sound of traffic and the familiar smell of exhaust fumes, the pavements shiny with damp even though the rain had stopped.

'Perhaps we should go our separate ways here. My young lady is waiting up for me! Please excuse me. I'm sure you understand. I must dash away. Thank you so much for an excellent meal. We really must meet again soon.' Words and thanks tumbled from him hurriedly and, Ouyang thought, insincerely.

'Certainly,' replied Ouyang. As they turned away from the restaurant, he left his guest to walk in the opposite direction, making sure he wasn't being followed. Ouyang was struck by Hanqi's secrecy about his movements that night.

Things had gone well so far, and since the timing could not have been more favourable, Ouyang soon started to pass low-interest pieces of information to Hanqi, mainly about Shanghai's Social Democrats and their foreign links. For his part, Hanqi readily accepted Ouyang's requests for specific and more important pieces of intelligence about the Chinese Communist Party, but in return for money. All the time Hanqi believed the information was destined to pass through Ouyang to other key non-Communists.

As the operation continued to go well, Yong congratulated Ouyang on his handling of Hanqi. Several times Hanqi had asked Ouyang more searching questions.

'Where do the funds come from for your work?' he queried once.

'Mostly from anonymous friends. Private benefactors,' Ouyang replied smoothly.

'Frankly, Ouyang, I don't much care where the money comes from as long as I'm paid! I need to maintain my lavish lifestyle. You know women are wonderful, but so expensive and demanding!'

'You're a lucky man! Why complain? You seem to be well set up. Up to now you've given me routine background information based largely on old defectors. Now I need hard, up-to-date intelligence about our Party, based on the testimony of newly-arrested Party members and Kuomin-tang agents still in place inside our Party.'

'Don't worry, Ouyang, I'll get whatever you want. I've recently recruited my own private sources of informers in the Kuomintang as well as within the International Settlement police; they will pass me highly sensitive intelligence from their own sources inside the Communist Party.'

'Excellent!' replied Ouyang.

Yong was fairly confident that through Ouyang he would soon be able to identify Communist Party traitors. In time for the next meeting with Ouyang, he drew up a list of the turncoats. 'These people will be reassigned away from sensitive and important Party work, used either to feed disinformation to the Kuomintang or they'll be murdered,' he announced, showing a streak of ruthlessness, his dark eyes looking straight into Ouyang's. He was deadly serious, determined to turn any setback to his own and the Service's advantage.

'This could be one of our more successful counter-intelligence operations. Keep up the good work, Ouyang, and keep me briefed on progress. I've told Chou En-lai about your work, and he wants me to thank you personally.'

6

'To know the road ahead, ask those coming back.'

Using an alias, Yong was nominated as the official signatory to an agreement with the Fujian rebel army. The rebels had formed in 1932 following the resignation of the Fujian provincial government; Chiang feared that the southern province was moving left politically, attracting other dissident Kuomintang forces. The choice of Yong as the leading negotiator had been a good one, as he already knew his opposite numbers. At the same time within the Chinese Communist Party a leadership battle was developing between Mao Tse-tung and Chou En-lai. Each had their followers inside the organisation.

'What do you think of this agreement?' Yong asked one of his colleagues later. Sometimes, as a negotiator, he was worried that he had been too closely involved and hadn't always been able to see the wood for the trees.

His office was a couple of rooms attached to the army headquarters, giving him access to vital security and communications equipment as well as all the resources that a military headquarters could provide.

He looked out of the open window and saw groups of soldiers parading in plain light green fatigues at one end of the tarmac square, and at the other end uniformed men exercised their skills stripping rifles and filling magazines at speed and repeating the drills blindfolded. Their fitness, bearing and discipline were impressive. When he reported back to his superiors, Yong had certain reservations about the security of information within the Rebel Route Army, believing them to be as leaky as sieves.

'We know already that Kuomintang military intelligence has high-level sources inside the general staff of the Fujian rebels 19th Route Army, and that they have planted several agents provocateurs in key units of the army and the provincial government. I expect the intentions of the Fujian rebels and details of their contacts with the Chinese Communist Party are an open secret to Chiang Kai-shek, and that he plans to defeat the rebels before they openly declare independence from his government in Nanjing.

'There is concern, too, that the agreements won't stick. So much so that in two days' time the Central Soviet have asked for me to be sent to Fuzhou as their top representative, with unlimited powers. I'll be travelling overland with two others and two escorts. Both my secretary and myself have been taught secret writing techniques by Chou En-lai's wife, and I've had basic wireless training from a Red Army signaller.'

From the moment that they entered Fujian territory they were under constant surveillance. During the day, Yong spent his time negotiating with the Fujian representative, while his assistant walked the streets gathering whatever information he could from the press and local residents.

'Tonight we'll meet up with my secretary, under the cover of a public bathhouse and a snooker hall, to discuss the progress of the day's negotiations, compare notes, draft and encipher telegrams for Ruijin,' he told his assistant, with whom he often talked over his concerns; the Chinese Communist Party Central Soviet headquarters was based in Ruijin.

'Despite having our own cipher we don't have an independent wireless communication link with Ruijin. We have to rely instead on the goodwill of the 19th Route Army signals office to transmit and receive our traffic. It's annoying, I know. An alternative could be to send messages in invisible ink via known Communist commercial agents travelling between Fuzhou and Ruijin.'

All this time he was collecting high quality intelligence about the rebels' intentions from his old Shanghai Secret

Service contacts who were still in place within the Fujian organisation. Despite the fragile agreement with the rebels, Yong continued to have strong reservations about the Fujian situation.

One evening, while playing snooker together, he confided in his assistant.

'The 19th Route Army is no different from any other Kuomintang unit. It shares the same objective of destroying the Red Army and pretends to believe that its land-reform programme is an evil trick designed to perpetuate the interests of the ruling classes that the Kuomintang represents.'

Yong's views were well respected by the high command, and in no time the rebels received a formal letter from the Chinese Communist Party Central Committee:

We believe that the Fujian Government represents the despotic gentry-landlord capitalist class and as such it is no different from the Kuomintang. The 19th Route Army is merely its armed force, with no intention of conducting land reform or arming the masses against the Japanese and Chiang Kai-shek. We therefore require you to begin mobilising the masses forthwith.

From then on the situation rapidly deteriorated. Kuomintang aircraft strafed the streets and bombed tactical military targets. Some feared they might use poison gas. At sea the rebel navy surrendered to the Kuomintang, and the 19th Route Army was in retreat to the south as Chiang Kai-shek deployed 150,000 troops against it. Substantial defections from the rebel leadership to the Kuomintang brought the town of Fuzhou into chaos, and Yong desperately needed to escape from there as soon as he could.

Remembering the tradecraft skills he had been taught, he managed to send an invisible ink signal back to his headquarters, via a secure courier, which simply said:

> The Kuomintang know that I am in town, and I believe I rank highly on Chiang Kai-shek's wanted list as a search target for his advancing troops. In addition, several Fujian leaders believed the rebellion to have been betrayed by the Chinese Communist Party in the form of my fellow negotiators and myself. The rebel government is in chaos and there are informers everywhere. I have no choice but to make my own evacuation arrangements.

He had seen for himself the nightly bombing raids as aircraft flew overhead, releasing their deadly cargo on to the streets and the innocent inhabitants. He looked up and saw bombs dropping indiscriminately everywhere. Fires erupted in buildings and the night sky became lit up by successive explosions and the leaping flames of the secondary burning. Ambulances and fire engines raced to the scene of the devastation, but there were far too many fronts for the authorities to operate on at any one time.

Making use of the distractions, Yong decided that was the very moment to break out. He ran as fast as he could from his quarters under cover of the chaos. He looked for the home of a former Chinese Communist Party member he'd met in Shanghai, now a businessman living in Fuzhou's commercial district, who had promised to help him escape.

Yong kept running as fast as he could, dodging the falling debris, stopping once as a piece of burning wood fell onto his foot, bruising and burning it, but he was undeterred. He breathed heavily but fear focused his mind on just one thing: to keep going. On and on he ran, hoping that good luck would stay with him until he arrived at his destination. At last he made it: a colonial style house, the home of a well-to-do merchant. Banging with his clenched fist on the heavy wooden front door welded together with steel rivets, he waited for what seemed a lifetime. A light came from the window above, and he made out the silhouette of his friend as he leant out and spoke to him.

'Who's that?' queried the voice softly, in the manner of someone expecting a caller but wanted to be certain that it wasn't a trap.

'Your friend!'

'I'll be right down.'

The door was unbolted hastily from within and his host warmly welcomed him inside. From the large stone paved hall, strewn with Oriental carpets, they moved into the drawing room with its tall blue china Ming vases, lamps, delicately painted watercolours and charcoal drawings depicting Chinese rural scenes. The chairs were low with white antimacassars, and the polished light wooden floors were covered here and there with colourful handmade wool and silk traditional Chinese rugs. The impression was one of luxury, and clearly it was the house of a prosperous businessman.

'This is very grand!' commented Yong as he was offered a chair and a pot of tea.

'I suppose it is. In the days when I was in the Chinese Communist Party underground movement in Shanghai, you'll remember I was very poor. Even now I'm still loyal to the cause, despite the fact that I make money smuggling goods to the Central Soviet! I purchase the goods cheaply here and sell them on at a profit and for cash settlement. It's quite simple really. I trade between Fuzhou and the Guangdung port of Shantou, which gives me the cover I need for trips to Guangdung itself and Hong Kong. Of course, this route is the only way of evading Kuomintang troops closing in on Fuzhou. It's all a bit hairy, but it makes me a living!'

'Can you help me get away now?'

'I hope so. I've managed – with great difficulty, I can tell you, and it required a large bribe – to get you a passenger ticket on a Japanese coaster due to leave here for Shantou tomorrow. I warn you, it won't be easy for you to move on from Shantou. The Kuomintang authorities are examining every passenger who has travelled from Fuzhou.'

'Well done, comrade. I am so grateful for your help.'

The following morning Yong left his contact's house, alone, via the back-garden exit and walked the half-mile to the port where he checked in and boarded the stinking unpainted coaster.

He managed to bluff his way ashore when the coaster docked at Shantou, and eventually crossed the short distance through storms and rough seas to arrive safely in Hong Kong. Three months later he set off back to Ruijin, travelling via Shanghai to be reunited with his family.

Fu-fang and Chin-yee welcomed him back with open arms. Yong measured Chin-yee's height against a doorframe, noticing how much she had grown while he'd been away. The family had been safe enough, but exasperated without news. The first night back he told them stories of Hong Kong and some incidents of his journey. They listened with wide innocent eyes. Chin-yee was allowed to stay up a little later that night, as the excitement at seeing her father again kept her awake way beyond her normal bedtime.

7

'One man tells a lie ... dozens repeat it as the truth.'

I was three years old when the Japanese invaded and occupied China in 1937, but it wasn't until 1938 that my father returned to the family in Shanghai. My grandmother had died and as an acknowledged senior Party official, my father was allocated an appropriate grade of living quarters for himself and the family.

The Japanese occupation with its systematic rape and slaughter of the population of Nanjing was one of the worst acts of bestiality ever recorded. It is said that wars sharpen senses; both physical and mental awareness is heightened by the constant closeness to death. Everywhere were reminders of the effects of conflict. That was the climate in Shanghai in the early years of my childhood.

Mass crowds of peasant women thronged the streets around the Western shops and wayward street-sellers' carts collided with each other. Pedicabs and rickshaws swarmed the already congested streets, forcing motor cars to a standstill, their arrogant and impatient drivers pressing their horns in frustration. The city noise was a chaos as cars and lorries spewed exhaust fumes.

The motor vehicles battled ceaselessly with the rickshaws, each seeking their share of the scarce space. Aggressive rickshaw coolies aimed to crowd out the foreign cars from the Bubbling Wells Road. Cruising bar-girls showed off smart American handbags and jostled for pavement space with elderly grey-haired amahs in dark shapeless tunics, their backs hunched by the weight of produce suspended from bamboo poles across their shoulders. It wasn't at all unusual to see lorries carrying executioners at speed towards the Old Chinese City to administer public hangings. Young beggars persistently demanded money, pleading homelessness and poverty, sometimes leaping onto the polished bonnets of wealthy-looking foreign cars.

At night, despite the Japanese occupation, the centre of Shanghai was still extravagant in its use of electricity, illuminating brash, American-style advertising hoardings which blazed out world famous brand names.

My sister Chin-yee, being older than I, took delight in bossing me about. She was a cunning girl. In front of my parents she would be pleasant towards me, showing affection and care. But as soon as they were out of sight, her personality changed completely. She became another character, bullying and bossy. Sometimes she hit me, but her attacks didn't last long as I soon learnt to defend myself.

Because she had impressed my parents with her caring attitude towards me, she was allowed to take me on short walks around the city. I never knew then if she was jealous of me being a boy and the youngest of the family, but she took delight in demeaning my remarks, and her comments were mostly spliced with sarcasm.

When I was older I remembered very clearly my sister's arrogance and her raucous laugh was repulsive, forced rather than amused. Her eyes seemed almost lost in another sphere. By then I was allowed out at night, and I was fascinated by the darkness down the Bubbling Wells Road with the multi-coloured lightbulbs of the garishly-lit nightclubs, their scantily dressed bar-girls hanging around the doorways. The gambling dens echoed with the distinctive 'click clack' of dice and mahjong pieces. I watched the glamorous Eurasian girls sitting in the lines of rickshaws outside The Park Hotel, dressed in ankle-length fur coats, whistling enticingly at the residents as they sauntered through the revolving doors.

I had noticed my father wasn't his usual self. He seemed preoccupied and withdrawn, and the lines on his face were more deeply etched than normal. His eyes took in much, but gave little away. If I talked to him he snapped back at me impatiently, preferring to stay in his own world. He was clearly worried about something. Even my mother had noticed the change in him, but she could get nothing out of him and we believed him to be overworked. Although I was unaware of his real occupation, I did know he was involved in dangerous work with the Party and that his work was causing a high and constant level of stress. He talked very little and smiled only occasionally, but I sensed a harder resolve.

One weekday many years later, at a time when I thought my father's powers had returned to him, I was at home alone when the telephone rang. It had a shrill, demanding bell tone which made me jump, as it was such an infrequent occurrence for us to receive calls. Our telephone was sparingly used, just to make essential social arrangements, even less so since my sister was then living away from Shanghai.

'Hello. Am I speaking to the son of Yong?' enquired an official-sounding voice.

'Yes.' I replied somewhat brusquely. I preferred to keep my telephone conversations short.

'I'll come to the point quickly. I'm from your father's office. I'm sorry to report that your father is in custody. He's been arrested for plotting and conspiring against the Communist Party leadership. I very much regret having to break the news to you in this way. He'll be held in the main city prison. You are free to visit him at any time; only immediate family, though for the time being.'

I was stunned, but remained in control of my emotions, trying to take in the information and the implications. It was a bolt from the blue.

'How is my father?' I asked, trying to visualise my father's awful and lonely predicament.

'He's as well as can be expected and has asked especially to send his concerns to his family.'

'Please tell him we are thinking of him too,' I replied, knowing how important it was for my father to know his family was behind him.

'Can you tell me more about the case?'

'I'm afraid not. You'll have to come to the prison to ask your father himself. As a political prisoner, he may receive visits from his family. That's all I can say at the moment. Goodbye.'

It had been a difficult call to take and I was thankful to be alone in the house to collect my thoughts. My immediate reaction was to sit quietly thinking, just thinking. I realised that my father must have been under intolerable stress for some time, possibly years, and I wondered for how long he had borne the weight of possible arrest.

The newspapers the following day carried the front-page headline 'Power plot foiled – suspect held'. I'd spotted the headline and cautiously showed it to my mother. It was foolish of me, as it did nothing to improve her state of mind. She was in deep shock, unable to concentrate, tearful and much in need of comfort.

The following day my mother and I went to the prison. My sister had been summoned home, but it was another day's journey for her. The stark grey concrete building reminded me of an army barracks, but even more unfriendly. Dirty square windows, too small for a man to squeeze through, featured with heavy iron bars sunk into the grimy stonework. Two huge double wooden doors, heavily guarded, marked the entrance.

We noticed that my father had been designated the best accommodation: a single cell to himself. Otherwise the facilities were crude, with a jug of cold water, a tin bowl and a rusty bucket into which he urinated and defecated; the contents due to be slung out stank. He wore a prisoner's uniform made of light grey cotton, baggy trousers and a jacket buttoned up high to the neck, which gave him a more distinguished appearance than was intended. I had expected to find him heavy about the eyes.

The three of us hugged each other and remained clasped together tightly for several seconds. It was an emotional moment for us all. I tried to keep back my tears and noticed that he was upset too. I knew then that the visit was likely to deeply affect each one of us for a long time to come.

'What happened, father?'

'I don't know what I am allowed to tell you, but I can't see the point of the authorities stopping me telling you now that I'm incarcerated here!'

'Take your time,' I said, reassuring him. His embarrassment returned and his words came slowly.

'It won't take long. I don't think there's any doubt about my being a loyal Communist.' His head hung low as he drew a heavy breath. 'For some time the Party leadership has been in the grip of intense internal struggles between the main contenders. There's been factional plotting which, because of my intelligence work, I've been fully aware of. I can only suspect that the leadership thought I knew too much – I was made a scapegoat in order to further the leader's own ends entirely to demonstrate that he still has a firm grip on the Party. It's an old ploy often used by autocratic leaders who actually fear their control over the Party is slipping.'

'So someone in high office had to be sacrificed?' I asked.

'Yes, that's how it works,' my father confirmed without any sign of anger.

'I suppose Mao Tse-tung, despite the debacle of the Long March and his emergence as supreme leader of the Party since 1949, is still likely to be challenged for the leadership from time to time?'

'Yes,' replied my father. My mother listened but said

nothing, still dazed, nervously turning the button of her jacket between her right forefinger and thumb.

8

'Don't send a small boat for such heavy cargo.'

On a cold, cloudy night in November, Tak-yan, an only child, was taken by her parents to join others at the rendezvous planned a month in advance by the escape committee. The group had mustered to its full capacity of twenty, all of them wearing their everyday working clothes and wrapped in sheets of black plastic to protect them from the worst of the rain. Underneath the loose wrappings each adult carried a small suitcase of minimal belongings.

'If you're not committed, then don't come. There's only one chance for freedom! The waters are still patrolled by the Hong Kong Marine Police, always on the lookout for illegal immigrants. I've done this route before, so I know it can be successful,' said Chang, the one-eyed local committee leader known as Rat Face, who, in return for money, had painstakingly planned this escape mission. For over three months he had prepared for this moment, getting the right equipment together. He had left nothing to chance and was very much on his guard, having taken the added risk of getting so many people out at one time. Escapes he knew were risky, best undertaken by smaller groups. But he had been paid, and now he had to deliver them safely away from the mainland.

Young children, wrapped in extra clothes with plastic sheets tied around them secured by string, clung obediently and quietly to the comfort of their mothers' bosoms. Either standing or sitting still at the rendezvous for a good hour or more had left their faces numb and chilled by the increasingly bitter wind and heavy rain showers that lashed across the bay. Finally, a whispering guide escorted them to the shoreline. Groups of four at a time slithered down the rain-sodden bank where the grassy field met the shingle beach.

Straining their eyes into the pitch-black squally night, each group stepped as quietly as they could in single file towards a small tender, held still in the shallow but choppy water. As soon as it was fully loaded, with great effort a lone oarsman rowed the tender out through the mist towards the junk. To help everyone to board the junk a boatman lowered a scrambling net and released rudimentary ladders hooked onto the side. Women passed their children up to the men who, being stronger, clambered up using one hand for themselves and the other to hold the child. Silence was ordered and no lights were allowed. The ferrying continued back and forth until all escapees were on board, and having counted heads Chang weighed anchor.

So far the operation had gone smoothly. No lights had been used as they sailed off into the squall-ridden night, the murky swell of the South China waters and an uncertain future. There were no regrets, only concern for loved ones left behind. No adult feared for their own life even though few could swim. It was the prize of a brighter future in another country that was the spur.

A northwesterly wind had filled the tall tawny sails. Chang glanced up from the wheel and saw what he feared most: the silhouette of a launch speeding a good 500 metres to the right of the junk. Strapping the wheel tightly to the housing he leapt forward to where the immigrants were huddled together, whispering to each other through chattering teeth. A child at that moment became unsettled and cried out.

'Shh, shh! Quiet!' Chang warned urgently, placing his forefinger against his harelip. 'Don't move! Keep your heads down. Pull the plastic sheets to cover you up. There's a fast launch snooping about.'

Tak-yan's mother clasped her tightly and rocked her

gently, reassuring her back to sleep. Her eyes focused on a piece of ribbon attached to her child's hat; pink and silky. Her own mother had sewn it on, especially strong to withstand the rigours of the journey, not knowing if she would ever see her granddaughter again. That ribbon became a symbol of hope, a deepening reminder of the family she had left behind, and the strength needed to sustain her during the escape. The ribbon had two long ends, which fluttered in the wind in spite of the drenching sea spray.

Having alerted everyone, Chang ran crouching back to the wheel, resumed control of the junk and deftly trimmed the angle of the sails. By now the launch was directly in line with the junk but hadn't come any closer to them. Chang straining his eyes in the darkness saw that the launch had moved further away from them. Soon it would be out of sight. Fifteen minutes later he went forward to give the immigrants the all clear.

'Phew! That was a close shave!' muttered Chang, mightily relieved the danger and possible discovery had for the moment passed. The first glimmer of dawn light would soon appear on the eastern horizon and rise up from behind the hills as they approached land. He desperately wanted to get everyone ashore before first light.

零 零 零

Meanwhile in England Algernon Stanhope, known as Algie to his friends, took life casually, especially his numerous love affairs. There was something open and aristocratic about his chiselled features and the steady gaze of his deep blue eyes. When he left school at eighteen he was allowed to return to his prep school for a term to fill in before going up to university. He was asked to teach a narrow range of subjects to the lower forms, but more importantly helped out with bowling in the cricket nets.

Cynthia was ten years older than Algie and a permanent member of the teaching staff. As mistress of the lower form, she was charged with bringing pastoral comfort to the boys experiencing their first year at boarding school. Both she and Algie lived in the staff quarters in a lodge in the grounds of the school. A high-spirited woman, Cynthia was clearly frustrated by the lack of brio among her fellow staff members. Having worked for the Foreign Office, she had travelled widely and the narrow confines of school life inevitably irked her. Because their rooms were almost next door to each other, she and Algie often met to have a cup of tea or a glass of whisky. As the term progressed, they got into the habit of going out for the day together, sometimes by bus to the seaside, and in the evenings eating out at local restaurants.

Algie was savouring his first taste of freedom, earning and spending his own money. He had developed a liking for whisky, which made him feel randy and brave and he enjoyed the exotic flat Turkish cigarettes which Cynthia had introduced him to.

'Let's have a drink in my room!' Cynthia suggested one evening as they walked back together to their quarters in the staff lodge.

'I'll be along, if I may, when I've had a quick wash. I feel rather sticky today. It must be this hot weather,' replied Algie.

That afternoon they'd been for a spin in his pre-war Rover. He needed a shave, too; he was already a two-shaves-a-day man, especially if he was going out in the evening.

It didn't take him long. Soon he was ready and knocked on Cynthia's door.

'Come in!' she said cheerfully. She had changed into a black-and-white check summer frock, belted at the waist, the pencil slim skirt showing off her long slim legs to their best advantage. Algie couldn't fail to notice the stylish merits of her dress and the seductive fragrance.

'Do sit down, Algie, and make yourself comfortable.'

The room possessed only two chairs. The rest of the space was taken up with a large double bed, a wardrobe and a dressing table. Despite the plain furnishings, Cynthia had made it feminine and cheerful, impressing her personality on it in a variety of subtle ways: curtains tied back by large bows, pictures on the walls, photo frames and perfume bottles on the dressing table and a lace mat under a small vase of freshly picked flowers.

'Water with yours?' she asked, already knowing the answer.

'Yes, please,' replied Algie. She poured two shots from the almost full bottle, topping up both glasses with water from the tap at the washbasin.

'There you are. Cheers!'

Cynthia talked on excitedly and interestingly about her life abroad. Algie was fascinated. Soon they were on to their second, third and then fourth drinks.

Algie was emboldened by the proximity of Cynthia and the effect of the alcohol. Her scent and the sight of her bare legs were beginning to stir him. Cynthia, sensing this, egged him on and brazenly mustered her feminine charms. She flaunted her voluptuousness. Rising from her chair she came tantalisingly close to where he was sitting. Algie moved towards her, his deep blue eyes clouding with lust. He slid his arm round her legs and moved his hand up her skirt to caress the silken flesh of her thighs. It was a totally instinctive gesture.

'Ooh – that's nice – very nice!' murmured Cynthia appreciatively. She encouraged him to go further by opening her legs and pushing herself against him so that his face became buried in her soft belly. Aroused, Algie's untested manhood was ready for action. Cynthia knew this and she wanted him as urgently as he wanted her.

'Come and lie on the bed!' directed Cynthia gently, not

for the first time taking control of the situation.

Algie was grateful for the older woman's experience. Gently she undid his trousers and peeled off his shirt. When she had pulled down his pants and tickled his scrotum he was eager and ready for her.

'Help me out of this dress!' she said demanding urgency. Then she giggled – making a pretence at being coy.

It was a while before they spoke again. Up until then the only sounds were of passionate groans. The first thing he noticed when they eventually uncoupled was the last of the midsummer's daylight through the open window and a wood pigeon cooing nearby.

'Not bad for the first time! You clever boy. You're going to steal a few hearts, that's for sure but for now I have you all to myself.' Cynthia purred as she lay on her side, supporting her head in one hand, the other playing with his hairy chest. Algie lay on his back covering the damp patch they had made together. There had been no awkward fumbling, no premature ejaculation. Then she leant across him to the bedside table and took out from the crumpled packet a cigarette, which Algie lit for her with the lighter lying beside it.

From then on Cynthia and Algie severely distracted each other away from school duties. Every possible moment they could manage, they were together. Except for when Cynthia had her period, they made urgent and passionate love and sometimes during that inconvenient time of the month too. Algie was glad for a break from her insatiable appetite to recharge his batteries, but Cynthia still wanted him. She had taught him well, how to love, how to please and how a woman's body worked. He never really understood how their minds worked, but he wasn't bothered with that for the time being.

He wasn't coming back to the school the next term. As the long hot summer term drew to a close, so too the days when Cynthia and Algie could be together were numbered.

'Once you leave here you'll meet a younger woman more your own age and you won't want to be seen around with me. I'll have to let you go. Just think of me here next term in the winter – in my lonely bed, dreaming about you at university and missing you terribly,' said Cynthia with dread in her heart.

'Let's meet in the holidays? How about a day in London together?' suggested Algie enthusiastically.

'Do you really think so? It's up to you. You know I'd love to,' Cynthia replied, hoping to see him one more time, a glimmer of light for her in the darkness of inevitability. So they set a place and date.

When Algie and Cynthia did meet up on a damp early autumn day in London, they soon became aware that the magic engendered by their former proximity and their affair at the school had simply evaporated. They gamely went through the motions and lunched in an uninspiring café down the Kings Road, and afterwards they pointlessly trailed around Peter Jones and WH Smith. Later, as the early afternoon twilight set in, they strolled into Hyde Park, passing Harvey Nichols on the way.

'Let's have a final fling!' she turned impulsively to Andrew. 'Let's go into those bushes over there. No one will see us and we'll lie on my raincoat.'

'Is there much point?' protested Algie, knowing full well that he had no enthusiasm left for prolonging the end of the affair. It had been great while it lasted, but it had run its course.

'You fucking bastard! You spoilt little shit! You want to finish with me don't you? I knew it would end sometime. Well, you're damn well not going to get away just like that. I haven't finished with you yet, my boy. Come with me!' she spat out at him, eyes shining, nostrils flared.

Disappearing from view they lay awkwardly on the reversed raincoat attempting to make love partly clothed, hurriedly, uncomfortably and feeling chilly. The moment came and went without passion, messily and far too quickly. Adjusting their clothing before anyone came near them, but still dishevelled, they picked up the heavily creased raincoat and walked together to the nearest tube station, saying little.

9

'From a gabled roof the rolling melon has two choices.'

Jane Kwok had two names: that was her proper one, but her professional name was Nancy Fook. She thought it sounded more interesting than her real one, which she used to conceal her true identity, essential when dealing with the most intimate details of clients' lives.

Born of an English mother and a Chinese father, she had been married and divorced, and had two children. At fifty-two years old, her life had encompassed years of studying and practising fortune-telling, writing the occasional short articles for both English and Chinese language magazines, and being interviewed on Hong Kong television.

Recently she had made herself available for private interviews in rented rooms in a dull block off the Nathan Road on Hong Kong's Kowloon side. She spaced out appointments, made by telephone only, but to her own convenience. She specifically asked clients – a mixture of Western and Oriental – not to tell her their surnames. Several clients were highly placed officials and businessmen who regularly sought her advice, expectant that important business or political decisions might rely on her ability to forecast the future. It was especially true of her more highly superstitious Chinese clients, who readily surrendered to her powers, verging on her becoming a serious influence in their lives. Other clients were well-off Westerners, white trash otherwise known as gweilos, and tourists answering discreet advertisements displayed in hotel foyers.

She wore exotic jewels dangling from her ears and ridiculous flouncy cotton dresses, daring enough to reveal and accentuate her large breasts and stomach. This bizarre creature was interesting and jolly, and her regularly dyed black hair still looked thick, strategically covering up a thinning patch on the crown. Her dark brown inscrutable Oriental eyes met her clients' honestly but shrewdly calculating, full of worldly and no doubt otherworldly knowledge. In no way was she overpowering or mysterious and many an apparently strait-laced person had fallen for her psychic powers.

'Isn't it going to be scary?' friends asked as soon as they had learnt Tak-yan was having her fortune told. They were suspicious because she was only seventeen years old. Perhaps some thought her a little young to be concerned about her future to that extent. But Tak-yan didn't care. She had come to a crossroads in her life and needed someone to show her which way to go but she didn't want every week in her life forecasted. She felt quite capable of handling the everyday decisions, hopes, errors, fears and expectations and the essential element of the unknown. It was just that she wanted some inkling about the likely direction of her life.

Tak-yan had saved money for the fee from casual work before she telephoned Nancy to make an appointment at her office. She quoted her price for her forty-minute consultation in Hong Kong dollars, US dollars and in sterling, which included a tape if she wanted it.

'What if she has bad news?', 'Supposing you're going to die young?', 'What will happen then – won't it upset you?', 'Tak-yan, you're really brave!' were comments from her friends, with varying degrees of scepticism.

She wished sometimes that she hadn't started on this, but her mother had got hold of Nancy's telephone number from a Chinese-language paper.

As the day of the meeting got closer, she never once felt apprehensive or fearful. She was ready to have her fortune told, and her past too. She was looking forward to it, wondering what mysteries might lurk in the pathway of the rest of her life, however long or short it might be.

She travelled across the harbour on the Star Ferry. Reaching the Kowloon side she walked through the bustling streets ending up at the top end of the Nathan Road and then turned right to Nancy's address. The multi-coloured neon advertising strips and hoardings in English and Chinese hung, it seemed, from each building, on top of and alongside one another.

Outside Nancy's building, much like any other in the vicinity, the ground floor was given over to a leather goods shop and entry to Nancy's quarters was up the dull grey concrete staircase to the second floor. There was no lift, and the old unpainted building stank of overflowing urinals mixed with incense.

Tak-yan was a little early but passed the time browsing round the leather goods shop. She summoned her courage and walked up the stairs and knocked on Nancy's door. Hearing a woman's voice reply, 'Come in', she pushed the door open and walked expectantly and humbly into Nancy's office.

The room was lit by one stark lightbulb suspended from the ceiling on a long worn-out flex and without any shading. Thin sticks of joss placed in old jamjars smouldered slowly, and the strong aroma gave the room a soothing spiritual atmosphere. Nancy sat in the far corner of the room. A cheerful red cotton tablecloth depicting star signs covered the table in front of her. She smiled and beckoned Tak-yan towards her.

'Hello!' she said.

'I'm Tak-yan.'

'Yes, I know. How are you?'

'Fine, thanks.'

'Shall we start? You can choose any three methods from this menu.'

'Will it make any difference which ones I choose?'

'Not a bit. It will come out the same!'

'I'll have palmistry, tarot cards and clairvoyance.'

'Good. Now can I look at both your palms? Just put them out in front of you,' Nancy asked gently, softly, kindly. Her voice alone was enough to send Tak-yan into a trance!

'Like this?' Tak-yan asked as she obediently turned the palms of her rather delicate, slim-fingered hands upwards, placing them before Nancy and looking into her eyes expectantly.

'I'm going to concentrate on the right hand.' As she did so, Nancy sensually caressed her hand, and giving Tak-yan her undivided attention, she read what she saw in the life line.

'You will live beyond fifty. . . You will die suddenly from illness.' Then she moved to the head line. 'Your head rules your heart and you make calculated judgements. The heart line is interesting and shows you will marry. Just put your hand into a fist like this. Yes. At the side here I see a child. It looks like one. You haven't got a child already, have you?'

'No!' Tak-yan replied.

'Are you married?'

'No! Not yet!' Tak-yan said, wondering if Nancy thought she was older than she really was. Could she have been mistaken?

'It's all there in the hand. Sometimes it's difficult for us fortune-tellers to interpret time, so I have to ask you to confirm your present situation.'

She moved her fingers to examine her Mount of Jupiter. 'Yes, here I see a prominent bump indicating that you have a strong character. You're better working on your own. There's only one boss as far as you're concerned! So you must be aware of that whenever you work with other people.' By now Nancy had gained Tak-yan's complete confidence and her undivided attention.

'One more thing, before we leave the palm. I can see that you have had turbulence in your life so far. I see a long journey when you were young, and different homes. Did you come over here as an immigrant? You're an only child too.'

'Yes. I came over with my parents when I was very young.'

'Just as I thought! Do you know, Tak-yan, we are all born with the various characteristics already imprinted on our hands. If I had read your palm several years ago, I would have identified exactly the same readings.'

'I'm so impressed,' Tak-yan replied, trying hard not to get drawn into too much conversation, which might have given Nancy useful clues to make her job easier.

'Now I'm going to identify your concern. Let's see. Yes, you're not sure what you will be doing with your life. Like most of us!. . . Yes. I see bright lights, music, men and dancing. You like dancing. You will be financially secure, eventually but not straightaway. I see a meeting that will change your life quite dramatically – there will be a journey overseas. Now I will use tarot cards. Please shuffle them: I'll read them and use clairvoyance to help me more.'

'I'm amazed!' Tak-yan exclaimed quite genuinely. Even though Nancy appreciated the feedback, she suspected she could see right through her anyway!

'Please take these cards and shuffle them.'

'They're rather large aren't they? Does it matter how many times I shuffle?' Tak-yan noticed Nancy had rather too much make-up on her face. The outsized earrings made her look exotic and her dress with the light behind it revealed a great deal of her body.

'No, not all. It won't make any difference what you do. When you've finished, divide the shuffled pack into three piles, gather them up and return them to me as a whole pack.'

'Like this?' Tak-yan asked.

'That's good.'

Tak-yan applied an old-fashioned shuffle to the large, unwieldy and heavily worn cards. While Tak-yan concentrated hard on the shuffle, Nancy took the chance for a few seconds of relaxation, clearing her mind, looking for a temporary distraction, however trivial. She focused on an old sepia photograph, hung in such a way that the glass reflected a shaft of sunlight, possibly a timely omen. Tak-yan had already handed over her inexpensive wristwatch, which Nancy pressed hard against the cards. With her eyes closed, she softly asked the question, 'Will Tak-yan have a happy and prosperous life?' and then repeated the question twice.

Nancy laid out the cards taken from the top of the pack in an order which enabled her to read out her interpretation. She paused.

'Hmm. You'll be successful but there'll be conflict. . . It won't be easy. Your life will change dramatically when you marry. . . I see lovers. There is intrigue surrounding your life in another country. I see treachery.'

'Thank you,' Tak-yan responded, confused, quite unable to connect her present with the future that Nancy had predicted. Her knees shook and her head swam with confusion. The strong smell of burning incense had heightened her feeling of unreality.

'Don't worry! Everything will turn out fine, but it'll be an adventurous life, not without danger,' Nancy said kindly, with those all-knowing eyes, twinkling wickedly, which so enchanted and fascinated her clients.

'Now, Tak-yan, is there anything you want to ask me?'

'Can you tell me more about the child?'

'Please shuffle the tarot cards again and we'll see,' Nancy replied.

Tak-yan put the giant cards down in much the same way as she had done before.

'I see a boy child. He will be a creative boy and will go to university. He will be a businessman connected with design, and he'll be happy and successful.'

'Will my marriage be successful?'

'You must be aware that your marriage will be under strain from time to time. Is there anything else you want to know?' said Nancy. So many times she knew more but said less, not wanting to elaborate.

'No. I think that's all, thank you.' Tak-yan replied, handing over the Hong Kong dollars in payment.

'Would you like the tape?' Nancy asked as she turned off the machine and took it out of the slot.

'Yes, please.'

'Here's your watch back too. It's rather warm! Sorry about that!'

When Tak-yan left Nancy's exotic room, she rejoined the masses of people shopping and going about their normal business. She felt detached from them, stunned by Nancy's skill at reading both her past and her future. She found the experience spooky and a little scary, and there was something in Nancy's eyes and voice as she spoke which told her that she was keeping something back, something which made her uneasy.

Nancy's face was constantly in her mind and when Tak-yan told her friends they were intrigued.

'I'm going to ring up Nancy and make an appointment right now!' they said.

10

'One lamp cannot light two houses.'

My sources told me much about Algie's life. His three years' studying mathematics and science at Cambridge had been enjoyable; he'd taken full advantage of the scholastic and social life of the university and of his college, and he had devoted a part of his life to pleasures and distractions that appealed to his unrestrained and sometimes dangerous character, an aberration conveniently put down to his Celtic ancestry. In his student days he possessed an unrestrained passion and flair to deliberately seek out the situations that bordered on being downright dangerous.

At one wedding he was invited to, Algie met Philippa. He spotted her across the length of the marquee – both being tall, they had an advantage over others in the crowd. Immediately striking, slim with dark features and a mysteriously pale skin, her green eyes danced expressively above her warm, generous and smiling mouth, Philippa had about her an air of vulnerability. Algie remembered for years afterwards what she wore when they first met; it was a light blue fitted coat with matching hat of light blue petals that she had made herself.

'May I introduce myself? I'm Algie,' he announced confidently after the first couple of glasses of champagne.

'I'm Philippa. Are you local?' She had been stuck with an elderly group and was delighted that Algie had come along to rescue her. Having exchanged encouraging glances several times, it only needed Algie to summon up the necessary courage to go across to her.

'Yes, I'm a fireman!' said Algie, waiting to see how the reply went down. It amused Algie to give way to a sudden impulse.

'Gosh! That sounds interesting!' exclaimed Philippa enthusiastically.

'Oh, it is!'

'How long have you been doing this for? What made you become a fireman? I'd love to know much more, do tell me!' asked Philippa so enthusiastically that Algie continued to concoct a plausible story as he went along.

'Now tell me about yourself, are you from London?' asked Algie.

'Yes, I've known the bride for years. Her father and mine both had farms where we grew up in Suffolk. We had such fun. Daisy is such good news, and I'm mad about her husband too. Have you known Daisy long?' asked Philippa, talking in a distinctly breathless way, hardly a moment to draw in breath, all outward!

'Actually, no – only a few months. We met at a cocktail party, and then out of the blue she kindly invited me to her wedding. So here we are!'

'You must have made quite an impression on her. By the way, thanks for rescuing me. I was getting rather hemmed in and very bored. Tell me, do you free a lot of damsels in distress?'

'Too many to count!' replied Algie with twinkling eyes.

They stayed close together for the rest of the reception, in harmony and at ease with each other from the first moment of their meeting. Afterwards they went out to dinner, buoyed up by the effects of an afternoon's champagne drinking. Since Philippa was staying with Daisy's parents, she managed to get Algie invited to lunch there the following day. After a jolly lunch she went back to London by train, but not before Algie had arranged to meet her the following weekend.

She shared a ground floor flat with two other girls in a large purpose-built Victorian mansion block in South Kensington, a few minutes' walk from the tube station. It was her grandmother's flat and the two girls effectively paid rent to Philippa.

Algie arrived up from the country on the Friday night and pressed the doorbell in eager anticipation. He had planned to take her out to dinner and then play it by ear. Philippa answered the door.

'Hello, Algie, do come in! Good journey? Let's have a drink. Whisky all right for you?' she asked.

Wearing a short black dress she looked stunning and Algie caught a whiff of expensive perfume. She wrapped her arms round him as they hugged closely and firmly and then with elegant strides she led the way down a corridor into the sitting room. On the side table a tray of bottles and glasses stood ready. Philippa poured them both two fingers' worth of scotch into heavy crystal tumblers.

'Your good health! It's really good to see you!' They toasted each other enthusiastically and then sat down. Philippa took a chair opposite Algie and crossed her long elegant legs.

'This whisky is just the job and the way I like it. I thought we'd go to the Bistro d'Art tonight. Could I possibly use your telephone to book a table?'

'It's right here. Help yourself. Do you know the number? It sounds a lovely idea. Algie, while I remember, I've been dying to ask you something.'

'Go on.'

'You promise to tell the truth?'

'Yes, I promise,' he replied warily.

'I don't think you're a fireman at all!'

'What makes you think that?'

'Put it down to feminine intuition, if you like! Come on, you promised to tell me the truth.' Philippa pressed for the answer.

'Don't you think I make a good fireman?' he asked.

'I've no idea. I'll be very angry if you're having me on. Now stop mucking me about,' she demanded, suddenly changing her mood, a touch of annoyance in her voice signalling Algie to respond.

'You're absolutely right. I'm an undergraduate at Cambridge!'

'There you are, I thought so! Good try, Algie. All the same, I was convinced for quite a time.'

He made the table booking using the number in the little black book in which he kept the telephone numbers and addresses of friends, girlfriends and restaurants.

They had a happy evening together and returned to the flat having taken a taxi back. In the darkness they cuddled and kissed and held each other passionately. As the taxi drew up to the mansion block, Philippa unwound her legs from across Algie's lap, gathered herself together and smoothed down her dress, which had risen up to her thighs. Adjusting her twisted black stockings and without the slightest inhibition she turned to him. 'Come up for a nightcap?' She looked him straight in the eyes and with a hint of mischief and a conspiratorial smile, kissed him possessively on the lips. It was her way of getting him to make up his mind.

'Is that OK?' he asked, pretending to be calm.

'Of course! I wouldn't have asked you if it weren't!'

He paid off the taxi and hand-in-hand the couple went into the flat. Philippa put the kettle on and as she did so, the couple hugged and kissed, pressing their bodies tightly against each other. They couldn't leave each other alone. Before the kettle had boiled he lifted her up in his straining arms and carried her without the slightest protest into the bedroom.

Algie stayed the rest of the night with her in her double bed and they became lovers. This time he was spared having to sleep in the waiting room at Liverpool Street Station, stranded, as he often was, until the milk train left for Cambridge, particularly when he had blown his modest allowance.

After that Algie came to London to see Philippa almost

every weekend. The flat was usually empty except for Philippa, and they enjoyed having the place to themselves. By the time the weekends came round, they were hungry for each other and lived only for the present.

Three months passed quickly and the relationship was becoming so strong that they were regarded as 'a couple' among their friends, invited together to weddings and dinner parties. One night after a rather boozy supper party they staggered back to her flat.

'You bastard! Why were you chatting up my best friend like that? I was so embarrassed,' she shouted, blazing with anger, standing close up to Algie, her blue eyes flashing, staring straight at him, hands on her hips like a fishwife. This wasn't the Philippa he knew.

'What do you mean?' asked Algie, totally unaware that he had caused offence.

'You know what I bloody mean! I hate men! You're all the same. I suppose you thought you would get into her knickers when you've finished with me?'

'Don't be so damn silly. Look here, darling, I don't know what's got into you but you're behaving most irrationally.'

'Don't patronise me with your 'darling this' and 'irrational that', who the fuck do you think you are?'

'I am the person who loves you. There's no one else, so get that into your head!'

Her arms had come off her hips and there was a sign that she was running out of steam, but it was taking time and there was no way he could rush her.

'So d-a-r-l-i-n-g,' she drawled with a strong hint of sarcasm, imitating Algie, 'I have news for you!'

'What's that?' enquired Algie eagerly.

'You'd better sit down!'

'Come on, what is it?' Algie was expecting a summons to Scotland to meet her parents and he wasn't looking forward to that. Perhaps she had found someone else and wanted to break off the affair.

'I'm pregnant!' said Philippa proudly.

'Christ!'

'Can't you think of anything better to say?'

'What a surprise! Oh, darling, that's marvellous. Are you pleased?'

'I think so. Are you?'

'You know I am.' Algie went forward to her, gathered her in his arms and held her protectively. He thought she was wonderful and he told her so.

'You are a clever girl!' he said reassuringly, understanding that the spat of a few minutes ago had probably been brought on by Philippa's insecurity about the baby and worry about how he would take the news.

'You had quite a lot to do with it! I suppose it was inevitable. We never take any precautions, do we?'

'I suppose so.'

They had been reckless but they were happy. There was a good measure of pride too that they had created something together. It was only later, as the days went by and Philippa's parents were told, that the economic reality of their situation started to sink in. Her parents were in deep shock, knowing that Algie had little money and was still an undergraduate. There was concern, too, about what friends and relatives might think. Despite the negative reactions, the couple loved each other and had a blind faith that all would be well.

They strolled hand in hand through Hyde Park, starting at the southern end of Kensington Gardens, past the Albert Memorial, the Peter Pan statue and across the Serpentine. The route took them to the north end of the park, leaving Bayswater on their right, pausing to look at the paintings hanging on the railings, down past Kensington Palace and the kite-flyers around the pond.

'It's fascinating seeing so many large dogs. Do you think they're all kept in flats?'

'I don't know. I see what you mean though. I've never

thought of that before.'

'Look at the young kids playing football with their dads. That's what you'll be doing soon! And look at the young ones in those rather special prams. So adorable.'

The attitude of her family, which turned decidedly against them marrying and having the baby, hadn't been properly taken into account by the couple. Harsh realities had to be faced, but as each obstacle was pointed out to them they stuck firmly to the belief that they could manage. There was only a short time left if Philippa was to have an abortion safely; a decision had to be made, and fast.

Without much consultation, her mother took matters into her own hands and suddenly packed Philippa off to Switzerland alone, to have an abortion. Despite her protests Philippa succumbed, as usual, to her mother's demands.

From a telephone box in Cambridge, armed with a mass of coins, Algie called Philippa at the clinic in Switzerland. He had lived every moment of her agony, both real and imagined.

'Darling, how are you? I've been so worried about you. Are you OK?' He shouted down the line, thinking she might hear better in Switzerland.

'I'm fine, just a bit tired. Tomorrow I'll be back and then I'll see you at the weekend. Everything's gone well, except that my hormones are erratic and I feel very tired.'

He wondered if she was feeling the same sense of loss as he was and the same feeling of resentment that all the arrangements had been made without any real agreement.

'I can't wait to see you on Friday,' said Philippa, as if nothing had happened.

'Same here. I've got to go now, darling, I'm running out of coins. Lots of love, and take care.' They blew kisses down the telephone and he hung up the receiver. Pensively, he returned to his college rooms.

When the weekend came, Philippa couldn't have been more loving. They hugged for several minutes, then she started to cry and shake uncontrollably. The tension and emotion of the last few days had come to a head. He took out his handkerchief and dabbed her eyes, cradling her head in the crook of his free arm.

'Darling, you're so brave. I still love you, even more than before – if that's possible!'

'You're so sweet,' she sobbed back, 'wouldn't you have wanted the baby really?'

'Of course, but we had no alternative, did we? Everything happened so quickly with you going off to Switzerland.'

'When I was in Switzerland I thought about it a lot, and I had time alone without the family breathing down my neck. I am bitter and resentful that we couldn't have had the baby. I thought of the tiny embryo being taken out of me and flushed down some plughole in Switzerland. A part of me went with it, you see, and that will be with me all my life. Then I wondered how it would be between us when I got back to London. Would you still love me? Would you blame me for getting rid of the baby? Would you be wondering if it might have been a boy or a girl? Would it have looked like you? All those sort of things.'

'What do you imagine I've been thinking?' he asked, holding her closely to him. Her sobbing had stopped now. She was talking openly about the abortion, relieving the pent-up tension, the sorrow and sense of loss.

'I know, darling, but it is different for men. Let's have a drink!' she said, wanting to change the subject.

'You get it and then come back and sit beside me. I want to cuddle up to you. Keep me warm. I keep getting the shivers, like someone is walking over my grave.'

Any worries he had that she might have blamed him for what she had been through and making her frigid towards him had been unfounded. Getting through the ordeal together had somehow strengthened their relationship, quite the reverse of what her parents had intended.

After a few months, pressure was put on Philippa by her mother to return to Scotland to live up there for a while to regain her strength. Philippa agreed. Her mother had long ago separated from Philippa's father and took pleasure in ruthlessly intercepting Algie's letters as though all men were to be wary of. The couple ingeniously countered this by putting in place a system for Philippa to collect his letters from a poste restante address in Glasgow. For a time this tactic worked, but with increasingly determined vigilance on her mother's part Algie knew it would be tricky for Philippa whenever they met in Glasgow.

It had become increasingly more difficult for them to communicate, so that when they finally made arrangements for a rendezvous, they had so little time together. They managed a picnic right outside the city of bought sandwiches and a cheap bottle of dry white wine, and later that afternoon they returned for a snatched moment of passion in the inexpensive bed and breakfast place that Philippa had booked for him close to the city centre.

It had been so good seeing her, and rather satisfying to have broken through the obstacles her mother had put in their way. But, over time, Algie's ability to travel to Glasgow and Philippa's letter-writing efforts gradually diminished. He knew she was under intense pressure from her mother, wearing her down to end the affair and he well understood the exhausting subterfuge involved in keeping the relationship alive. Her mother deliberately arranged for Philippa to accept a constant programme of invitations to dances, balls and parties in Scotland with the serious hope that she would meet a more eligible bachelor.

It was only a question of time before Algie received a letter from Philippa saying that she had met someone who looked much like him, even down to the hairy chest! A few weeks later yet another letter came, telling him that she was engaged. Algie was devastated. It took him a long time to adjust to a life without her. There had always been a glimmer of hope, so long as she didn't meet someone else, and particularly someone approved of by her mother but a man she might not love. Now that possibility was dashed for good.

零 零 零

Several years elapsed before their paths crossed again. Algie was staying in Northampton with Daisy, by now divorced and remarried, when Philippa's name came up. Daisy had told him she was living quite near to them, and that Philippa had asked if he would call in on her on his way back to London. Algie suspected that Daisy and Philippa had typically conspired between them to set him up.

He drove back to London the next morning, his mind a whirl of past memories that he had kept locked away in his mind and were now reopened. The rawness of the emotions distracted him from driving safely. Daisy had called Philippa to say he would drop in for coffee at around ten o'clock. The traffic was light and he had made good time. When he got there he found that Philippa was quite unchanged. She greeted him warmly at the door with that same look of enchantment he so vividly remembered at their first meeting, but they did not kiss.

'It's so good to see you, Algie! Do come in. You look just the same! You haven't changed an inch. We have the house to ourselves. My husband is at work and the children are at school, so we can catch up on the news without any fear,' Philippa told him without drawing breath, excited and nervous. She had lost none of that disarming air of vulnerability, and he was relieved that her abortion had not stopped her from having more children.

They chatted about nothing and everything, but not their past together, and soon it was time for him to leave.

But there was still an underlying tension, an attraction which the years apart had done nothing to diminish. Their chemistry was dangerous.

'Look, Algie, this is my telephone number. Let's meet in London sometime? It would be such fun to do that. Like old times,' she said quite blatantly.

'Why not? This is my number if you need it,' he replied in answer to the challenge. He had nothing to lose.

'It would be really lovely to meet,' Philippa continued to press for an agreement.

She had come back into his life again and it didn't surprise him when he got a call from her only a few days later to arrange a clandestine meeting. He had to keep it very much to himself.

On the agreed day, he arrived in London sufficiently early to book a table at the restaurant he had chosen for their lunch together, discrete, friendly and romantic, in Walton Street, close to Harrods. He earmarked just the table he wanted, for two in the corner, away from the window and the glance of casual passers-by. Then he walked back to Harrods, his heartbeat quickening in anticipation. He found her immediately, waiting in the banking-hall just off the famous food section on the ground floor, looking her usual tall, beautiful and elegant self. Suddenly he was aware that her vulnerability was more pronounced as he greeted her and escorted her down Walton Street, hoping they wouldn't be spotted together. He was very much aware of the considerable risk she was taking, and not for the first time he admired her pluck.

'Good afternoon, sir and madam. What can I do for you?' asked the manager in a strong foreign accent as he received them at the door. Algie was annoyed that he hadn't been recognised.

'I booked a table with you personally only an hour ago! The table I chose is over there!' replied Algie testily.

'I do apologise, sir. Please follow me. Can I take madam's

coat? Would you care for the menu and wine list?'

'Yes, please.'

When they were settled down, it was just like old times. Sitting opposite each other at a small circular table, Algie gingerly clamped his legs round Philippa's and she didn't resist him. They ordered two gin and tonics followed by a main course of seared salmon with white wine, served by attentive young Mediterranean waiters who seemed to have sensed the romantic occasion. No doubt they were used to lunching lovers, illicit or otherwise!

The restaurant, despite the agreeable atmosphere, was empty at first but it soon filled up. They chatted away and the combination of the drinks and the ambience helped them both to relax. She wore a tightly fitting polo-neck top with a long string of pearls beneath a tailored suit. Either deliberately or by chance, she was wearing exactly the style of clothes he had liked her in best. He wondered sentimentally if she had remembered his taste from all those years ago.

After the meal she was due to catch a train from Waterloo to Basingstoke, where she was staying with her parents-in-law. Algie took her to the station in his car and when he had found somewhere to park he turned off the engine. Appealingly she cuddled up close to him and started to cry.

'Darling, it's been so lovely today. Thank you so much. I know it must sound strange, but I still love you, you know. I also love my husband, and I just wish I could have you both. Please let's do it again!'

Algie produced his handkerchief from the top pocket of his best suit and wiped her eyes tenderly. Her make-up was beginning to smudge and he carefully cleaned her face as one might a child's. It reminded them both of the special moment in the past when she had just returned from Switzerland and their first weekend back together in the flat.

'If you were married too, we could all meet up without this subterfuge and then I could see you more often!' she sobbed.

He escorted her gently onto the train and they settled into an empty compartment. At the last minute Algie decided to travel with her. At Basingstoke station they planned to leave the train separately, he to cross over to the other platform and return to London. It was extra time together and despite the improbability of a future together, he had no wish to leave her feeling sad and tearful.

In the compartment they sat like Siamese twins, joined at as many points as was decently possible. She put one hand in his and the other she pushed down deep into his trouser pocket, caressing and squeezing him as he held her to him. Her sobbing died down for the first part of the journey, but as the train got nearer to Basingstoke she just clung to him helplessly and without a word. There was nothing more to be said. Algie envied her husband – he was a lucky man. Algie wondered what sort of a man and a husband he was. The train came inevitably to Basingstoke station. In a moment she was out of the train and through the ticket barrier without ever looking back. Having deliberately let her get ahead of him, Algie left the train himself from a door farther down the carriage and made his lone return to London.

11

'If heaven made him, earth can find some use for him.'

I grew up bright enough to get a place at the prestigious St John's University in Shanghai, where I studied science subjects and met a cross section of undergraduates who later in my life became useful contacts. It was somehow natural, given the influence of my father's professional reputation in the Secret Service that I would follow in his footsteps, destined for the Service by family tradition. I had no wish to be a lawyer or businessman and the life of a Secret Service official really appealed to me. Despite the episode of my father's arrest, I was accepted into the service and vowed to avenge the wrong done to his honour and to our family's reputation.

In the 1970s I was appointed to work in the Chinese Secret Service department in Beijing, on the Hong Kong Desk. My department had been most thorough in its research; once we had decided on a target we took time looking into the smallest detail that might reveal the character and weaknesses of our prey. We joked whenever our chief asked if we knew the colour and size of our target's underpants! If we didn't know, he became angry and sent us away to find out.

I had been called into the briefing officer's room to receive the background information on Hong Kong ahead of the more detailed and secret briefings about Secret Service strategy and targets.

'As you know, British Forces are stationed in Hong Kong to assist the Hong Kong government in maintaining the security and stability of the Colony. The peace of the Colony has been threatened several times by civil disturbances, most notably by the violent rioting in the streets, which we inspired. The domination of our mainland by the Party under our Chairman Mao Tse-tung has made relations between China and Hong Kong difficult. Illegal immigrants cross over the land or sea borders from the mainland into Hong Kong at an alarming rate. It is not unusual for our people to swim, quite illegally, across the expanse of sea supported only by inflated footballs, so great has been their desperation. Not all of them are strong swimmers and the bodies of the weak and unsuccessful are regularly found washed up on the northern and western shores of the New Territories.

'Since the British government's policy of "substantial withdrawal of British forces from east of Suez" came into operation, Hong Kong's administration came in line for reorganisation and will report direct to the Ministry of Defence in London. Singapore, until now the main Far East headquarters for British Forces deployed in the Far East, is to be run down too. The British Army deploys mainly Gurkha troops, so-called mercenaries from Nepal, to patrol the area in the north of the New Territories, which borders the mainland of China. Elsewhere, there are many other troops and units from the British Navy and Air Force scattered around the Island and the New Territories. Of course, all this will change when the lease runs out and Hong Kong reverts to China.

'The economic heartland of Hong Kong is the magnificent natural harbour, which lies between Hong Kong Island and the tip of the Kowloon Peninsular on the mainland. Severe gales caused by tropical cyclones are expected annually in any of the months from May to November, but most likely from July to September. Gales have been experienced once a year on average. Sometimes the centre or 'eye' of a mature typhoon passes sufficiently close to the Colony to produce winds of hurricane force, which severely endangers both life and property. The 'eye' of one relatively small typhoon can cause hundreds to be killed or injured and thousands made homeless. Ocean-going vessels have been sunk or washed aground; hundreds of small craft have been sunk or damaged; several hydrofoils and cross-harbour ferries have been put out of action.

'Kai Tak, the airfield and its runway, have been built much like Hong Kong itself; in response to demand, reclaiming land from the sea. This civil engineering process involves pouring rubble into the sea to create a firm and solid landmass. The runway at Kai Tak was built out from the Kowloon mainland piecemeal in this way, continuously heading further and further out to sea.'

The briefing went on for an hour and I was getting bored. I was interested in some background information, particularly in the changes that had taken place since my father was there and over the intervening years, which he had already told me about, but I wanted to focus on the main target of our covert operation.

零　零　零

Algie's career move at Science International to the overseas business division began when he was twenty-five. Since leaving Cambridge, he had been involved with the UK-based company at their Surrey headquarters, liaising with the British Ministry of Defence in Whitehall over the type of weapons his firm could provide for the British Armed Forces. The company made assessments both in terms of the technical and commercial feasibility of projects and its own ability to meet specifications and deadlines. It took a long time for an idea to become reality, for a weapon system to be put into production, tested and eventually brought into service in the armed forces.

It was some time, too, before Algie was considered for an overseas posting to the company's Hong Kong office, the key Far East base for the promotion of weapon sales and technology to countries around the Pacific Basin. It had been a well-established convention that the incumbent head of the company's Hong Kong office would also be a bona fide agent of the British Secret Service, passing back valuable weapon secrets.

His life in a small flat close to the Central district of Hong Kong Island was ideal for a bachelor. It was much like being in the centre of London, so well positioned for everything, particularly easy for shopping and crossing over the harbour by ferry, either on foot or by car. His bedroom had a view across the harbour to Kowloon and the mainland. He could see the busy harbour with ships of all sizes, the constant movement and energy, the dominant mooring of the American Navy's giant aircraft carriers stopping off on their way back from Vietnam. American sailors in best uniform spewed out of the hulks to enjoy rest and recuperative shore leave in the glittering girlie bars of Wanchai. He saw junks and sampans littering the harbour ready to attach themselves like limpets to any large ship in harbour, either to repaint the rusting vessels as they lay still or to offload cargo to the 'go-downs' as the wharf warehouses are called. Because his quarters weren't air-conditioned, Algie was always aware of the mewing and hooting sounds of the busy harbour and the onshore traffic activity.

Hong Kong life, despite the intense work and social activity could become claustrophobic. Well-educated British girls went to Hong Kong much as they might have gone in earlier years to India in the days of the Raj, drawn to the excitement of the place, the possibility of having fun far away from home and the search for a husband. Some were on a posting with the Foreign Office and others arrived with only a slight connection they used to find themselves accommodation and work.

Algie first met Barbara in Hong Kong. She had come out alone to make a life for herself. Her father had died recently and she needed to get away from her over-reliant mother. She was employed as a secretary in another non-sensitive part of the military headquarters. Working closely with the military, Algie had his own office tucked away in the headquarters, which he used as his base and provided him with the necessary cover.

One day, soon after her arrival, Barbara was walking down the corridor looking for his office to deliver a message from her boss. At first, she walked straight past Algie's open door, giving him a glimpse of the yellow mini dress which, even at a quick glance, accentuated her shapely legs and full figure and set off her long blonde hair. She smiled and as she turned away from him Algie noticed marks from the wicker typing seat she had been sitting on, engraved like lattice work on the backs of her tanned legs. Short skirts were the fashion and Hong Kong was always well up to date with the latest designs, mostly copied cheaply from the leading fashion houses of Europe.

She returned to Algie's door. 'Hello, I'm Barbara, secretary to one of the civilian departments here. My boss asked me to give you this message.'

'Come in, please. Do sit down,' he said getting up from behind his desk and trying hard to appear unflustered. Normally his office door was securely locked whenever he was away, but she had caught him 'at home'. Algie kept her talking for as long as possible, searching hard to find an excuse to see her again.

'So you're new to Hong Kong – would you like to come to a party with me tomorrow night?' he asked outright.

'That would be nice. Thanks, what's the form?' she asked enthusiastically.

'A friend of mine is giving the party and I'm sure he won't mind me bringing you. It'll be a good chance for you to meet some people. Shall I pick you up at 6.30? Oh yes, you'd better tell me your address.'

He had managed a full social life in Hong Kong without

jeopardising his cover. To those who did not know him, Algie gave an outward impression of callousness and indifference. Even though it was some years in the past, it was a self-protective mechanism he had developed after the let-down with Philippa. Determined to deny his deeply sensitive nature, he was reluctant to get too close to anyone emotionally. It didn't mean that he didn't fancy women or that he didn't have affairs, it was just that he was guarded about making any commitment.

Algie knew intuitively that with Barbara he might be on dangerous ground. She had made him recognise his own vulnerability. Something about her told him she had experienced tragedy in her life and that like him she was avoiding hurt. He wondered if she had come to Hong Kong not only to get away from her mother but also an ending love affair. It was often the case with people who moved to Hong Kong, but he didn't think she would be without a man for long.

Expeditions to a bungalow in the New Territories were a favourite pastime, usually made up of specially invited groups of friends of both sexes. It was quite a drive, making it best to visit for a long weekend or a public holiday. Cars were loaded up with essential supplies at Victoria on the Island before crossing the harbour on the ferry. From the Kowloon side, the road took them north along the coast via Castle Peak, deep into the peaceful and sparsely populated countryside of the New Territories.

Guests would bring provisions and comforts capable of being carried on the back. The men brought drinks and cold boxes while the women, under an appointed and experienced 'head girl' – often Barbara – planned meals and brought the ingredients. Each person was allocated a job so that everyone made a contribution. All supplies had to be packed such that they could be carried for the last mile along the concrete paths skirting the paddy fields and up the final steep climb to the bungalow itself. It wasn't a weekend for the faint-hearted, especially with the lack of mod cons. The girls shared a dormitory with bunk beds, and the men lay out either on the veranda or inside on the floor in sleeping bags on lilos.

'Why the hell aren't you ready?' Barbara demanded of Algie in a bad temper when he answered the flat door to her. She had parked her car at the underground parking bay normally reserved for the residents and in a place they could transfer her supplies to his car more easily.

'Sorry I'm late. Running a bit behind, I'm afraid,' said Algie irritably, having just woken up with a start from the incessant ringing of the doorbell. With a towel hastily wrapped round his waist he looked in poor shape, dirty, unshaven and his hair unbrushed.

'Come in! Help yourself to coffee. I need to shave but I won't be long,' he said casually.

'You look a bloody mess! What have you been up to?' she asked bluntly, still hung-over herself from a different party she had been to the night before.

'Just a late Friday night session in the Wanchai. I can't remember much!'

'I thought so. I'll wait. Do you mind if I put on the radio?'

'Carry on,' he shouted from the bathroom above the sound of hot water running into the basin. A wet shave soon gave him vigour. He dressed quickly and went to the kitchen to put a couple of pieces of bread into the toaster.

'Sure you don't want to join me in a coffee or something else, toast? It's going to be a long drive and it'll be some time before we get settled the other end.'

'Alright, you know best,' she said icily, and came into the small kitchen where there was little room for either of them to move about. Refreshed, Algie saw the world in a different light. Even though he was still drunk from the night before, the sight of Barbara in her loose-fitting and short shift dress made him feel randy.

'Come here!' he demanded clumsily.

'Why?' she asked.

'Because – because I want to put my arms around you,' he said, trying to sound appealing. An urge had come over him.

'Come off it, Algie, we've got no time for that now! Hurry up, we must get going to meet the others at the ferry,' she responded, deftly seeing off a tricky situation and putting Algie down without much difficulty. She hadn't given him the slightest hint that he even had a chance with her.

He tried his luck once more in the car before they set off having transferred her stuff into his now fully-loaded car. From then on there would be other people about and moments of being alone together would be minimal. As he started the engine and with Barbara settled in the passenger seat, he suddenly lunged across and kissed her full on her scarlet lips.

'What was all that for?' she asked angrily, hitting out at him aggressively, catching him on the side of his face with her ring. 'I've already told you to pack it in. Are you going to leave me alone or do I try and get a lift with someone else when we all meet up at the ferry?'

'Sorry,' he replied, easing back into the driver's seat of his Sunbeam Alpine sports car and checking with his hand that she hadn't drawn blood from his face. She had, and looking in the mirror he saw to his horror a deep gash down the length of his cheek.

'You bitch!' he said, 'look what you've done!'

'You asked for it!' she replied, quite unrepentant.

When they met up with the rest of the party, they sensed that Algie and Barbara had had a row and one bright spark who noticed the scratches said, 'Good to see you both, just in time. Been in a cat fight Algie?'

'Yes, 'fraid so,' he replied reddening, feeling rather obvious. He suspected it wouldn't be long before Barbara told the other females in the group what had happened.

That night, sitting around a hastily gathered wood fire, the glow from it showed up Algie's troubled, frustrated blue eyes.

Barbara was an outdoor girl, and sometimes at the cottage when eating round a table with the group she would drift into a dreamlike state. She seemed in a world of her own, unaware of the conversation around her. Men would follow her unquestioningly, and as she cast a spell of fascination over them, she gave the impression that she didn't give a damn for any of them.

If ever the weather was bad at the cottage the visitors played party games and there was plenty to drink and much loud snoring at night. Lovemaking and pairing off was discouraged, making the atmosphere more relaxed; any undercurrent of passion had to be held in check until the return to the Island at the end of the weekend.

Back on the Island, throughout the summer, there were tennis parties at Government House, launch picnics and water-skiing. At Christmas many in Hong Kong started wearing dinner jackets, making an early start to the festive season from the first week of December. But by the time Christmas came, many were prematurely exhausted.

Curiously Algie and Barbara were often seen around together; many regarded them as a couple. Although they were good friends, neither had actually expressed strong feelings for the other. Each was there for the other, but that was as far as it went. They never did move to a more intimate relationship after the incident in the car.

In London, Sergeant Jerry Flood was feeling frustrated as he'd been in the rank for three years now and hadn't yet been given some of the more juicy cases that came to Special Branch. Married with two young children, he was tempted to move out of England to join the Hong Kong Police Force. The pay and conditions were good and he would be promoted to Inspector. He wrestled with the possibility which occupied his thoughts day and night.

'Why do you want to leave England?' asked his wife, who wasn't keen to move and disrupt the children's education, but more importantly she would miss her mother.

'I'm bloody pissed off, that's why!' he replied.

12

'A whale in shallow water amuses the shrimps.'

Tak-yan by now shared a rented flat in the Wanchai with a friend who had introduced her to the mamasan of a popular girlie-bar in the red light district of Hong Kong. She knew she could earn good money there. She thought it might be fun too, infinitely preferable to working in a humdrum office. Many young Chinese girls were being recruited into this rapidly expanding and lucrative business. It was a popular attraction for the sex-hungry and cash-rich American servicemen coming to the Colony for rest and recuperation leave on their way back from the Vietnam War.

'It's easy! You start work here at 11.30 am, just in time for the lunchtime customers – they're mostly foreigners, sex starved gweilos – and you continue on until midnight. I pay you a basic wage. On top of that, I pay you a percentage of what your customers spend on you. You must treat your customers nicely, talk to them sweetly and encourage them to drink more. If a customer is so enamoured with you that he wants to take you out of the bar before time, he must negotiate a 'buying out price' with me first, you understand?' The mamasan had a touch of the exotic about her as she sat with a long cigarette holder in her hand and blew a cloud of smoke, which she watched disappear upwards to meet the nicotine-stained ceiling.

'Yes,' Tak-yan replied.

'Good. We like to create a cosy atmosphere here, welcoming and always given a hint of sex being available to our customers, far from home, longing for female company. American sailors have more money than good sense and they are easily seduced into spending cash.'

'Won't they want sex?' Tak-yan asked matter-of-factly.

'Almost certainly, they usually do! Particularly as they become more drunk. By the time they've blown all their money, their minds may be willing, but often the flesh is not! All the time we aim to entice these people by constantly hinting at the possibility of a good time. I like my girls to look sexy all the time they're on duty in my bar. You must wear very short skirts, low-fronted blouses and high-heeled shoes. I see you have a good figure. Men will go potty over you so you must show off your assets to their best advantage. I tell all my girls to cuddle up to the customers, take them into a cosy dark corner, relax them, stroke them gently down the inside of their thighs and look adoringly into their eyes. Make them think that they're the only person in the whole universe. It never fails! Don't forget they come to our bar for magic, to be taken away from the real world for a few hours.'

'It sounds fairly straightforward.' Tak-yan retorted.

'It is! Men are so easy to manipulate; you'll find that out very quickly. If they ask for sex while you're working in the bar, they must buy you out first. I've already told you that. You can charge whatever you like once you're alone with your customer away from my establishment. But there's nothing to stop your customers from waiting in the bar until you've finished work. It'll avoid them paying the buy-out price. Whatever happens, I make money and so do you. I know you will be a great success here at the Pussycat Bar. We have the best girls in Hong Kong. Don't forget, I want to see a doctor's certificate at the end of each week to say you are clean. I have a reputation for clean and pretty girls. You understand that, don't you?'

'Yes, mamasan.'

'And from now on you will be called Fleur.'

Triad gangs from the mainland, making good money from them and in hard foreign currency, operated many girlie-bars in the Wanchai. In order to maintain an unofficial operating platform on mainland China, Triads had given generously to Communist Party funds. It was a mutually beneficial exercise and a cynical way for Chinese Communists to extort funds out of the money-grabbing racketeers. So many of the hedonistic pursuits offered in Hong Kong were racket-ridden, run for the benefit of the mainland Communists.

The mamasan had once been a working bar girl herself, but promoted through age and experience to manage the air-conditioned Pussycat Bar with its dark, inviting, lavishly furnished, womb-like interior, a heavy metal-studded front door, entered only with intercom approval. Outside in the busy street a cylindrical sign, much like an old-fashioned barber's pole, illuminated the suggestive picture of a scantily clad bar girl in the guise of a black cat, which revolved garishly, saucily taunting punters.

Fleur became accustomed to the working hours and settled into the routine of sleeping between 1.00 am and 10.30 pm when she was alone. If she had a punter for sex, she usually took him to a small hotel round the corner from the bar, down a poorly-lit side street. There, smelling of carbolic, small but adequate rooms with undersized double beds, clean sheets and cramped en suite bathrooms were rented out by the hour at her client's expense.

She liked her work and better still she was beginning to save money, even after paying her portion of rent for the shared room with the smelly communal lavatory down the corridor. She planned to save enough to rent an apartment and she wondered for how much longer she could continue working like that, before her looks faded. She wondered what would become of her when she was older. She understood well enough how the earning power of a bar-girl depended upon her physical attractiveness to men. There was a no sadder sight to her mind than an ageing, once beautiful bar-girl working long after her looks had dimmed. She had seen these over-made-up, face-lined women up at the bar, sitting alone, morosely dangling from high barstools, bored, unmotivated, attracting little attention other than a mocking glance or a pitying whispered comment. They had seen better days. No longer able to attract customers, they were a poignant reminder to their younger more glamorous colleagues, settled comfortably on soft red sofas cuddling up to eager customers with the prospect of a busy night ahead, making money for themselves and the bar.

'Fleur, I think you're happy here, aren't you?' asked the mamasan one day.

'Oh yes, mamasan,' Fleur replied respectfully, genuinely happy with her lot.

'Good. Come here, my dear, you're looking very lovely today. Incidentally, have you got the doctor's certificate for this week? You know the regular fanny inspection.'

'Sorry, mamasan, I forgot to get inspected,' Fleur replied.

'I want the certificate tomorrow morning. Don't forget will you? Otherwise I will have to take stern measures.'

'You will definitely have it, mamasan.' Fleur didn't want to be asked again, especially in front of her colleagues at the bar. She had genuinely forgotten to be inspected. Sometimes she was so tired she could hardly think straight. But she was confident she would be found clean by the doctor. The past week's clients mostly had difficulty with erections or had messy premature ejaculations, but she had charged the full amount all the same.

The mamasan guided her through an open green baize door into a small room at the back of the bar. This was the place where she kept the cash, locked away in a heavy safe. Adding machines, ledgers opened at pages of figures, piles of paper and a telephone all competed for space on the littered surface of the desk. Two large glass ashtrays, filled to the brim with discarded filter cigarette butts, held down the highest piles of papers and invoices. Faded photographs of pretty young Chinese girls, some in frames, others mounted collage-style on cardboard, were hung on the walls giving life and colour to the otherwise dusty nicotine-stained spaces. This was the hub of the mamasan's empire, the place she did the books, counted cash and slipped away to for a few minutes to enjoy a cigarette before re-entering the noisy bar and the infernal beating of pop and rock music. The noise was deafening but the girls and their customers liked it. Sometimes, Fleur asked for the volume to be turned down if it interfered with her ability to entertain customers, those who wanted to talk to a female and drink in peace.

Several months passed. Fleur and the mamasan got to know each other better and before long the mamasan called her into her private back room. When she sat down, Fleur noticed the mamasan wearing a string of pearls round her neck, close to the skin. She had been told that the skin enriched pearls and she imagined she took them to bed with her. The mamasan was flicking through the social pages of the latest *Hong Kong Tatler* lying on her desk. Beneath her coarse exterior beat the heart of a social climber.

'I have an interesting proposition for you, Fleur. It could open up a new life for you. Do you want to hear what it is?' asked the mamasan mysteriously.

'Yes, mamasan' Fleur replied, wary of any proposition put to her.

'This is a very serious and important request and I want you to treat this discussion with the utmost secrecy. Do you understand? Otherwise, there could be a nasty accident,' she said, drawing her extended finger murderously across her throat.

'Yes, mamasan.'

'I told you when you first joined me that money from here goes back to the mainland. By working here all my life, I've believed I have done more for the Party by being away from the home country. Since you've been here, I've seriously thought that, with the success you have in the bar, your good looks and intelligence, you would make a first-class secret agent. It probably sounds like an idea out of the blue, one you're not at all prepared for.'

'I'll consider anything you ask, mamasan,' Fleur replied obediently without any further thought. Her reply showed that she came from a culture where younger women respected and obeyed their elders. It also showed how important her economic reliance was on the continuing favour of the mamasan.

'Very good. I had hoped you'd say that. Even so, you must think on it for a few days. Then we'll talk again. Remember, not a word to anyone.'

It didn't take long for her to make up her mind. Fleur reported back to mamasan two days later. She was businesslike as she welcomed Fleur back into her office, professional, dressed in a smart embroidered olive green silk chongsan with black flat patent leather slip-ons and her greying hair tied up on top of her head like a beehive. There was rather too much powder on her face and heavy make-up round her eyes.

'The plan is for you to meet a friend of mine, called Chin-yee, who, if you agree, will be your case officer. She will come here one night this week to discuss how you might work together. At first, you will continue to work here in the normal way, learning to extract information from customers by using your feminine charms. You will pass any information back to Chin-yee by whatever method of communication she recommends and teaches you. It could be a coded letter, coded telephone message, dead letter box, or a courier using a false address. She will probably change the method from time to time. In due course, she will have a specific target for you to get to grips with. When the moment is right, she will arrange through her contact inside Lane Crawfurd's for you to be employed there. It will get you away from the bar world and give you more prestige. Don't forget you can always come back to work for me in the evenings if ever you want to earn more money! The Lane Crawfurd cover will be better for you when you're targeting more high-class Westerners. Incidentally, Chin-yee has already recruited and infiltrated a good Party member into the famous department store in uptown Central.'

'Will I lose money by doing this?' asked Fleur, thinking practically. Despite her acquiescence, she was in this for her own benefit too, and if she didn't like it she would have said so.

'No. It should remain about the same. But if you get short I'll always employ you on a part-time basis. A few grateful customers from time to time should keep your cash topped up! The work you'll be involved in will be very important to the Party and that should override the financial considerations. You'll not go short; we'll make sure of that. We want you to be content.'

'Thank you, mamasan.'

'The Party desperately needs you. Please be prepared to meet Chin-yee next Wednesday, here. I'm confident you'll get on well with her.'

Chin-yee turned out to be a skilful case officer, working from her deep cover job at the Chinese Emporium on Kowloon side. She was so nearly ready to spring her trap on the target. She remembered in her childhood how her father used to set very simple mouse traps using a bait of meat morsel with the spring-loaded wire held back, poised ready to be snapped shut on its victim. That was how it was going to be, she thought. After much research and surveillance by her colleagues, the target had been thoroughly researched. Furthermore this would be the moment when she would get even with her brother, so long jealous of his career. She was recruited to the Service before him, yet he had been promoted and was now at a senior level to her. The thought constantly aggravated her.

零 零 零

Algie was sent to Malaysia as an observer with a commando unit based in Singapore. He had taken part in an exercise in jungle-warfare training conducted from the commando carrier off the coast of Malaysia. He had hardly sufficient notice of the trip to take the anti-malarial pills before he arrived in Singapore.

He leapt from helicopters, climbed and descended from ropes and spent the next few days and nights deep in the Malaysian jungle. Mosquitoes were rife, particularly near the still-water pools, and it was well known that this particular part of the Malaysian jungle was malarial.

A few days after his return to Hong Kong he developed flu-type symptoms with a high fever. At first the medical officer diagnosed a 'swinging temperature'. But, as the days went on, the fever became more intense and the temperature soared. He lay weak and drenched in sweat, chilled and shivering under piles of blankets. Whenever he became delirious he was dangerously near to drifting into a coma. Being in such a state, alternating between extremes of temperatures affected his brain and led to frequent bouts of dementia. He was getting weaker by the hour and no one had diagnosed his problem correctly.

During one of the lulls in his fevers, still shivering and soaking wet, he used what little strength he had left to crawl out of his bed to seek some positive help. His next-door neighbour hurriedly called an ambulance, which sped him on the car ferry as quickly as possible across the harbour to the British military hospital on the Kowloon side.

The military hospital was large, but its resources were

usually devoted to delivering an endless stream of babies to the fertile wives of British servicemen stationed in the Colony. The doctors welcomed a new challenge and made heavy weather of Algie's condition. They took endless tests, posturing in their white coats in the corner of the room with their backs to him, muttering in hushed and secretive tones. After a few days and numerous tests, the characteristic imbalance of white and red corpuscles and a typically swollen spleen was revealed. The inevitable conclusion was malaria. Despite having taken precautions, it seemed the Paludrine tablets weren't proof against certain strains of virulent mosquitoes.

'Good-morning,' said the medical officer cheerfully and with a noticeable changed note of confidence. 'At last we have found the answer. We don't expect to have to treat malaria here in Hong Kong these days. It's becoming a much rarer disease throughout the world. In fact, few general practitioners in the UK have any experience of the disease at all. Unfortunately, because it has taken some time to diagnose the problem, you're now in an extremely weak state. You've lost a lot of weight. The white and red corpuscles in your blood have got out of balance and we need to correct this with a course of treatment aimed at getting more iron into you and returning your spleen to its normal state. All this will take some time, so you'll be with us for a while, I'm afraid. It's going to be boring for you after a week or so. Right now I expect you're too weak to do anything, but that will soon change, so please be patient.'

'Thanks. At least you've found out what is the matter with me!' replied Algie limply, relieved that the waiting for a diagnosis was over. He was beginning to feel more like a guinea-pig, the object of medical curiosity and debate. More than anything he felt cut off, a prisoner in some ways, heavily controlled, his mind and his energy dulled.

He received a few telephone calls from his friends. By

now the message about his condition had been passed around. As soon as the investigations were concluded he was allowed visitors and one of the first was Barbara, bearing grapes wrapped in a brown paper bag. She swept into his room exuding vitality, with her blonde hair tangled, blown by the wind on the ferry across the harbour.

'Algie, how are you? What on earth have you been up to? We've missed you at the parties!'

'The medics have taken ages to diagnose malaria,' he replied.

'Thank goodness they've discovered what it is! It's such a pity you're in hospital because you won't be able to come to my farewell party. I'm leaving Hong Kong next week to go to Australia: I really feel I must move on. I'm joining the *Canberra* when it comes into Hong Kong.'

'What the – bloody hell, this is all very sudden! When did you decide this? It's going to be very different in Hong Kong without you,' Algie said with feeling and taken by surprise.

'Don't be silly! It'll be just the same! There are plenty of other people,' Barbara said typically dismissive, deliberately avoiding an emotional situation and deftly changing the subject.

'So what's the news?'

'You just won't believe this: yesterday I crashed my car! Actually, someone else did, which is a real bore, but it's unlikely to be repaired before I leave the Colony. It's more likely to be a write off.'

'Why don't you borrow mine? It's not doing anything while I'm stuck in this god-forsaken place.' He reached over to his bedside locker and passed her the keys. 'It's parked under my apartment block at mid levels. You know where that is. It's where you gouged my face! Look after it will you and leave it where you find it. Just get the keys to me somehow before you start your travels.'

'Do you really mean it?' she asked, looking irresistibly

appealing. It was a look that had melted him on previous occasions.

'Of course I do.'

They talked together for a while and she told him the latest gossip. When he started getting tired she left him, assuring him that she would come back to see him again before she left for the Antipodes.

'Bye, take care,' she said softly as she took his hand in hers, then hugged him and left his bedside.

He had loved seeing her and there was an emptiness when she was gone, but she managed several more visits. On her departure day, he watched from his hospital window as the vast hulk of the *Canberra* slowly glided out of Hong Kong harbour and away into the open seas, taking Barbara to an unknown future. He waved at the great ship with many tiny figures on board and wondered if he would ever see or hear from her again. It had struck him rather late, like a delayed time-fuse, that of all the girls he had met since he first came to Hong Kong, Barbara had meant the most to him.

13

*'Slander cannot destroy an honest man. . . when the
flood recedes, the rock is there.'*

The early days of Algie's life in the Far East saw him
working with the military but as a civilian with the benefits
of both worlds. He enjoyed the social scene in Hong Kong
and his work had moved into researching the different
types of weapons the Chinese military were using. His
ability to gain the trust of the British Secret Intelligence
Service had gained him access to ever more sensitive top-
secret information, acquired mostly from highly secret
sources from across the border on the mainland. Secret
agents had infiltrated the inner workings of the Chinese
military and took considerable personal risks in reporting
back. Algie's skill in interpreting the scientific nature of the
information had helped both the British military and his
employer Science International. This enabled both parties
to assess their own needs in the West's scramble to develop
weapons designed to outperform their Communist counter-
parts, an imperative in the arms race which obsessed
leaders in both the West and the East.

零 零 零

I was climbing the promotion ladder in the Chinese Secret
Service and following quite naturally in my father's –
Yong's – footsteps. He had been unwell and wasn't
expected to last another year. His heavy smoking habit
had brought on a severe lung infection, diagnosed after
tests as cancer. My long-suffering mother, Fu-fang, fussed
and guarded over his bed in their modest retirement home
in Shanghai, making sure the oxygen cylinder and
breathing mask were close to hand. Since my father had

been used as a scapegoat by the leading Maoist elements of the Chinese Communist Party, he had learnt not to take too seriously the accusations that he had mismanaged certain clandestine operations. He was well aware that the case against him had been cynically engineered. But my mother and I feared that deep inside my father's subconsciousness he was profoundly hurt, particularly at the loss of face he had been forced to endure so close to the end of his career and after so many years of loyal and distinguished service.

He had a bad winter of declining health. His breathing pained him. He got up without any energy, forced himself through the day and went back to bed utterly drained. There wasn't a moment when he wasn't aware of his body's increasing failure. When spring came he was disappointed that instead of giving him fresh energy he was even more washed-out. He started to experience night fevers too, which left him even more debilitated in the morning.

Day by day with minimal food his gaunt body became emaciated, the skin stretching across his jutting bones, his face hollow, eyes staring. He took in oxygen, gasping rather than breathing, fighting. . . fighting the unequal battle to gain a few more days and hours of life. In the final hours his body shut down slowly, methodically, feet chilling first then like a shadow it moved up the body colder. . . colder, eyes unseeing, glazed, heart pumping, ever heavier gasps; oxygen was of no use. It was only a question of time – the final moment of the struggle was in the hands of the Maker – nothing could turn him back. Then the final gasp, a rattle down the throat and he was no more: an inert body ready to be mourned over, buried and put to rest.

However well prepared the family might have been, they were shocked. My father was sadly missed, the happiest recollections flooded back. Unpleasant ones never surfaced; they never did, except by the mean spirited. There were tears and a mass of very private thoughts, the scale of the grief diverted by the immediate practicalities of the administration of death.

'I think it was the accusations that really hurt him and finally killed him,' I told my mother and sister, rather gently.

The victimisation of my father hadn't so far affected my career, certainly not in any way that I knew of. I firmly believed that I had in my blood the natural aptitude for the tricks and deception required of a professional spy. It was obvious to everyone in the Service that I was my father's son, and it was universally acknowledged that the accusations against him had been trumped up to enhance the Chairman's flagging reputation. Vindication of my father's honour became my driving force, which ignited my motivation to doubly prove my family's worth.

One day I was called to my chief's office at the old Secret Service headquarters building in Beijing, which butted on to the back of the Bank of China building. Long gone were the days when the headquarters was in a briquette factory in Shanghai, the cover my father had set up. The close connection with the Bank of China provided the necessary cloak for Chinese Secret Service operatives at home and abroad. Although I had recently received several briefings about Hong Kong, I was left up in the air about the nature of my interview with the chief.

I took the ponderous lift, noticing how it resembled a bright metallic box with mirrors and how they reflected the shininess of the metal even more. Being rather old, judging from the groaning sound of the pulleys and wires above me, it dragged me rather reluctantly to the top floor where the chief's office looked out over the dull expanse of the dirt-stained rooftops of Shanghai.

I mused on how Chairman Mao had virtually sealed off China from the outside world but still ruled a huge population by oppressive means. Perhaps the mere idea of oppression connected with something in my brain, making me claustrophobic as I ascended each floor laboriously in the small shuddering metal box.

I knocked on the chief's door. It was slightly open, allowing the familiar smell of tobacco smoke to waft into the corridor.

'Come in, Wu,' said the chief in his gravel-throated tone. I walked in showing the necessary respect. He was standing at the window pensively gazing out over the dreary urban landscape; lines of undulating tiled roofs, islands of belching smoke, rare pockets of green. Black smoke spirals stained the grey sky. A toxic cloud hung over the city, gathering in more fumes from the unclean atmosphere belched out by chimneys serving the city's energy needs.

The chief was an ambitious man and had known my father well, having served under him and he had a high regard for his skills. Having said that, the chief couldn't overtly support me for fear of upsetting the Party leadership; there was an uneasy truce prevailing signalling that the chief and the Party hierarchy were getting along fine together.

The chief turned to me in an especially benign manner, his eyes twinkling behind half-frame spectacles.

'Sit down here, Wu, will you?'

'Thank you, chief.' I deliberately gave the impression of an obedient puppy dog. The chief both expected and liked that.

'I'm sorry to hear about your father's death. Lung cancer can be very painful at the end. Perhaps it's all for the best that his agony is finally over. Your father was a very fine man, he taught me a lot.'

'So I understand, he spoke well of you.'

'Don't forget that you're working for the good of the Party. One of our problems in China at the moment is that we have a huge army. There's never a shortage of manpower in China but we are concerned – and I know the Party Chairman is – that Russia has gone ahead too far and too fast in the arms race. Frankly, we're starved of technological know-how about the West's weapons. Whenever the West introduces a new weapon, we should be just behind them introducing something similar of our own, but we are not! As you know, the Russians have managed it for years, greatly helping to maintain the balance of power in the Cold War. We are a massive country and we simply can't afford to be left behind. Supposing Russia is weakened in the next few years? Where will we be without our own expertise? By deploying KGB agents, the USSR has been very successful in acquiring Western weapons secrets, if necessary by the most ruthless means. You may recall the recent cases in Britain of Soviet spies being caught and imprisoned. Risks have to be taken, Wu, I can't deny that.' The chief had a great leader's gift of communicating his thoughts simply.

'I agree entirely.' I had listened to the monologue before.

'Good. Now let's turn to your mission in Hong Kong. You'll remember that your late father perfected many of the espionage techniques we still use today, so they won't be new to you. In my experience, you'll find it's often easier to be more creative, plan and carry out certain high-risk operations well away from your home country. I was posted to Hong Kong once and I'd give my eye teeth to be back there again – right now!'

The chief spoke slowly in a rasp-throated drawl but he had a formidable reputation for heading up some remarkable Secret Service operations against the West. His experience as a ruthless operative had given him the authority to plan strategies for the Service as a whole, against targets all over the world. If, to the outsider, the chief looked benign and portly, being of short and stocky build, it was a camouflage, deliberately acquired to disguise a sharp-brained spymaster whose successes far outnumbered his failures.

125

He looked out of the window again and paused to light up another cigarette of coarse tobacco, wrapped surprisingly delicately with his stubby fingers in the thin rice paper. The simplicity and the unaffected style were so typical of him. Behind his chair, the obligatory framed photograph of Chairman Mao looked down, deceptively cheerful and avuncular. Apart from that single framed photograph, the chief's bleak office had no other adornments. The impression was one of ruthless and stark efficiency with no hint of the comforts of high office a person in his position might have enjoyed. Single-minded dedication to the cause shone out as he turned his bald wide forehead and jowly face towards me. His dark grey Maoist-style tunic appeared typically unsophisticated yet practical. The chief paused to collect his thoughts, preparing to resume his instructions to me.

'As you know, your sister works as the manageress of the Communist-owned Chinese Emporium in Kowloon. Because she has long been an agent of ours doing some excellent work for us in Hong Kong, my intention is to send you there too, but as an official of the Service. I want you to work closely with her to develop more sub-agents, preferably women, who are loyal to us and who can be relied on to exploit selected targets, mainly British or American, who have access to important Western military secrets. You should consider heterosexual entrapment techniques, using the best-looking girls who speak English and will be at ease in the more sophisticated European culture and social life.'

'I see,' I said, feeling a slight awkwardness in his presence.

'After some thorough research we've identified your target. That's the first important step. With the help of your sister you must select and recruit a suitable female agent for entrapment purposes. Brief her personally and run her as your own agent. I think you'll find this a very interesting assignment, as well as a good career move.'

'Thank you again, chief, for this opportunity. I'll do my best. Do I have any other duties in Hong Kong?'

'Absolutely not. You're to be completely focused on this operation. In my view, even a medium to long term payback will be what the Party Chairman is looking for. Between you and me, he's very concerned that we're already so seriously behind in the arms race, beyond the point of no return as it were.'

'Right,' I replied. It was best not to argue with the chief and to say as little as possible. He was prone to a short temper and irritability, depending upon the state of his gout; it was easy to spot because he limped, pained by the build up of uric acid forming crystals around the joints of his big toes. Sometimes it was one foot then the other, sometimes both at the same time. Around the tops of his ears were the telltale signs of small, hard and uneven deposits which had disturbed the normally smooth line of the skin. The chief's face down to the last puckered lines around his mouth reflected his character, an intriguing life and one of heavy cigarette smoking.

'Oh, yes, one more thing. I know your work has kept you long hours and the Service has dragged you away from a home life of your own. Hong Kong may well be the ideal environment for you to change your bachelor ways. It's time you had the comfort of a good and loving woman. Believe me, it's essential to a happy, productive and fulfilling life. A man needs female companionship as he gets older.'

I then realised that when he chose, the chief could behave like a caring human being.

'Yes, chief,' I reacted meekly, wondering if the chief had been talking to my mother who was constantly dropping hints about how she would like me to settle down with a nice woman. My sister had married a boring bespectacled official in the Bank of China five years before and still there had been no children. I speculated rather wickedly that it was more likely that her husband wasn't up to it; I had failed to see how my sister could ever have been physically attracted to him, a puny little man without professional or financial standing

I admit I had become narrow in my outlook and possibly too absorbed with my work. I was too tied up with the business of the Service to even consider outside distractions. I knew the chief was giving me sensible advice.

I bowed my head and left the room, my mind awash with interesting operational possibilities.

It was easy for me as a single man to pack my bags and move at short notice. Before I left for my new posting, I spent the night in my mother's house saying goodbye and enjoying a deliciously tasty meal she had prepared specially for me of boiled rice with slices of fish and duck with bean shoots and green vegetables, the spicy aromas filling the small apartment. It was a simple but special farewell supper. I promised my mother that I wouldn't be going too far away and that I'd be back from time to time. She had grown accustomed to family separations in the Service, and she never deviated from the firm belief that the Communist Party cause was the highest calling for which personal and family sacrifice was worth making.

I was going to the posting with my self-confidence high, but I recognised that my lifestyle was too solitary; I was not an easily sociable man and neither did I take to small talk and idle chatter. Perhaps a wife would take care of this side of things.

14

'A white-washed crow soon shows black again.'

I remembered what my father and some of his former colleagues, who were still alive, had told me about the time when he and his team had dreamt up a succession of imaginative operations. He had told me so many things about the early days of the Service and how he used to sit at his functional desk in a dreary office overlooking the coal yard of the factory at the new headquarters.

零　零　零

The weather was hot and a swathe of greasy hair fell down over one side of Yong's face, just enough to shield his right eye altogether but leaving the remainder of his hair swept back smoothly. The escaping strand was incongruous and a rather welcomed imperfection in the orderly official in the minds of his subordinates.

'I won't be in the office tomorrow morning,' he shouted across the room at his underlings, 'I have to report to Chou En-lai at the Party headquarters. He's taking a close interest in our operations. As you know, our activities form an important part in the Party's mission to neutralise the Kuomintang. Only last week he told me there must be no let up in our efforts.'

'We'll look after the shop while you're away,' said his deputy who covered for him in his absence. How much of the work rate was due to Yong and the affection in which his staff held him or whether it was blind loyalty to the Party and the Service was not clear. Yong certainly was loyal to his staff and they returned that loyalty, so trust and respect were easily maintained.

'I'm lucky to have such a good team. We live in a treacherous world, an insecure one where we don't always know who our enemies are. A friend can become an enemy within an instant. Among my comrades here I admit I feel a degree of safety, but don't any of you ever give me reason to question that loyalty.'

In a ruthless occupation, Yong's admission of feelings of insecurity warmed him to his staff. It wasn't taken as a weakness, because they had seen how single minded he could be when necessary.

'Now I want to brief you on a fresh target.'

At that moment an assistant stood up to open the windows letting in fresh warm air and the sounds of heavy lorries reversing, loading and moving off.

'The background to this operation is interesting. A few years ago the Service recruited Zhao Zibo, a superintendent in the French Concession Police Force. Our real target, however, is not Zhao but a young lawyer called Chen Zhigao who practises in the French Concession district of the city. He has been involved in many cases leading to the imprisonment of left-wing activists by the French authorities. His skill is derived from briefs provided by the China Mutual Aid Society and in the course of this business he has managed to secure the release of many Communists. Chen's contact at the Mutual Aid Society is a strikingly beautiful woman called Huang Shulan. She is head of the company's Claims Department.'

Yong was in his element, fluent and enthusiastic, not allowing any interruption until he was ready.

'Any questions so far, comrades?' he asked.

There were none. Each assistant looked attentively while he delivered the brief, standing up behind his desk, a large stained linen-backed street map hanging on the wall behind him. The pause allowed the smokers a moment in which to light up.

'Chen does not know that the company is really a Party-controlled organisation, or that Huang is a Party martyr, her reputation considerably reinforced by her recent marriage to a member of the Chinese Communist Party Central Committee. Chen's work gives him easy access to the police, prison and judicial authorities in the French Concession, a ready-made and thoroughly worthwhile focus for recruitment. I've been involved in this case from the very beginning and I'm aware that he probably won't provide high-grade intelligence, but he's well placed to talent-spot targets within the French police and prison service. He might even introduce potential recruits to our Service!'

'Excuse me, Yong, but may I ask if you know Chen personally?' asked one of the assistants.

'I don't, and he might well be wary of a direct approach by us. On the other hand, Huang Shulan knows Chen very well and has reported back to her superiors that Chen seems attracted to her. So far she has rejected his advances and withheld telling him of her true background. Tomorrow evening after I've reported to Chou En-lai – I expect his meeting to be brief – I've arranged a secret meeting with Huang in the city to discuss the way forward.'

At a safe house the following evening Yong noted how tall and statuesque Huang was, wearing a long black dress, rather formal and European in style, with a low front. Her stylishly simple but effective necklace of artificial pearls contrasted with the darkness of her dress and her long black hair. She was a beauty, and in common with many women in Shanghai make-up had turned her sallow skin unnaturally white and geisha-like. Special cosmetic pencils had been applied to her mysterious almond-shaped eyes, transforming her into the looks of a sophisticated Western woman. She fascinated Yong and it took all his powers of self-control to concentrate on his professional task, her sensuality and fragrant scent conspiring to distract him. He didn't recognise the brand, being unfamiliar with such refinements, but he guessed it came from one of the Western department stores on the Bund.

'I've got permission to transfer your work to my department aimed at helping you turn Chen's obvious feelings for you to our best advantage. You might find this approach rather direct, but I've been fully briefed on your background and we believe you're now in a key position to help us. What do you say?'

'I'll be happy to help in whatever way I can, you know that. May I call you Yong?'

'Please do. I want you to play heavily on Chen's emotions. I don't know how far you are prepared to go sexually; that's your decision. I don't think I should dictate how to deploy your sexuality to the best effect – you'll know that far better than I do! When you've gained his confidence, ask him as a friend to introduce you to French Concession officials, who could help you in your work with the Mutual Aid Society.'

'I understand. Can you give me any more background that might be helpful?' she asked.

'I've quite a mass of information, but I'll tell you only what I think you need to know.'

He looked across at her and gazed into the dark recesses of her eyes. She was very beautiful. It occurred to him that Chen might not be up to making a play for her after all, but he was banking on him being persistent.

'We think Chen will introduce you to his friend Zhao Zibo and then he'll become the main target of the operation. Being a senior Chinese official in the French Concession police he'll have the confidence of his French superiors and access to high-grade intelligence,' continued Yong.

'Is there any more background information on Zhao?'

'He was born in Shandong, but he has lived in Shanghai

for many years. He has some useful contacts, both inside and outside the legal system. On the surface he seems conventional, but our records show he is coarse and poorly educated. He's a playboy. He mixes with criminal gangs and exploits his position to accept bribes, particularly favouring friends and relatives who run various illegal rackets in the city. For sure he's a slippery character with no known affection for the Chinese Communist Party, so we must be careful. Despite this, we believe he will co-operate if approached carefully, and we think you, Huang, will achieve this for us. But I can't pretend it will be an easy operation.'

Huang got up from the armchair and smoothed down her dress. She shook Yong's hand. In return he bowed his head in the usual respectful gesture and let her out through the back door of the house. He left by the same exit fifteen minutes later.

Chen, obedient to the instructions he had received, set up a supper party to which he invited Huang and Zhao. It was held in a private room at one of the many smart Shanghai restaurants, a fashionable French-managed hostelry called Pierre's. He thought the choice rather appropriate, especially as he was totally familiar with the layout and the French, English and Chinese menus, keeping him in control throughout.

A few minutes before the appointed time Chen arrived to check that the arrangements were in order, particularly the position of the table and the place setting. He quickly familiarised himself with the menu. At 7.45 pm Zhao strolled in and was greeted by his host who shook his hand vigorously. Chen immediately detected that Zhao was nervous and he smelt alcohol on his breath.

'Hello, Chen! I got caught up with some friends for a quick drink. Sorry I'm late! The lady hasn't arrived yet, has she?' he asked breathlessly.

'No,' replied Chen stiffly. There was no way Chen could have known how many drinks Zhao had had, but he was hoping for the best.

They sat chatting for a few minutes before the star herself glided in. Zhao spotted her straight away and Chen watched his reaction closely.

'My goodness, she's stunning,' he whispered under his breath, sucking in air through a gap in his teeth. Chen had anticipated perfectly the effect Huang would have on Zhao.

'That's our lady! Impressive, isn't she?'

Reinforcing her good looks she elegantly walked towards them. She wore a simple dark green sheath dress cut to her neck, Chinese style in the front and slit seductively high up the side of her right leg. She wore little jewellery except a dress watch and a gold bracelet on her left wrist.

'May I introduce my friend Zhao to you, Huang?' said Chen having first greeted her with a formal handshake, gently taking her right hand in both of his and holding her for a second longer than necessary. This was meant to indicate to Zhao his less formal relationship with her.

Zhao leapt to his feet, moved to the side of the round table and pulled out a chair to help Huang into it. Chen smiled to himself as Zhao did everything he could to make an impression on Huang.

'Do you live near here?' asked Zhao rather too early on in the conversation, no doubt spurred on by a false sense of bravery acquired from his pre-dinner drinking session. As he waited for the answer he leant on the table, clumsily upsetting knives and forks and the carafe of iced water placed at the centre of the table.

'Oh dear!' said Huang, avoiding answering the question. Instead, she turned her full attention to the sodden mess that the upturned carafe had made on the starched white linen cloth which threatened to flow onto her lap. But she was quick to react; she jumped up and with her napkin jabbed at the soggy patch. 'What an arsehole!' she thought to herself, but at no time belying her true feelings of displeasure.

'Madam, please accept my apologies,' begged Zhao.

'Waiter! Can you please clear this up?' asked Chen much put out by Zhao's antics.

Once the commotion had subsided, Zhao recovered his composure and couldn't do enough to restore his image in the eyes of Huang. He tried to please her, passing the freshly filled water carafe, passing sauces, asking her if she was enjoying the meal. He had become her blatant admirer. Huang meanwhile had continued to enchant both her male companions, treating each equitably, mixing seductive glances with the occasional gentle placing of her hand on the arm of each, without ever giving the impression of affection for one more than the other. Her mind was made up about Zhao. She knew how to get the best out of men without giving away her own feelings.

They finished the meal of *paté de foie gras* followed by roast *petit poulet* with a bottle of white Burgundy. Afterwards they relaxed over coffee and cigarettes, and a cigar for Zhao. By the end of the evening Zhao was well fortified, his daring even more enhanced by alcohol and the luxurious ambience.

'Madam, may I present my business card? Please don't hesitate to contact me if you ever need a favour,' he gushed obsequiously, full of flamboyance and brandishing the smouldering cigar between the forefinger and thumb of his left hand.

'Thank you. There could well be some Mutual Aid Society matters you might be able to help me with. I'll certainly make contact with you,' replied Huang calmly. 'Now if you will forgive me, gentlemen, I must get back home.'

'Let's meet up again in a few days' time; shall we say this time next week?' offered Zhao enthusiastically, hardly able to bear not seeing Huang for another whole week.

No agreement was made. Lame excuses that she needed to consult her diaries seemed to keep his eagerness at bay. Breaking up the party, Huang left the men to gossip, once Chen had seen her safely to her transport home. While Chen was away from the table, Zhao came over faint from the excess of cigars and drink and rushed to the lavatory just in time to vomit the multi-coloured contents of his meal into the basin, blocking it up and leaving behind a foul stench.

At her meeting with Yong a few days later, Huang reported every detail of the meal and the meeting hosted by Chen.

'Do you know that creep, Zhao, nearly ate me alive instead of his meal! He has suggested another meeting soon, next week in fact. I stalled for time. What do you think?'

'Try not to put Zhao's nose out of joint. He must believe that he is your suitor too and you should play along with him. Why don't you contact Chen and suggest another meal with him and Zhao, saying you're happy to meet him and hope he'll become a friend? This will show you're not romantically attracted to Zhao. I suggest you slow the pace down a bit and play a little hard to get, in order to gauge the depth of Zhao's yearning for you. We know he is a wastrel who constantly patronises brothels, so we want to be sure his interest in you is not just a superficial flash in the pan.'

One week after their first threesome at Pierre's, Zhao called Chen.

'Why has Huang failed to contact me as promised? Can you call her to get us together again?'

'Certainly, but I'll have to leave early as I have another important meeting to go to.'

The next meeting was set up shortly after the call.

'I'm so sorry, I've been terribly busy. I should have

contacted you to meet up again earlier. Please forgive me, gentlemen,' purred Huang, deploying feminine guile as though to seek forgiveness.

'Don't worry, that's no problem,' said Chen casually. During the meal he noticed that Zhao had looked silent and morose, uncertain that his affections were being reciprocated. When Chen took early leave of his guests, Zhao and Huang stayed behind and it didn't take Zhao a moment before he tried to make headway with Huang.

'Huang, will you let me have your address and telephone number?'

'I'm sorry, Zhao, it's rather difficult at the moment. I live with relatives and it would be most inconvenient for you to contact me there,' she replied fluently.

'If you would prefer, I can offer you private accommodation in the French Concession?' said Zhao desperately, so besotted with Huang, searching for a way to gain her affection and avoid a rebuff.

'I'm fine for the moment, but thanks for the offer.'

'Don't forget my offer of assistance whenever you want it, will you?'

'Of course not, but I'd prefer to take up your offer of help directly, instead of seeing you in Chen's company each time,' said Huang in a way that Zhao might read as favouring him. He was so close now to both recruitment and seduction that it was a close run thing which would come first.

15

'Wise bees sip not from fallen flowers.'

Algie went into a decline when Barbara left Hong Kong and judging from the increasingly less frequent letters she wrote to him, it was clear that her interests and affections were engaged elsewhere. He was getting sick and tired of Hong Kong. Many of his friends had come to the end of their postings and had left for other places. He was hardly motivated to make new friends. Algie was tired of life generally. Instead of keeping up his former busy social programme, he became morose and solitary. As an acknowledged expert in his profession he had put his energies into his work, but he still took part in rare and now uninspired trips to the cottage in the New Territories. In his current state of mind any real enjoyment evaded him by reminders of happier times he and Barbara had once spent there, far away from the bustle of Hong Kong Island. Now he was a man lost in his own world, bordering on self-pity.

In his spare time he often made his way across the harbour on the Star Ferry, which never ceased to fascinate him as it tirelessly ploughed its way across the harbour waters to the Kowloon side and back again to the Island side. He had done the trip so many times with Barbara so that too brought back memories. He went shopping, not so much to buy but more to look at the vast range of products in the fashionable stores and to experience the excitement and buzz of the varied Oriental crowds. He took in the pungent street aromas along the Nathan Road, which ran north from the very grand Peninsular Hotel, with the fleet of British racing-green Rolls Royces parked outside, opulent and ready to transport guests on demand and in supreme luxury.

On one of those days after calling in to the modern shopping mall at the Ocean Terminal with its labyrinth of high-class retail shops he continued on, as he usually did, down Nathan Road and headed for the China Emporium on the left. The Emporium, managed effectively by the Chinese Communist Party, exploited cheap labour enabling them to undercut other outlets of similar goods. It was a whim that beckoned Algie into the shop to look for Chinese mandarin sleeves, his thoughts on presents to send home, something that would travel easily by post. Surveying the goods on display, he looked a touch helpless. Pausing at the Chinese mandarin sleeves, he wondered how well they might look at home, hanging from a wall or in a nice frame. A young Chinese woman came up to him, slightly older than Algie dressed in the pillar-box red uniform of the Emporium with matching blouse and skirt, cut to a fashionable length slightly above the knee.

'Good morning, can I help you?' The assistant smiled in a friendly way and spoke such good English that Algie was taken aback.

'I'm looking for something to send home for Christmas,' Algie replied, using the Emporium to take refuge off the streets from the searing heat and humidity of mid summer.

'We have some very suitable things here. Please come with me.' There was a persuasive persistence about the woman.

She led him to a part of the store that dealt with prints and maps, things that would travel easily by post. She pulled out several trays of prints and together they discussed what might be appropriate. Then she led him to her office to carefully pack up the modest purchases for him.

'Please excuse my small office. I'm the manageress here. Do you live in Kowloon or on the Island?'

'I'm on the island,' replied Algie, with a shade of hesitation, deliberately vague.

Algie returned to the Emporium several times after that and each time the manageress was there, efficient, patrolling her department's floors, checking salespeople and helping customers. She and Algie got to know each other better after each encounter, and he became more at ease with every visit.

'Do you have any Chinese friends? I presume you're not married otherwise your wife would be helping you now?' she asked light-heartedly.

'The answer is no, on both counts.'

'I have spoken to my husband about you. We would like to welcome you to our home for a meal. Perhaps you have never been to a Chinese home before?'

'You're right, I haven't. It's very kind of you,' replied Algie, who welcomed the opportunity of an entirely different social scene and a distraction from the irrational thoughts of Barbara, getting him nowhere.

'I'm sorry, what's your name?' Chin-yee asked, although she already knew it well enough.

'Algie.'

'That's a nice English name.'

'Yes. What's yours?'

'I am Chin-yee,' she said sweetly. 'I have a business card here in Chinese and English; it gives my home and work details. Why not come to see us next Saturday evening? Saturday is a better day for us; my husband is a bank clerk and he doesn't work on Sundays. We'll try to get a few other English-speaking Chinese friends to join us.'

'That would be lovely. What time would you like me to come?' asked Algie.

'About seven o'clock. We live on Kowloon side up the far end of Nathan Road? It's easy to get a taxi from the Star Ferry terminal.'

Chin-yee decided that Algie had an old-fashioned innocence about him. Some women found that attractive, especially the mothering kind. It was this side of him that had attracted Chin-yee.

Algie was flattered and fascinated about the possibility of entering more deeply into a Chinese social world that few Europeans were able to do.

Collecting up more new purchases wrapped personally by Chin-yee, and armed with her card, he left the store but not before giving her his home telephone number in case of complications about the invitation from her end. As he walked down the bustling Nathan Road, he skilfully negotiated the throng of harassed Chinese and sweating white faced shoppers swarming over the hot dusty pavements in search of bargains. High summer and the afternoon's humidity were about to herald a mighty storm. The local radio had reported that hurricane 'Bertie' was in the area of the Philippines and heading towards Hong Kong, but it was just possible that favourable winds might divert it at the very last minute. A fortuitous change of course had happened before.

Earnest storm warnings were issued around the Colony, with regular announcements over the wireless and on television advising everyone, onshore or at sea, to take appropriate action. Small boats and sampans rushed to specially built storm-shelters. On land, cars were parked well away from the possible danger of being swept up by the force. Protective bars were placed across windows of dwellings. Food was stockpiled against the prospect of being housebound for the few days it would take for the storm to blow over. Ferries were secured to their hefty moorings and aircraft grounded. Large cargo, military and passenger ships either sailed off to make for calmer waters or resigned themselves to riding out the storm where they were, straining hard at anchor for several hours.

I was becoming well established in Hong Kong and had put a tail on Algie; building up a picture of his way of life, his habits, routes, that sort of thing. Taking the Star Ferry back to the Island, Algie had queued briefly to allow the incoming passengers off first. When the signal light turned green, the returning passengers, orderly and without fuss, sloped on to the old ferry-boat. Before occupying their seats, the newly-boarded passengers flipped the reversible seat backs so that they faced the magnificent view of Hong Kong Island. At night, it was a breathtaking sight with the lights glittering from the shoreline high up into the dark sky. The giant neon advertisements shone out from the tall commercial buildings in the central part of the Island, reflecting in the shimmering and dark swirling waters of the harbour. Behind the high-rise buildings reared the mountains and the Peak itself, the wealthy residential area that dominated the Island. Taipans and gweilos, the non-Chinese heads of business, lived there in great splendour away from the exhausting heat and pollution below. To the left and right the harbour teemed with boats of all sizes: sampans and dredgers, ocean liners, tankers, cargo vessels with intriguing registrations, military ships, all adding to the frantic bustle, the vitality of the Colony.

Unfathomable Chinese of all ages spat in their inimitable way, spewing without inhibition their phlegmy contents on to the pavement. Old people, their faces deeply lined by sun, time and life, dressed traditionally for the most part. Younger people opted for the garish, cheaper European styles, the well-to-do young Chinese wearing the very best of European fashion.

Once across by the ferry, Algie walked to the terminus and took the red public taxi to his apartment up at mid-levels overlooking Victoria Harbour. It was small. Rents were high in that area, but it was well enough furnished for his own comfort as a bachelor. Each day his amah, who – unknown to Algie – was one of our agents, came to clean and look after his laundry and sort out his domestic needs. They communicated rather desperately in pidgin English but over time a master-servant type trust had grown between them. Algie's only problem was that she was bossy and autocratic. Despite her nagging and grinning, which showed off her missing teeth and a few gold filled ones, he insisted on some things being done his way and not hers!

On the amah's day off that week, Algie put his feet up and watched television with a bottle or two of cold beers he kept in the fridge. He contemplated his personal situation and was relieved to feel the previous depression giving way to a new optimism.

The following Saturday came round soon enough. Time passed quickly in Hong Kong; during the week he had spent time on Repulse Bay beach, swimming and sunbathing. It was less crowded then. He had a good day combining a swim with topping up his rather pasty suntan, and having towelled himself down and brushed away the gritty sand he went back to the flat to prepare himself for the evening ahead. He showered to wash away those awkward particles of sand that stuck in orifices. Once dried off, from his built-in wardrobe he chose a blue shirt with single cuffs secured by a pair of plain metal links open neck and dark grey slacks with dark suede chukka boots. He slicked down his wild lavatory-brush fair hair with lotion and dabbed on some aftershave to clean up some minor nicks from his wet shave. He felt an eager anticipation, an excitement for the evening ahead of him, totally unpredictable, an element of risk, perhaps danger too.

To get to Chin-yee's flat, Algie crossed the harbour by car ferry. On the Kowloon side after making wrong turns, he eventually found Chin-yee's flat at the end of the Nathan Road. At first sight, it looked a typically dreary Hong Kong tenement block, but once inside, he saw that it was basic but adequate, devoid of luxurious furnishings and fittings. Chin-yee opened the dark wooden door and warmly welcomed him inside. Having introduced her husband, she ushered him into a larger than expected sitting-room, where in the corner a table was laid for six. At each place setting a china bowl, a set of wooden chopsticks and a tumbler with a small Chinese flower delicately floating in it. He was the first guest to arrive and Chin-yee offered him rice wine. In no time the other guests arrived, and at first Algie couldn't comprehend their complicated Chinese names but it soon became obvious he was the only *gweilo* or white person.

Chin-yee had been true to her word. He would only meet Chinese that night.

'Now, Fleur, I want you to meet Algie,' said Chin-yee. Fleur was looking petite and appealing in her tightly fitting cream silk chongsam. 'Fleur works in Lane Crawfurd's store on Hong Kong Island and speaks English, don't you, Fleur?'

'Hello, Algie. I'm sorry, my English is not that good, as you will find out. It's more like American, I think!'

'Fleur, that's a nice name but not very Chinese,' ventured Algie.

'I'm always being asked about that. I think my mother fell in love with a French sailor once, but my father is Chinese as far as I know!'

The exploratory conversation continued; Where do you live? How long have you been in Hong Kong? What do you do? Algie answered them all, even down to his cover occupation in metal manufacturing. He found her easy company, and Chin-yee thoughtfully arranged for them to sit next to each other so that Fleur could explain some of the Chinese traditions. He was an eager pupil, toasting or 'yam singing' his hosts and fellow guests as the deceptively strong rice wine began to take effect.

Six courses of varying hot and spicy aromatic dishes were produced by Chin-yee, placing them on special warmers in the centre of the table. Each guest stretched forward, working their chopsticks skilfully to secure portions of food from the serving dishes to add to their bowls of rice. Algie noticed how expert they were, how intent they were on their food and he was aware of his own lack of skill with Chinese food. The other guests in between mouthfuls looked across at him and smiled as if they felt pity for him. After a while they started talking among themselves, except for Fleur who continued to direct her attention at Algie.

'You must make sure you have a bed of rice in your bowl. Then you use your chopsticks like this,' she said helpfully.

'Someone showed me how to do this before, but I've been idle so now I'm unpractised.'

'It's easy, just watch me! Help yourself to a bit from each of the dishes, like this – like the others are doing. Chin-yee will refill the dishes when they are empty. Rice symbolises life and noodles longevity. If you see eggs coloured red they are for happiness and good luck. Small sweet cakes are usually round to symbolise harmony and fresh fruit, particularly oranges and pineapples, symbolise gold and good fortune. An orange will signal the end of the meal.'

The meal did end with oranges, mixed together with lychees in a bowl. Algie by then was in a carefree mood. He needed to make a move with Fleur, the right one. He offered her a lift home, which to his utter surprise she accepted with an equal measure of coyness and appreciation. He was glad of the hot jasmine tea before he left, sobering him up sufficiently to drive back across the harbour.

They caught the last ferry by the skin of their teeth, parking well forward on the car deck. They got out of the car and leant against the bonnet to take advantage of the coolness coming from the water and to admire the magic of the Island as it came to meet them. The dark sky was alive with stars. They watched the moon peering over the hills.

'You know, Fleur, I never tire of this view,' Algie murmured, his hair ruffled in the hot night breeze. There was a certain raw energy about Fleur, eyes dark brown with reflections in them, which heightened the intensity of the colour. To Algie, she was like some exotic bird struggling against unknown elements. The ferry approached the quayside in the shining water reflecting the multicoloured extravagance of lights from the shore, some from neon beaming out from high-rise blocks.

'We're so lucky to be living here,' she replied as Algie took a chance and put his arm around her protectively. She snuggled into him quite willingly and put her head in the crook of his arm. She was short compared with Algie, only coming up to his chest. In the darkness she looked up at him and her lips quivered playfully. For a moment they were silent, there was no need to talk.

'Would you like to come to my flat for a coffee?' Algie asked, sensing Fleur's willingness, as far as he was able to gauge anything with a Chinese person. He knew nothing of her background that made her what she was now.

'That would be nice,' she replied compliantly. Already Algie was thinking ahead, wondering what her slight body would be like in bed. He hadn't been with a woman for some time. Life, he decided, was looking up.

Waiting for the kettle to boil, Algie set the mood by putting on soft music and turning down the lights, leaving only a small table lamp to cast its soft shadow over the proceedings. Fleur sat on the sofa as he quickly made the arrangements before the water boiled.

'I haven't been to many European flats before,' she said cheerfully.

'What do you think of it?' asked Algie without the slightest fear of criticism.

'It's very nice and so typically European, I think. Not that I really know! I see you have a few Chinese bits and pieces too.'

'How do you like your coffee – strong, with milk, sugar?' he called out from the kitchen.

'Black, please, no sugar,' she replied.

When he came out from the kitchen, he brought two mugs of coffee made from a tin of 'instant'. The tape music was softly playing Rachmaninov and the lights were dimmed low. He flopped down beside her on the sofa and moved to take her into his arms. She didn't resist him. She looked into his eyes and kissed him on the lips. She stroked the front of his trousers, which already betrayed excitement.

Compliant in his arms, she let him gently undo her chongsam. It fell to the floor and as his need increased Algie released the hooks of her bra, supporting breasts whose nipples stuck out sharply like little nuts. He peeled off her white lace briefs and with his help it was her turn to undress him. Drawing her to him he slid his leg between hers, playing with her slight body like a cuddly toy. Lying on her back he felt between her legs. He found the sparsely-haired triangle. As he stroked she moaned appreciatively at first, and then with increasing impatience she helped him enter her; firmly, smoothly and then more deeply. Her legs parted wide and locked together behind his back as he rocked her backwards and forwards until they reached a perfectly timed gasping climax.

'Now I've got him!' She thought to herself as they rested, calm and sated.

Their bodies had generated considerable heat. After a while they showered, soaping each other sensually under the water that cascaded down their soft skins. Then they lay side by side on his bed with the overhead fan rotating slowly, giving a cooling down draught, bringing tiny goose pimples to their flesh. Sleeping in each other's arms for the few remaining hours of darkness, they awoke cool, legs still entwined, face to face while the early-morning sun filtered sharply through the thinly-curtained windows. She caught him smiling and she smiled back a little self-consciously. The hurricane still hadn't come; there was hope of being spared. In those few moments he was aware of something new in him. The feeling of apathy had vanished. He had been brought back to life.

'I like you, Algie – you like me too perhaps?' Fleur asked, not for the first time she searched Algie's soul, hoping to enchant him with her almond-shaped eyes. She didn't talk much but she showed her affection quietly; so different to the constant nagging and nattering of Western women.

'Fleur, thank you for everything. When shall we meet again?' asked Algie, smitten with longing and not wanting her to leave him for a moment.

'Are you free next Saturday?' she asked.

'Yes, but can't it be sooner?'

'It could be, except I work late at night during the week.'

Fleur schemed that the best way to hold his interest was to keep him uncertain of her, initially rationing their meetings. She thought him a kind, clean, passionate Englishman with a strong body and considerate manners.

16

'Happy people never count hours as they pass.'

Every moment of the day and night when they were not working, Algie and Fleur spent their time together. Physically and mentally they fitted well together. Emotionally, too, they gave each other support whenever it was needed.

'We must ask Algie with Fleur. It's so good to see Algie happy again. He seems so much more content now, and she's such an intelligent, lively and attractive girl,' was the unanimous, slightly patronising opinion of his friends still in Hong Kong.

'Lucky chap, I rather fancy her myself! She's certainly a bit of all right. I wonder what old Algie's got that glues her to him?' speculated others, mostly his male friends with far from pure thoughts.

'Darling, I love you so much,' he whispered in her ear, nibbling it lightly as he held her in his arms, besotted.

'I love you too, Algie, you lovely, romantic and old-fashioned Englishman.'

'That's just the way I am.'

'You have all those British traditions and special ways of behaving based on years of class divisions.'

'So what! That's what I represent. You Chinese have a history that's much older than ours.'

'OK, OK! Don't let's spoil our evening by arguing.'

They took the car, the old Sunbeam Alpine with the roof down, after work and drove over the hills along winding hill roads, past his old haunt at Repulse Bay and on to Stanley Bay to relax on the beach, swim and picnic. There were few other people about. They raced each other into the sea. Algie hit the water first and swam towards Fleur's floral-bikinied body, knowing she was still learning to swim and stopping her from getting out of her depth.

'Darling, this is the most wonderful place to be. Look back at the hills littered with rich houses and blocks of flats,' he said, holding her tightly to him and cradling her in his arms, the sea taking some of her weight.

'Don't drop me!'

'Will you marry me, Fleur?' he asked so suddenly without warning.

'Phew!' she gasped and paused. 'What do you mean?' she asked taken by surprise, unable to collect her thoughts. 'What did you say again?'

'I said, will you marry me? Surely it means the same the world over!' Embarrassment had come over him and his words came slowly.

'Am I meant to think about it before giving you the answer?' she asked impishly.

'You can if you want, but it isn't a business transaction! You Chinese might well think it is. Will you be my wife and spend the rest of your life with me? So what's your answer?' The tide had gone out quite a way and Algie sifted sand nervously through his fingers.

'Now I understand! Yes. Yes. I'm sorry, I'm so slow, but it is a big shock to me – out of the blue, I think you say.'

'Now you have made me the happiest man in the whole world! I will always love you and care for you.'

'I hope so!' exclaimed Fleur as they kissed deeply, embracing and squeezing each other until they needed air.

'Let's go back to the flat. Then I'll show you how much I love you!' Fleur said spontaneously, knowing just how to please her fiancé.

To make the marriage ceremony more meaningful and mainly to please Algie, Fleur undertook Church of England religious studies to become a member of the

Christian Church in Hong Kong, and planned to be married at St John's Cathedral.

On her wedding day Fleur looked stunning, dressed in a traditional white gown with her veil shimmering in the early September sunshine. The ceremony had few guests other than those friends of Algie's still in the Colony and Fleur's parents and Chinese friends who weren't necessarily Christians. Chin-yee was there too, and all the women made a special effort to dress up in fashionable clothes. Tight-fitting pastel silk suits were the order of the day, with chic hats perched precariously on their heads, under which mysterious Oriental eyes observed every detail of the happy scene without giving anything away.

The Chinese ladies, small in stature compared with the Europeans, looked a little incongruous inside the vastness of the cathedral. Algie admired the work of the early missionaries and priests undertaken in the early years of the Colony, over a hundred years before, converting so many Chinese to Christianity. Tightly packed rows of tombstones in scarce graveyards, allocated from commercially valuable building ground, bore testimony to the numbers of Chinese Christians buried in Hong Kong over the years. It seemed entirely natural to Algie and Fleur that they should have been blessed in the Anglican way, supported by their friends from both communities.

Algie's father, Thomas Stanhope, on the other hand hadn't taken the news well and had written his son a short sharp letter leaving him in no doubt what his views were about mixed race marriages.

Gateways

Dear Algernon,

   Thank you for letting me know about your engagement to Fleur. I hope it will be a happy time for you both but I must warn you against a mixed marriage, in your case to a Chinese lady. No doubt she is worthy of you and you of her, but I have seen too many of these types of marriages in India and frankly I'm sorry to have to say that in my experience they don't always work out for the best. You see, it's easy to be caught up and enamoured with locals when you are so far from home but in years to come the reality might set in, especially when you have children. They will be half English, half Chinese and there is nothing you can do to disguise that. The problem will be more for them than for you. They will possibly not be accepted by either of their fellows. It is a sad and cruel fact of life but I would be failing in my duty as a father if I did not point this out to you. You are also the only male successor to the family line and it is your duty to try to continue that line. I expect you will give me many examples of successful Anglo-Chinese marriages but I can only talk from my own experience.

I am wheelchair bound at present. If you will forgive me, I won't be attending the wedding but I look forward to receiving you both at home on your next leave or whenever.

Your ever loving father.

Algie was upset with his father's unexpectedly forthright message. He put it down to him being grumpy in his old age and constipated from too much sitting in a wheelchair. In a fit of pique and to show support to his future wife, Algie wrote back vehemently arguing with his father and expressing disappointment in his attitude.

In the dark watches of the night his father, a light sleeper ever since his wife died, faced the prospect of his grandchildren being Eurasian and generations of Stanhopes carrying Oriental blood for evermore. He cheered himself up with the memory from his own youthful times out East, recalling how attractive some of the Eurasian girls were. With that thought on his mind, he usually fell asleep, calm, a faint smile on his face until the dawn broke and the birds started their orchestrated chatter in the hedgerow right outside his bedroom window.

After a year's marriage, which started with Fleur moving in to Algie's flat, much to the annoyance of the amah, Algie received a telex from his head office in Weybridge, England. He read it and reread it to make sure it was really addressed to him. Later that day when he got home, he waited somewhat impatiently for Fleur to get back from her work at Lane Crawfurd's.

'Halloo!' Fleur called out, pulling the key from the lock and putting it back into her handbag. Algie had already opened a bottle of well chilled champagne, an extravagance earmarked only for special occasions.

'Darling!' he exclaimed, throwing his arms around her as he lifted her up off the ground with his bear hug.

'What's going on? What's the special occasion?'

'I've some really good news. I've poured out something special for you. Here's a glass. Now sit down!' Algie paused dramatically and patted the sofa.

'Come on, Algie, you're keeping me in dreadful suspense!'

'How would you like to come with me to America? I had a telex from my head office this morning asking if I would go – with you, of course – on an attachment to the Los Alamos National Laboratory in New Mexico. Apparently the Americans are sharing some of their nuclear weapons technology with us Brits. I've been appointed to send the up-to-date information back to my firm in England. Both the British Ministry of Defence and the Foreign Office have approved the posting. You always pretend not be interested in my work, but this posting should be good fun and a great experience for us both, particularly at this stage of our married life. As far as I can tell, we will live in the secure base there. Knowing the Americans, it'll be very congenial and the work will be very exciting and interesting. You'll love it there too, the warm climate, the people and the experience. It's too good to be true!'

'Oh, Algie, it sounds wonderful! When would we go?'

'Steady on! I have to get back to them tomorrow, once I've discussed it with you, then they'll give me dates and so on. I'd like us to go home to England for a few weeks' leave before going on to America. This is highly confidential, so you mustn't tell anyone until it's all tied up and agreed. Just say I'm going on a secondment to America for scientific work.'

零 零 零

As soon as she could, Fleur passed on the information about Algie's posting to Chin-yee, who in turn passed it on to me. I couldn't believe my luck. Up to this point, Fleur hadn't given us any significant information about Algie's work, other than dates, hotels, countries and the names of people he had visited when he went away on a business trip. She had looked more and more like a longer-term investment. At last, after more than a year, the Chinese Secret Service was poised to pull off a substantial coup.

I needed to brief Chin-yee on the best way to run Fleur as an agent-in-place while she was in America with Algie. To protect Chin-yee's cover, I decided to take the ferry to Lantau Island, passing ourselves off as a Chinese couple on a sightseeing day trip, paying homage to the Buddhist temple and generally walking round the island. I needed to be alone with my sister as I had come to feel pity for her. I had noticed how her hard exterior and her inability to relax, avoiding any frivolousness, had created a protective shell to conceal a miserable soul.

'Chin-yee, we must play this very carefully. Firstly, we have to hand Fleur over to our people in America so they can control her while Algie is posted in Los Alamos. I want to be kept informed of the couple's whereabouts and activities because sooner or later I believe they will be returned to England. You will remember what I said at the beginning of this operation; how I saw the Stanhope couple as a long-term project. Please remind Fleur how she has to be extremely careful not to arouse her husband's suspicions. We want him to remain entirely innocent of the activities she carries out on our behalf, forever, if possible. Tell her too that she should make contact in Los Alamos with other Chinese or half-Chinese people. By cultivating them socially she will have a natural Chinese cover. You've really hit gold, sister! It's such a pity we have to hand Fleur over to our colleagues in America, just when it's getting exciting!'

'You know best, Wu. I'll arrange to meet her at lunchtime. That is the best time for her. She has a break from her work around midday in Lane Crawfurd's. This is pretty sensational, but we must keep calm! Let's take a stroll round the island before catching the ferry back, I could do with the fresh air to cool me down.'

We scrambled over small grassy hills and enjoyed the views across the surrounding waters on our way climbing up to the Buddhist temple to light a stick of joss, planting it in a rudimentary container full of sand. The smell of the mass of burning embers was soporific and the fragrant smoke stung our eyes. It was a relief to step outside the temple into the fresh air again and listen to the gentle tinkling of the Buddhist objects swaying in the light breeze. My emotionally numb and spartan existence amid those beautiful surroundings was immersed with a moment of warmth and colour. I hadn't slept well lately and I hoped the fresh air would settle me later that night to help regain a pattern of slumber.

'Fancy after all these years you and me working together on a secret operation. What would our father have thought? Do you think he would be proud of us?' I asked my sister reflectively.

'I'm sure he would,' she replied without the slightest hesitation in her voice.

'Perhaps we will be less aggressive towards each other

now that we have been brought together like this?' I suggested.

'I'd like to believe that too, Wu. I know we haven't got on well in the past. I've found you so serious and old beyond your years, and I often wondered if you ever had a childhood. You don't fool me, I know that you really have a core of steel under the oh-so-soft covering that you show the world. The closest I ever got to you was when I comforted you as a baby when you had bad dreams, but that was a long time ago. Let's try now to improve things between us? Shall we do that?' she beseeched him.

'For years I've thought you resented me as the son in our family, particularly when I followed so closely in our father's footsteps into the Secret Service. You probably thought life was too easy for me, and I was being favoured in some way?'

'I admit I was mean to you, jealous I suppose. That was only natural, but I won't do anything to prejudice the Party or the family. I'm not blind to the imperfections in the Party at the moment, which one can see more clearly away from the mainland.'

'What do you mean? You can talk quite freely with me.'

'Mao has focused on a programme of suppression on the mainland. The lack of education has created an underclass, unable to produce educated people to run the country. It's almost as if he deliberately wants to keep everyone down. In some ways his inability to keep pace with Russia's arms race is a symptom of this inflexible policy.'

Chin-yee was getting on her high horse and starting to get aggressive. We hadn't had a conversation like this for some time. In her earlier years sarcasm had been her verbal tool, often cutting and cruel. Despite mellowing, her political ramblings soon aggravated me. Her short dumpy body was dressed in a shapeless cheap printed cotton frock, without style. Her flat feet looked red and swollen, strapped into ill-fitting sandals, but she maintained her dignity and impression of superiority by thrusting her hands deep into the side pockets of her dress. She looked up at me, unblinking, eyes flashing angrily: a discontented woman, unhappy with her lot.

From the top of the hill we started our way back down steadily to the jetty to catch the ferry back. The sea surrounding the island was dull grey, reflecting the low overcast clouds. Here and there pinpricks of distant ships splashed thin streaks of white in their wakes.

'I think I know how you feel, and you're not alone. One day an injection of new blood will change the Party. Then it will move forward in keeping up with the modern world rather than stagnating in the current antiquated and retrogressive control of a vast, backward and repressed population. You know that in my position it is difficult for me to say more. We'd better start back or we'll miss the ferry.'

'You always break off just when it's getting interesting! Tell me, Wu, what ever happened about that unfortunate secretary you got pregnant in Beijing? Did the Party spirit her and the baby away? Am I an auntie? Was that the real reason you were posted here so suddenly? Come on, give me answers now that we are alone together?' she pressed me directly, dredging deep in her reservoir of charm before the inevitable return to her normal aggressive self.

'I don't want to talk about it. Sorry,' I replied. There was a part of my life I didn't want to discuss with anyone.

'Typical!' She replied in a sulk, taking the rebuff personally. 'You give everyone the impression of a deep force, which keeps certain people away from you, it stops them getting close.'

'So?'

It was typical that she should get personal by trying to demean me. There was usually a trade-off with Chin-yee, which made it difficult for me to relax totally in her company.

17

'The house with an old grandparent harbours a jewel.'

The last weeks in Hong Kong went quickly for Algie and Fleur, culminating in a week-long round of farewell parties. They weren't so sad to leave; the time had come to move on. For Fleur it was also the realisation of a lifelong ambition to travel to the West.

Her elderly parents had been re-housed far away from the flimsy shantytown communities perched precariously on the hillsides. The Hong Kong government had decided on an ambitious project to build towering skyscrapers made up of hundreds of separate apartments into which immigrants were hurriedly transferred. The accommodation was modern and antiseptic, devoid of character, and in some ways the inhabitants became even more unhappy, isolated and depressed than before. Fleur had been told it was a known feature of life the world over that people would prefer to live in poor but friendly low-level buildings rather than in impersonal tower blocks. The spirit of comradeship and shared nostalgia for the old ways in the end proved more important to them than a clinically ordered existence in efficient low-cost, high-rise surroundings without traditional atmosphere or friendly neighbours.

Such was the environment in which Fleur left her parents, but there was no question that she should stay behind for them. She believed her parents to be adaptable and would make new friends. The people in the next-door flat on the tenth floor of their block were particularly helpful. It was a wrench for her, but she had her own life to lead and the opportunities offered to her and Algie didn't come up every day. She did worry, though, that her parents thought ill of her and judged her to be self-interested and ambitious, but they said nothing.

The couple's leave in England, with the exception of a few days, was spent almost entirely at Algie's father's house in Somerset. But they had a few days in an inexpensive three-star hotel off Queen's Gate in Kensington before that. After sightseeing and shopping they moved out for another couple of days to Weybridge so that Algie could report to his office.

'I want to introduce you to everyone here who affects my life,' Algie told her. 'My father is besotted with you, I can tell. Of course, he won't admit it! You must forgive him as he's rather doddery when he gets out of his wheelchair. He's getting on and now his hearing is going. But he means well. Darling, it must be so strange for you coming to England at long last?'

'In China, we have a tradition of honouring our old people. I think it's much stronger, that feeling of family unity in China than it is in England. Your country is much like I have read about in books. It's so odd seeing the mass of white rather than Chinese faces. I've seen very few Chinese over here so far. Do they really live in groups like small communities in London's Soho and China Town, and run fish and chip shops and restaurants?'

'I think so,' Algie replied.

During their time in England they enjoyed that very special but brief feeling of freedom without responsibility, experienced by those home from abroad during long leaves, especially after a long spell overseas. Algie told her there was a sense that as a couple they might have been more interesting to friends than when he was last on home shores as a mere bachelor. Some things never change, and Algie's father's home was comfortable and had retained a certain quintessential rural and very British charm.

To Fleur, Algie's father was the typical English gentleman, with a weather-beaten face, skin stretched tight over the cheekbones, pale misty deep-set eyes, a bushy grey moustache, shoulders stooped and back bent from years of standing outside.

One evening when they were all sitting at Archie's father's house, Fleur wanted to know more about her husband's family, particularly his late mother and his father. The earlier objection Algie's father had to their own marriage had been largely forgotten.

'Dad, do tell Fleur about mother. You know, the story about how you captured her heart,' asked Algie, leaning forward to put another log on the open fire, hoping to take the early chill away by adding a warming atmosphere to the low-beamed sitting-room where they nurtured their after-dinner drinks. Silver photograph frames crammed the tops of the polished antique furniture. One particularly large oil painting in a heavy ornate gilt frame was a portrait of a very beautiful woman. Fleur guessed it to be Algie's late mother, about whom he had spoken with great affection. Algie meanwhile was stroking the smooth head of his father's sleeping black labrador bitch.

'Oh, very well! Algie's mother was called Jennifer, known as Jenny to everyone outside her close family, but to us she was called "Bolly".'

'That's an interesting name,' Fleur said. She was sitting cross-legged on the floor in front of the fire. A guard stood in front of it to protect the Persian rug from spitting embers. They had been well fed with roast beef and Yorkshire pudding and Fleur was feeling relaxed.

'The reason she was called "Bolly" was a closely guarded secret, known to only a few of the close family,' continued Algie's father. 'Sometimes, if pressed by close and trusted friends, after much red wine and well into the evening when inhibitions and lips loosened, I have been known to let slip the secret!'

'Go on, Dad, Fleur is longing to know,' urged Algie, knowing well that his father deep down liked nothing better than to talk about his family and his adored late wife.

'It's rather silly, really,' said Algie's father in his self-deprecating way, hoping the mysterious build-up wouldn't become an anticlimax. 'It all goes back a very long way to when I first met Jenny. I was at University and as you would expect there was another chap on the scene. He was a rather smarmy bugger and had a private income, which enabled him to woo the girls, driving them around the country in his open-topped sports car. Needless to say, I didn't have two pence to rub together. Jenny, as the glamorous daughter of a senior diplomat, had been round the world and was much in demand at service parties. At nineteen she was sophisticated with a stunning beauty and vivaciousness which stayed with her all her life.'

'Really?' Fleur interjected quietly. She was thinking back to the contrast of her own life and how her parents had struggled on the mainland and then as illegal immigrants in Hong Kong.

零 零 零

When Fleur and her parents had recovered from the risky journey by sea from the mainland they made their way across Kowloon and on to Hong Kong Island. They joined scores of fellow refugees living in small wooden and paper shacks wedged into the folds of the hillside. Their home was dwarfed by the tower blocks whose residents had modern amenities. But these shacks were real homes at last for an invisible population for whom electricity, piped water and an address were unnecessary luxuries. They were squatters, living a first-base existence, having successfully run the gauntlet of the ever-vigilant patrols on both sides of the border.

As soon as the family arrived by boat in Hong Kong they disappeared without any official identity and reappeared as illicit job takers in cheap restaurants or on building sites, paid a pittance. This was the first rung of the ladder to their new life, and Fleur's parents were no exception. After a while, scores of immigrants moved into small poorly-equipped rooms into which whole families crammed themselves with little more than the roof over their heads. Both her parents worked hard to earn money by any means they knew, often stretching the borderline between entrepreneurial and illegal activity.

Each day Fleur's mother used to make her way across the ferry to Kai Tak airport to join the vast army of cleaners who worked on incoming passenger aircraft after their long-haul flights. On board were the remains of crumpled one-day-old newspapers from the West. She used to rush to grab the best ones, iron them out with a flat iron as quickly as she could, and within hours she had sold them on the streets or in hotels!

Meanwhile, her father worked as a chef in a noodle parlour in Causeway Bay and seldom came home till very late, then he was up again at six o'clock the next morning. Fleur grew up with hard working, loving parents in a close, loyal community. During the daytime, her early years were spent with other children in the block under the care of a nominated 'mother'. Even though they lived in abject poverty most of the immigrants from the mainland never for one moment regretted their decision to flee.

'I'm not boring you am I?' asked Algie's father.

'Not at all. Please go on, it's fascinating,' Fleur replied quickly, snapping out of her private thoughts, memories that had been put away, locked up in the attic of her mind. Then she looked across adoringly at Algie, who caught her eye and smiled. He was holding a half-filled crystal brandy glass in his left hand.

'Jenny shared a flat with her sister in London while they attended various schools,' Algie's father went on, 'She studied acting, taking after her mother in that way, quite unlike her sister who learnt cooking. I used to arrive in my scruffy jacket with leather patches at the elbows, straight from university, and clearly I was in a different league to smarty-pants with the sports car. So I saved up some money working as a barman and with the proceeds I arrived at Jenny's flat, carrying a most wonderful bottle of champagne. She was overcome with surprise and throwing her arms round my neck, cried out "Bolly! . . . You darling man – I love you!"'

'You see, darling, Bolly is the slang for the champagne called Bollinger!' explained Algie.

'Oh, I get it!'

'Quite right.' Algie's father was in full flight spurred on by an appreciative and attentive audience. 'It was the best investment I ever made and I never looked back from that day onwards! She was such a super woman, supporting both me and Algie. She was wonderful, too, at organising family reunions, Christmas and birthday parties, Sunday lunches, yet she still had time for good works in the village. Outside the front of the house signs were constantly being erected on long wooden poles, inviting participation in a cancer charity sale, or some such thing, of which Jenny was one of three on the committee. We always supported the Conservative Party candidate and put a sign out at the local and national elections.'

'I thought you voted for the Local Residents' Association?' asked Algie, now being reminded of much of the village life that he had forgotten.

Algie's father rambled on about the latest news in the village, 'I'm so sorry, I do bang on if encouraged!'

'Not at all. It helps me so much to know more about your way of life and Algie's too. Of course I've read books, but all this is new to me.'

166

'Are you sure I'm not boring you? You must stop me if it's too much. Algie, make sure Fleur's drink is topped up, and pass her those chocolates you kindly brought, they're delicious. Where was I? Oh, yes... '

He kept his polished Malacca walking stick between his legs and rested his hands on top of the smoothly curled handle with its engraved inscription on the silver band below the crook. His upturned grey and unkempt eyebrows made him look fiercer than he really was. He was a man whose life was ebbing away rather more quickly than he was prepared to admit, no longer caring much what he said or did. It simply didn't matter anymore. He got up frequently to go to the bathroom and he complained of disturbed nights in which he urinated rather too frequently for his liking. His doctor had told him it was prostate problems, but he took no notice and deliberately tried to ignore the inconvenience he obviously suffered.

'I used to help Jenny with the minutes of the meetings she attended which were appallingly recorded by the person appointed to the task. Sadly the art of minute-taking seems to be a thing of the past.'

'But you love all that stuff, Dad, being a stickler for detail and pedantic about the use of the English language. Mother always said that your fastidiousness kept everyone up to the mark,' said Algie, complimenting his father.

'Did she really? No committee in the village was complete without Jenny's presence; the Women's Institute, the over-sixties' outings group, the planning for a national celebration, the monthly quiz night in the village hall and many more. It was a good opportunity for me to do my own thing and slip away to the pub for a few pints with the chaps. You know, Fleur, the village pub in many parts of Britain is the centre of village life and information. If you think ladies gossip, you should attend an informal drinking session by a group of local chaps in the pub! There, all manner of village gossip, opinions and hearsay rumour is exchanged. Some quite personal, opinionated and prejudiced discussions take place, settling of old scores, that sort of thing.'

Algie looked across at Fleur lying down, cat-like, on the rug in front of the fire, head resting on her hands. Algie's father intrigued her.

'Christmas time was a big occasion when Mother was alive. Fleur, you must tell us about your family sometime.'

'I'd like to.'

'Good God! Is that the time? I must go to bed. We've got an early start tomorrow.'

18

'When the melon ripens it will fall itself.'

An impressionable male of Chinese-American parentage, John Poon told me how he was crucially affected by his early life. His father, Lee, had escaped mainland China in 1949 when the Communists took power. Fearing the regime of Mao Tse-tung, he had fled along with thousands of others to the newly-formed Chinese Nationalist stronghold on the island of Formosa, renamed Taiwan. Financial help had come to the island from the West, America in particular, who believed the way to combat Chinese Communism was by bolstering the Nationalists, helping them set up profitable manufacturing industries and providing covert military assistance.

Lee met Tessa, an American working with an international aid organisation set up to support the fledgling Republic of China under Chiang Kai-shek. The island badly needed Western help to protect it against the continuous threat of invasion from the mainland. Lee worked as a banker and was greatly attracted to Tessa; they decided to get married, and young John was born in 1952.

'Tell me, John, how are you getting on at Harvard? What is your life like there?' asked Lee, now living in Australia, of his son during a long vacation.

'It's great. Although I'm half-Chinese – which is pretty obvious from my features – I'm used to getting teased about being neither one thing nor the other,' replied John, who for several years had harboured a deep racial inferiority complex.

'I thought all that nonsense had stopped when you left high school. Your Chinese features have certainly become stronger as you've grown older, I've noticed that. I had hoped that people of your generation would be a more tolerant society.'

'It's really no problem, Dad. We have so many different colours and races at Harvard. It's really great there with the flower-power people all dressed as hippies. We join together to demonstrate against the American involvement in Vietnam. You would be surprised how many people have strong feelings over there, and I'm part of a not-so-small protest group. We like to think we're quite a force to be reckoned with! You might have read about some of our more dramatic demonstrations.'

'From time to time I do read about the campus revolutions, and sometimes I have wondered if you're a part of them! I know it's a natural student thing to rebel.'

'Definitely. I'm quite angry about so many things going on in the world at the moment. You could say I'm an idealist in the minority, but there are many others who see things the same way.'

'What sort of things?' asked Lee.

'The huge expenditure on weapons and loss of human lives in the Vietnam War, for a start. It's a typical example of the ruthless and bullying attempts by capitalist powers to dominate and overrun more helpless, poor countries, forcing innocent people in the paddy-fields to submit to their domination by inflicting terror with napalm bombing.'

'What about the capitalist system?'

'It encourages personal wealth creation in a way that is selfish. Actually, Dad, you yourself have benefited ever since you left the mainland. Because people like you are at the mercy of ruthless gamblers; markets change, speculators manipulate markets for their own good and countless lives are affected when crashes come and the ownership of assets change. As I see it, the ability to create personal wealth encourages a class-based society.'

'Is that so?' replied John's father, trying hard not to react to his son's extreme views, nor let their discussion get into a more personalised argument. John was hardly ever at home and he wanted to spend what little time there was together in harmony. John had been an intelligent child, prone to self-seeking tantrums and argumentative with his parents, severely stretching his parents' tolerance, sometimes forcing his father to box his ears.

'Yes, it certainly is. You, for one, are a prize example of decadent capitalism. You should be ashamed of yourself, especially knowing that you left your poor family behind on the mainland to go to a capitalist island. It's disloyal. The people on the mainland need our help.'

'You're entitled to your views, John. No doubt, there are strong socialist influences at work at Harvard spurring you on to challenge the capitalist order in America and the West, in favour of the down-trodden and poverty-stricken Communist countries. In simple terms, is that how you see the world split up?' asked Lee.

John was nervy, fidgety, crossing and uncrossing his legs, a man who might drum impatiently with his hands on the steering wheel of a car when driving in traffic. Always wanting to move on fast, not wanting the peace and calm of staying still for a moment, constantly needing a challenge, always on the go. His nerves demanded a constant activity, like a marathon runner, if he stood still he would probably fall down.

'Yes, but I like it at Harvard. The course is interesting and mentally challenging and I have a lot of friends, mainly in the Asian community there. We tend to stick together as a group.'

Father and son had talked quite freely. Lee worried that his own financial problems might have been responsible for tipping John over the edge, firing him up with subconscious anger and bitterness. But Lee believed in the merit of institutions like Harvard, where free speech and intellectual questioning were encouraged.

'It's a just a pity that no one preached back to the students about the terror tactics used by Communist regimes to hold on to power. You idealistic left-wing students seem hell-bent on creating a so-called classless society with everyone equal.'

'Actually, we're greatly encouraged by the sayings of Mao Tse-tung in his *Little Red Book*. It's fashionable reading at the moment among young university students everywhere.'

Lee had had several meetings at university where he was being actively recruited by a Communist spotter who had infiltrated the campus and was sedulously looking for potential agents for the Chinese Secret Service, the intelligence arm of the Chinese Communist Party itself. In the evenings, a far-left lecturer, Wang, gathered together a small cadre of well-targeted individuals to extol the virtues of Communism.

All over the American campuses, the Department of Energy was constantly on the lookout to recruit scientists from university to help with their ambitious nuclear development projects. John was easily attracted to this, and having been offered a scientific research career he was destined for either of the leading Lawrence Livermore or Los Alamos nuclear laboratories in the United States.

零　零　零

The BOAC flight from Heathrow to Dallas, although long, was easy and comfortable. Algie's company had allowed him and Fleur the privilege of flying business class, adding greatly to their comfort, which included more leg room and unlimited quantities of free champagne. The heavier luggage, containing their Chinese furnishings and personal bits and pieces the couple had collected in the first year of their marriage in Hong Kong, had gone on ahead in giant packing cases.

From Dallas they took the internal American Airlines flight to the airfield at Los Alamos, a community of some 18,000 residents which was there mainly in support of the Los Alamos National Laboratory, situated in the beautiful Jemez Mountains of northern New Mexico.

The summer heat of New Mexico shimmered above the bonnets of motor cars and hovered like a mirage above the tarmac roads, creating floating images of distant pools of water. But that was all they were, images. The landscape with its dusty, dry and sandy terrain reminded Algie so much of films he had seen of the desert. He was used to the heat but he had surprised himself by coping well with the effects of the journey. Fleur had wisely taken the precaution of taking her sunglasses and consumed quantities of water instead of alcohol on the aircraft. She had never followed the Western enthusiasm for alcohol and deliberately avoided dairy products like milk and cheese, seriously believing them to be a major cause of cancer in Western society.

At the airfield they were met by an American associate in his large and ostentatious 1960s Buick Oldsmobile. Algie was particularly intrigued by the steering-column gear-shift. It reminded him of his younger, single days, when he found the front bench-type seat, without the interference of the floor-mounted gear-change, a definite aid to sex. He wondered mischievously if that was the main attraction for Walt, his future guide and mentor. It was hard to gauge his personality in his vacant face, unruffled despite the heat and a full unkempt beard blanked out by eyes that lacked expression.

'So you guys had a good trip? Welcome to our world!' said Walt rather dourly, but trying to sound jolly; it didn't really suit him.

Walt was a long tall streak of a man, over six feet two

inches, with a thin, deceptively frail-looking frame. At thirty-five years of age, his sandy hair was cut close like a GI's and this accentuated the prominence of the startlingly bushy eyebrows which sheltered large, rarely-blinking green eyes. Walt intrigued them both. Fleur, true to form, set to work on assessing his character, relying mainly on her feminine intuition which Algie had come to respect. He anticipated that the two of them would pull Walt to pieces the moment they were alone together.

Walt shook hands limply and Algie, being the stronger of the two, was careful not to squeeze his colleague's thin and sharp-boned hand too hard.

'Thanks for coming to meet us,' said Algie appreciatively, sweating profusely under the strong sun. He felt the silky moisture trickling down the back of his shirt, forming a pool in the lumbar region and soaking the back of his shirt.

'It's a pleasure, no problem at all. We occasionally have a Brit come to visit for a couple of days but you are the first to be staying with us for as long as a year. I've been here for two years and next year I move across to the Lawrence Livermore National Laboratory in California. I'm one of the few scientists here who is still a bachelor, but we have a real good social life on the base.' Walt drawled on.

Loaded up with the baggage, Walt swung the heavy, glinting, aluminium-wrapped car out onto the highway, one hand resting nonchalantly on the left-hand-drive steering wheel that responded to the slightest touch. They headed out from the airfield and into the desert-like landscape with its backdrop of high parched mountains. The vast plain was home to some of the world's leading nuclear scientists, all feverishly straining mind and limb to keep America and the West ahead in the nuclear arms race. As they got closer to the base itself the forests grew close up to the perimeter fence, a fire hazard in times of drought Algie had read somewhere.

'We just have to check in at these security gates, it won't

take a moment,' said Walt as he brought the car to a smooth standstill on the outside of the perimeter fence, the entrance gates guarded by two armed security men. He took out a sheaf of papers from the glove compartment and with his loping stride sauntered up to the guardhouse. Algie and Fleur were summoned to join him to verify their identities before being allowed through the electronic gates.

'You guys will get used to the high security here. But once you're on the base, you'll find sports amenities, excellent PX stores and medical facilities. There's always some party going on. Hell, there's some few thousand of us! Just a warning, though: we all need to get out once in a while, but you'll find almost everything you need here on the base.'

'Where's our house, Walt?' Fleur asked. She was sitting in the front seat and had a good view of the surroundings.

'See over there? On the edge of the camp,' he pointed, 'That row of white-painted houses with nice front gardens; they have even bigger ones at the back. One of those is yours. You'll like it. All mod cons, I think you Brits say, and each house has a place at the back for a barbecue.' Walt pointed with his free arm as he drove towards the allocated house. As they got closer it became larger and the white wood boarding gave the house a pleasant rustic charm. It was freshly painted and everywhere, the garden and the street, was spotlessly clean and tidy.

Walt opened up the house and handed over the keys. An information pack about shopping facilities and so on had been left inside by the telephone in the hall. Walt had arranged for a camp car to be put at their disposal until they bought their own car. Algie was handed an efficient military style programme and immediately they were made to feel welcome.

Algie and Fleur wasted no time in getting used to their new surroundings and enthusiastically joined in the social scene and integrated with their new colleagues. Fleur met up with the few Anglo-Chinese scientists, thrilled to welcome her into the fold. They arranged to meet up regularly to get together and to explore their Oriental roots, usually to the exclusion of Algie who was quite happy to leave his wife to make her own social contacts.

零　零　零

John Poon's telephone answering machine flashed, indicating a waiting message. He pressed down the 'play' key. There was only one message. It was from Fleur. There was no denying he felt a rush of excitement. It was even more special since he hardly ever received calls. He had few friends compared with some of his colleagues on the base working at the laboratory. Perhaps her call would bring an end to his dull routine incarcerated on the base, unmotivated to move outside it, too lethargic and disinterested in much other than his scientific work. She was hardly ever out of his mind, with her arrogant self-confidence, bright chat and sudden calmness. He had human needs.

零　零　零

'Algie, I'm going out tonight to an Anglo-Chinese reunion. We're holding a special supper to celebrate Chinese New Year. Do you want to come?' Fleur asked her husband.

'Do you mind terribly if I pass this time? I have so much work to do trying to catch up on this advanced technology; frankly, most of it is way above my head. You go off and enjoy yourself,' replied Algie who had, unknown to her at the time, received a rare but most welcome letter from Barbara. She was married, had one young son and seemed to be living happily in Sydney. Although her letters were few, when they came they were full of news and Algie believed in some small way she cared for him. The opportunity of an evening to himself to compose his reply to her had come at a good time. He remembered how, in the Hong Kong days, Barbara had resented having her wings clipped. How was she coping with the tying nature of marriage and a baby? Despite the parting, he thought about her a lot and in his heart he still missed her.

'I won't be late,' Fleur replied, kissing her husband lightly on his forehead. She knew he didn't like Chinese New Year celebrations; he had had more than his fair share of them in Hong Kong. Away from Algie she was getting a reputation on the base of sweeping males off their feet and wives were getting jealous.

One morning, quite out of the blue, Fleur received a letter from a travel firm based in New York, specialising in tours to the Far East. The letter was written in Mandarin and had asked her to telephone a certain number to obtain further information. The brief telephone call she made from a box outside the base had established the link with her new case officer from the Chinese Secret Service, attached to the Chinese Embassy in New York. He wanted to brief her personally, especially as he had received encouraging handover notes from our Hong Kong office.

Using coded letters and invisible ink they made the arrangement to meet up at the Express Coffee Shop in downtown Los Alamos. It was opposite a parking lot on the road leading out of town towards the airport. They spotted each other easily; he with the snub nose and bullet head giving him an ugliness which should have protected him from passion-starved women. Having exchanged the recognition signals they changed cars and drove off into the desert, away from the direction of the laboratory camp.

'You've come with an excellent recommendation from Chin-yee and my colleague Wu in Hong Kong. We're so pleased you will continue to work for our cause here. One of the most important targets in the whole world is the camp over the hill; there is so much going on there that we need to know.'

'I realise that.'

'I'm sure you've been told not to make your husband suspicious. You should encourage John Poon to acquire secrets for you using whatever method you advise to achieve the result. We know he was born in Taiwan, the historic enemy of the People's Republic of China, but he has been allowed to work in the most secret laboratories here. We also know – and this is interesting – that when he was at Harvard University he held strong left-wing views like many Western students at that time. The authorities consider that period in young people's lives to have been nothing more than a harmless passing phase.'

'I get the picture so far,' replied Fleur, as her case officer edged closer on the front seat of the car and brushed his hand across her bare knees, which she had clamped firmly together to protect her modesty against the rising of her short cotton skirt. She wasn't at all surprised that he had tried to come onto her; men usually did. In her experience, those involved in dangerous espionage activities were pumped up with too much testosterone, but she was confident she could handle this one.

'We want you to run him as an agent – I don't know if running is the right word here! – you know what I mean. Get to know him well, if necessary intimately. Discover what his beliefs and motives are. Stress that you feel sympathetic to China and its plight as a poor country where you, and he too, have relatives living in harsh conditions. Say how heartily you deplore the gross imbalance of riches, which the West exploits, you think unfairly, guaranteeing them the leading position in the arms race. By acquiring secrets for China that imbalance could be redressed and a disastrous worldwide military confrontation averted,' suggested the case officer.

'I don't know how long this will take. First, I'll have to

get his total trust. In a way it is made easier for me. Being a bachelor, he's already shown his keenness to establish a Chinese identity with me, but it may well need some sexual input on my part,' Fleur announced quite unabashed. She noticed it was a hot day and her light clothing stuck to her. A fly had landed on the case officer's nose, which he flicked a couple of times but it landed on him repeatedly, easily getting the measure of the controller's ineffectual swatting technique.

'That may be so,' he continued, 'in which case he'll be a very lucky man!' Well into middle age, the case officer had fantasised about having an affair with someone like Fleur, but a fantasy it had to remain. She had given no hint of returning his enthusiasm, which depressed him. At fifty-six years of age, with his potbelly and bulging shortsighted eyes, he was reluctant to admit he had had his day. Now he was left to the fading memories of his more erotic youth. He had learnt to hold his libido in check, to avoid it affecting his judgement on operations, especially one as important as this one, which the Party Chairman himself was showing such a keen interest in.

'Here's the telephone number. Don't lose it. If there's any problem, just call this number in New York and ask for Jackson, my codename for this operation. The office is a small room in a Chinese Travel Agency, a Party investment through a complicated network of holding companies specialising in holiday trips to the Far East. They know how to get hold of me there.'

The couple sped back in the hired car, especially laid on by the local courier. Having wished her the best of luck, this time resisting making any further advances, the case officer said goodbye. They went separately in search of their own cars and mingled back into the normal world as unconnected people.

19

'He who was bitten by a snake avoids the tall grass.'

Fleur spent a few weeks getting to know John Poon before she felt confident he would meet her alone and away from the base. She remembered the point at which she had judged the moment to be right, the barometer read ninety degrees. At 2.15 pm on the dot, John walked into the coffee bar where she was sitting, dressed in a floral mini-skirt and white T-shirt, hoping to look cool in an unsophisticated but utterly feminine way. She had ordered herself a cappuccino and when John joined her he ordered the same. The introductory greetings were completed and after the coffees they strolled out to John's car and drove away from the camp, in the same direction Fleur had gone with her own spymaster barely a few weeks before.

'Let's pull off the road and park the car behind those trees and walk for a while,' she said spontaneously.

'Right,' replied John obediently. She knew well enough that John was a shy bachelor and not for the first time she might have to take charge of the situation. John was prone to absent-mindedness and she worried he might fall short on practicalities. He needed to be jerked out of the rut he had found himself in.

Having parked up well off the road and behind a small ridge topped with a thorn tree they walked together for a while. Fleur outwardly showed magnificent self-confidence but underneath there was fear and uncertainty. Despite her anxiety she was determined to go ahead with her plan. She suggested they sit down on the long dry grass under another thorn tree in the shade, as the afternoon sun was so strong. The only sound was of insects rubbing their tiny wings together and a few bees buzzing around, flitting from plant to plant, lingering in the nectar then moving on. Otherwise there was no movement, just the hard blue of the sky with occasional cotton wool clouds and the dead quiet of a wilderness.

'John, I like you very much. I was attracted to you from the very first time we met. It must be so lonely for you as a bachelor,' Fleur said putting her arm round his shoulder, awkwardly at first, then, sensing a need to calm him, she took his hand in hers and stroked it gently.

No woman had ever said that to him, nor had he felt that way about a woman. Had he missed out on life? Until now it had never crossed his mind. Revelling in this unaccustomed and energy-giving emotion he felt slightly confused, yet he welcomed it. He had ensconced himself in his own monotonous world, within the safety of his academic achievements and the laboratory compound, but it hadn't brought him warmth in his heart and often he was introspective to the verge of self pity.

John became more relaxed as Fleur put her hand on his tummy and stroked his face before kissing him lightly on the lips. He responded warmly to her gentle touch. She cuddled up to him more closely. It made him feel protective towards her, manly.

'You like me too, John?' She asked him outright, in a way that was reminiscent of her time in the Wanchai girlie bars. The lines were very similar.

'Yes, very much, but you're married,' he replied cautiously.

'Don't worry about that! I have an arrangement with my husband. We have an open marriage. He allows me to have affairs; in return I allow him freedom to do the same. You don't have to worry, he won't come after you with a meat cleaver! He just asks that I'm discreet, that's all. It's a good arrangement actually and it works well for us.' She sensed the pent-up passion building inside him but desperately needing the crucial trigger to release it.

Fleur leant over and placed her mouth close to his in an open invitation to him. His lips skimmed her peppermint-tasting lips, tentatively at first, then more purposefully, savouring the spittle as he probed his tongue along the roof of her mouth. The scarlet gash of lipstick had been licked and sucked away. Presently, he moved his head down and buried his head between her breasts.

Caressing his thighs slowly, Fleur found John's zipper, carefully pulled it down and felt inside. She knew she had aroused him sometime before. With her other hand she brought his hand towards her, guiding him to feel between her own legs. She placed his hand in the cleft, which was already moist. In a moment he was transformed by uncontrollable passion. He pulled urgently at her clothes. In a second he was out of his trousers. She helped him off with his shirt before he clumsily worked her flimsy pants down her legs. Fleur smiled to herself, knowing the power she now had over him in his state of clamouring vulnerability. She pulled her dress over her head, self-consciously revealing her small-breasted body, hairless but for a black sparse tuft of pubic hair.

She felt no guilt. A sudden animal passion had engulfed her, making her impatient too. She wanted him to take her forcefully. Desire and excitement erupted inside her, ignited by the rough touch of his flesh. Her eyes closed and she started to tremble. He lingered to savour, kiss, lick and marvel at the most sensitive parts of her body, hardly able to control the urgency of his desire. Fleur ran her fingers through his hair tenderly and guided him into her.

'John you're a big strong man. Come into me now!' she pleaded. He penetrated her easily; she lay face upwards on the parched ground, the entry silky smooth but tighter than he had expected. He took much of his own weight on top of her, working her legs spread wide as he thrust more deeply into her. She rolled her head from side to side as the sensation reached its height, flooding her whole being and pulling at the deepest parts of her anatomy.

When the immediate humping crescendo of passion had subsided, she opened her eyes. He was kneeling naked beside her, his uncircumcised flesh limp, a spent force. Leaning over her he lightly kissed her face and breasts, so tenderly that his lips hardly touched her flesh. He rolled back to lie beside her sprawled nakedness, both bodies glistening in the afternoon heat. Satisfied for the moment, they sank back into the long grass, stroking and caressing each other as they crept languidly into each other's arms, rested for a while, feeling at ease, but they said little other than the appreciative murmurs lovers make.

'John, that was so good,' she said dreamily.

They didn't speak for a while, then he stirred and traced his forefinger lightly over her body, starting at the toes and working up to her neck.

'That tickles, but please don't stop!' purred Fleur, eyes closed and a smile on her face. Then she sat up, changing her mood: more alert, steeling herself to move on to the main purpose of their rendezvous.

'What's it like being a Chinese at Los Alamos?' she asked softly, sounding genuinely interested in his welfare. She brought him to his senses but he found it hard to snap back into reality.

'Fine. Everyone's very helpful,' he replied.

'What do you do there?' she asked more directly than she had ever spoken to him before.

'I work in the laser and nuclear testing areas. It's quite interesting,' he replied, stifling a yawn, sounding anything but enthusiastic about his work.

'What do you think about the state of poor old China now and their position in the world?' She asked seemingly innocent questions as she stroked his hair back from his forehead and kissed his shoulder lightly, brushing her lips across his warm, salt-tasting flesh.

'I'm really sad that China is so poor and so far behind in

the arms race. It has far too many people to support and they were very badly treated in the Cultural Revolution. I suppose that's why so many defected to Hong Kong and Taiwan by any means possible. So brave, those people. They should never have been forced into that situation.'

'I agree, but what can we do about it?'

'You tell me!'

'Let's go for a walk.' Fleur suggested. She had recovered her energy rather more quickly than John and stood up. She pulled him to his feet and they put their clothing back on from the pile they had left in the long dry grass. Once they were dressed they strolled hand-in-hand towards the forest where the heady scent of softwoods was captured under the canopy of giant evergreens, their leafy branches keeping out the heat and sunlight. The forest was quite still and cool, a contrast to the heat in the open ground. As she walked Fleur's graceful, feline movements fascinated him.

'John, have you ever been married?' she asked breaking the silence.

'No,' he replied.

'The opportunity must have arisen?'

'Not really.'

'Come on! You must have had girlfriends in the past, tell me about them?'

'There's nothing to tell.'

'John, don't be such a bore! Do you mean to say you've been working so hard on all this technical stuff for the past few years that you haven't had time to get laid?'

'Yes.'

Just then she stumbled. Her shoe caught on a stone, turning her ankle awkwardly. But there was no reaction from her companion; it was slowly dawning on her that she was dealing with an automaton, and it was becoming difficult to keep up the pretence that she was fond of him. She was disappointed he didn't come forward to help her but managed to recover her step without his help.

'Thanks for your help!' Fleur said sarcastically.

'Oh!' he answered back unmoved by her scarcely concealed protest.

'Why do you think you love me all of a sudden? Before I got to know you better you seemed to be an unemotional man not wanting any commitment. You certainly showed feeling a few minutes ago! Is it just sex that releases your feelings? You can have that with anyone!'

'I suppose so – but you're special.'

'Too damn right I am!' she replied proudly, confident of her seduction skills.

'Perhaps you're frightened of women and relationships?' she challenged him again.

'Maybe,' he replied sullenly. He was non-committal in so many ways – a perfect agent – but she wondered if he would be fun to have as a lover after all! They turned round and walked out of the wood and met full on the heat coming off the open land. John scratched the mole on his right cheek, which tended to demand his attention whenever he was nervous.

'Do you still feel strongly about helping the mother country? Would you be prepared to take some risks for me?'

He looked at her curiously, surprised. One minute thinking of her as someone's wife, the next as a fellow conspirator. The long pampas grass slowed their progress and all the time she worked on him, breaking into his mind, testing his motivations, putting up possibilities that called for commitment to an enterprise.

'I expect so. How could I refuse you?' he added cautiously, 'It depends what it is.'

'Would you feel able to pass me Western weapons technology secrets? You could play such a valuable part in reducing the enormous lead the West has. It is a priceless gift you have.'

'Now I understand what you're asking, but what can I

do? I'm such a small cog in a big wheel.'

'You're a patriot, aren't you? I want you to pass me as much information as you can on whatever design or technological information you can lay your hands on. Anything in fact that will be useful for our masters in Beijing in the development of our own weapons of mass destruction. Would you be prepared to do that?'

She looked straight into his eyes, coaxing him, at the same time stroking the inside of his thigh lightly, sensually lingering, soothing him. She had perfected the technique with customers in the girlie-bars where she first learnt to seduce men regardless of her true feelings for them.

'I think so. Perhaps my work might at last take on a real purpose. I admit that recently I've felt as though I'm a machine, frying my brains, unnoticed and unappreciated, an insignificant part of a long-term project which might not even get fully funded by Congress.'

'Are you sure? This is a very serious and potentially dangerous operation,' Fleur asked, wanting him to be certain of the risks he would be taking.

'I realise that,' he replied unflinchingly.

'I'm so proud of you, John. I knew I had the right man when I first set eyes on you. I'm told the Party Chairman is particularly interested in getting the secrets out of Los Alamos, and he will certainly follow this operation with a very special interest.'

'It's as important as that, then?'

'Definitely. It's deadly serious and so vital to the peace not only of China but, I believe, of the whole world.'

It was still a challenge to get an emotion out of this boring man, but she was confident of her hold over him. Ignoring his pock-marked face, Fleur kissed him lightly on the mouth, lingering long enough to dart her tongue in between his lips. Her kisses became more intense and passionate as the minutes passed. Deliberately and very slowly she moved her right hand down his chest, stopping to grasp a nipple and roll it between her finger and thumb. Then she kissed his other nipple, nibbling it, making it stand proud. She moved on down, dragging her tongue softly over his limp, vulnerable body, licking him back into life.

She moved back to kiss him on his lips while holding and squeezing him in her hand. She had an urge to comfort him and in an uninhibited animal way she longed for him to be inside her again. Sensuous desire had now taken its hold on them both. He clasped her hair and head in his hands, this time more savagely than before.

Her eyes shut, she was in another world. He grasped her breast into the palm of his hand and she trembled. 'Come in me!' Fleur urged, stretching her hands down to stroke and fondle him again. She held him tightly and then guided him to the point of entry; half-naked he thrust into her. He pushed in hard but it was easier this time and the pressure made her gasp. He paused, so she squeezed him tight into the walls of her vagina. Their rocking movements gained speed until their lithe bodies arched in unison. The sheer power of primeval lust exploded and fused them together. She heard him cry out like a child in the final moment of ejaculation.

He rolled away and they lay side by side, panting. While their heartbeats subsided, they gazed up at the sky regaining sight of their surroundings slowly. They rested for a while before deciding to return to the camp, concerned not to attract suspicion with an overlong and unexplained absence. She stood up and pulled him to his feet. They checked and adjusted their clothing, both taking care to smooth and brush their hair. Fleur, always the one to pay attention to detail, plucked away bits of grass from their clothes as they casually made their way back to the car.

Back at the original meeting place they transferred to their own cars and set off for the base. They arrived separately and twenty minutes apart.

John was in his seventh heaven. For him sex had the added piquancy of having it with someone else's wife. More importantly, Fleur probed his deeper thoughts and gave him a worthwhile direction in life. She had taken the trouble to try to understand him. He had been drifting aimlessly before, but now he faced a heady mix of deception skills and bravery. Now his life was to become fuller and he was flattered that Fleur was pursuing him and was almost willing to be manipulated by her. He started to enjoy his work, too. People noticed a more lively spring in his step and he radiated cheerfulness. To reduce any feeling of isolation, she called him regularly, sharing as much of their lives as they could. The fresh impetus to his whole existence he owed to Fleur.

It wasn't long before John reported back to Fleur. He was keen for more passion and desperate to impress her. His first offerings consisted of secret letters divulging technical secrets about lasers and how the technology could be adapted for military use together with forecasted introduction to service dates.

He told her about the Americans experiencing serious problems and delays with their nuclear testing programme, holding up their strategic arms development. One highly-classified letter he had found was actually from the President himself, expressing a real worry that hold-ups in the programme could not be tolerated in view of the Russian nuclear programme being so close on their heels.

At first, the illegal removal of documents didn't come easily to John. He had found it difficult to conjure up a plausible excuse, a lie, for staying late in the office once everyone else had left for the day.

'So how did you manage?' asked Fleur, knowing he would find it difficult to express his feelings.

He explained how some people stayed late if they were behind in the work schedule. He stayed back deliberately pretending to work late, but just when he went to the safe he heard a sound outside down the corridor. He stopped in his tracks, his mind racing, desperately thinking how he could appear more natural. The more he thought, the more nervous he became. The mole on his cheek played up. It stood out livid. A single annoying strand of black hair sprung from its centre, demanding to be itched and plucked out. The mole was a distraction, but his hands shook and then the sound disappeared. Was someone nearer or further away than before? How would he react under stress? Will the person still be there when he leaves the building? Who the hell was it? Where were they now? He was panicking. Wet sweat patches appeared under his arms. He felt hot in the crutch, Y-fronts tight, restricting. Gurgling noises in his stomach interrupted the silence, uncontrollable and to him excruciatingly loud!

'So what happened then? Fleur asked, genuinely fascinated.

'I gathered the sensitive material I needed – rather clumsily, I'm afraid.'

'Well done,' she said.

'But my hands still shook. I felt sick. I thought I might vomit.'

'Poor you.'

'I broke out in a cold sweat. Having the valuable assets in my hands increased my fear of being caught and forced me to speed up my movements quite unnaturally.'

'I can see you now.'

'I was in a blind panic.'

'You are brilliant, John! It must have been such an ordeal and so scary.' She put her arm around his shoulder and stroked the back of his neck with her index finger.

John handed over the precious documents at a place where they were certain of not being seen. She immediately took the vital documents home to copy using the special camera and a strong light bulb.

'What happens now?' he asked.

'I'll return them to you this evening to make sure they're not out of the office for longer than necessary. After I've photocopied the material with a small but powerful mini camera, I'll place the film in an envelope and call the local courier's telephone number. He'll pick up the material, getting the envelope off the base as quickly as possible, even before you've returned the papers to where they belong in the office – or is it the safe?'

'Both. You won't be longer than necessary, will you?'

'Don't worry. I know it's a tense moment. I'll be as quick as I can. Meet me back here in half an hour.'

'Good luck.'

Her case officer had told her not to rely on post or commercial means as things could so easily go wrong. The human courier system was best. She decided to deposit the film in a dead letter box for the courier to pick up, lodged behind a loose brick in a wall well outside the base and virtually undetectable, out of range of the base's security cameras.

When the operation was over and the original papers were back in place, Fleur rewarded John with a walk and more sex. She convinced him of her feelings for him, ensuring his continuing commitment to more operations. So far John hadn't pushed for anything more from her, but she suspected it wouldn't be long before he pressed for a more permanent attachment, possibly wanting the exclusion of Algie from her life. She would deal with that eventuality if and when it arose.

At their next meeting she broached the subject of her relationship with Algie.

'John, you do realise that I and many other women are perfectly able to have a sexual relationship without it affecting the emotional equilibrium of their own marriages? Some women find it as easy as many men do to deceive their partners without raising damaging suspicions. I suppose it does rather challenge conventional attitudes towards the trust between partners.' John shrugged his shoulders as if it was none of his business, caring little.

She always praised John whenever he produced material for her, acutely aware of her need to keep him in a high state of motivation. She put in place a simple system with the designated courier, sometimes meeting him outside the base to hand over the film, at other times using the dead letter box procedure; never the same method, exactly. For many months this routine continued smoothly, as far as she was aware without interruption or detection. Her case officer had told her that the only problem with a well-established secret network for the passage of top-grade information was its vulnerability either to complacency or if one member in the chain fell ill, moved away or turned out to be a traitor.

John's self confidence had grown in the short time that Fleur had him under her control.

'Fleur, I'm getting bored!' he exclaimed unexpectedly one day. The new vigour had brought impatience, the least likely emotion she had expected from him.

'Not with me, I hope!'

'Of course not, I don't mean that. Do you know what I've done?'

'Tell me,' Fleur tensed to the possibility of any irrational behaviour that might compromise his cover and the operation.

'I've transferred data relating to nuclear weapons from a secret computer in Los Alamos to an outside computer. It can easily be accessed by virtually anyone!'

'You're so brilliant, John!' Fleur said excitedly and threw both her arms round him. She was ecstatic and planted a huge wet kiss on his lips. He grinned back at her. She paused in thought for a moment.

'Who can access this second computer?' she asked.

'From now on Chinese intelligence officers will be able to

retrieve vast amounts of information. From the data I've already put on there alone, it will be possible for the People's Liberation Army to develop their own miniaturised warheads in China!' he said excitedly.

'How amazing! Now you're really motoring! Tell me John, how is it so easy for you to do these things from inside such a top-secret establishment?'

'So far in life, I've learnt that nothing is what it appears to be. Scrape away the surface of most institutions – and most people too, for that matter – and you will find something quite different. Tear away the veneer of tight security at Los Alamos and you will discover glaringly obvious lapses. I guess a determined enemy has to find those holes and exploit them. Sorry, I'm sounding more like a general! You know what I mean though, don't you?'

'Yes, I follow you. I'm absolutely fascinated. So what's the trick with these computers?' she asked.

'You simply won't believe this, but luck seems to have been on my side for a change. There's been a fierce bureaucratic battle between the United States Department of Energy and the top-secret laboratory here at Los Alamos, which it supervises. The department said it was short of funds and has used that as an excuse to procure the necessary state-of-the-art computers the scientists have been crying out for. They were so hacked off by the penny pinching and bureaucratic attitude that they've reacted by downloading top-secret data on to newer, faster but much more insecure machines! So there you have it: I told you it was simple, didn't I?' He sighed and looked tired. He had been so obsessed with getting every detail just right.

'You're so brilliant! Could you possibly write me a summary of all this? We mustn't waste a moment to get a report up the chain to our intelligence people as soon as possible, before anyone suspects there is the slightest possibility of leakage through any unauthorised access.'

Fleur was confident that she could run her agent

effectively for a little longer. Immediately after her meeting with John she called the special number of her case officer from a coin box using the pre-arranged code words.

20

'Insects do not nest in a busy door-hinge.'

Walt was John Poon's dreamy and docile boss. In his laid-back, bump-on-the-head scientist manner, his mind often drifted into flights of highly intellectual eccentric erudition. Colleagues pulled his leg unmercifully about the practicalities of life passing him by and it had never occurred to him, despite numerous security briefings, that vital secrets might have been stolen from under his nose. Walt was far too trusting and innocent.

Algie had picked up – with difficulty, he had to admit – enough of the key technological factors relating to the future development of weapons in America to brief relevant interested parties both at the MOD in London and his firm in Weybridge. The content of his briefing had the potential to impact on the size and shape of the British armed services and the fiercely fought over military budgetary requirements. In terms of introducing any new nuclear-weapons capability, long lead-times had to be understood and accepted. By cutting out the time-consuming expense of research and development, Britain had decided it was more economical to share information with a reliable ally, followed by the procurement of the weapons they needed at favourable discounted rates. The purchase price would have included an element of shared cost in the American research and development.

When the couple returned to England at the end of Algie's secondment, Fleur's farewells to her case officer and to John Poon were necessarily low-key, discreet affairs but emotional on John's part. It surprised Fleur that in spite of their cultural differences, Algie had got on rather well with the Americans. He was the quieter of the two, more reserved. She still accompanied Algie to most of the parties they were invited to together, and they had returned hospitality in their own home, but Fleur had preferred to socialise with her kindred Chinese and half-Chinese friends on the base.

Farewell parties for them started after the heavy baggage had been packed and sent on in advance. Algie's father had been alerted that they would be coming home and that they would like to store some wooden crates in one of the outhouses until they found somewhere to live. They planned to rent at first, somewhere near Weybridge, while they looked round for a suitable property to buy.

零　零　零

Fleur's father had often told her about his early life in Shanghai where he grew up in tin-shacked compounds and where whole communities were housed along the muddy banks of the Yangtze River. A typical camp usually housed up to one hundred souls in cramped communes with little privacy. It wasn't at all unusual for a couple with five children to live in two rooms, taking it in turns to queue up in the street to collect water from the tap or fetch it in buckets from the river. The lack of privacy was most evident in the communal latrines, simple holes in the ground where defecation took place in full view and oblivious to those waiting their turn. The conditions often led to unrest, crime and violence, brought on by frustration. Lice and worms were commonplace, and so was the discovery of dead bodies washed up by the river's tidal flow. Despite the hardships, though, these robust, inscrutable and ingenious people carved out a sort of life for themselves.

The excited noise of the city was constant, with impatient motor cars, agitated bell-ringing cyclists and excited lorry drivers, all pressing their way ever faster and more dangerously through the busy streets. In the background ships hooted on their way out to an anchorage in Hankow Bay at the mouth of the mighty Yangtze River. Limpet ships and sampans bobbed through the choppy grey water to attach themselves to moored-up cargo vessels and join in the non-stop craning-off of goods shipped in from all over the world for transfer to the onshore warehouses and go-downs. The city, the river and the port never stopped and the sounds remained with Fleur's father for life. He used to hark back to the old days of Communist rule on the mainland.

'There was no running water in many of the old houses. As kids we used to play in the street for hours on end chasing hoops. Your grandmother used to wear a red armband and hobbled about the way old women do. The red armband signified that she was a vigilante, a member of the neighbourhood committee who kept an eagle eye on things. She was a grass-roots member of the Communist Party. They recruited retired people in those days to be the eyes and ears of the Party, watching everything and then reporting back. I remember the smell of coal smoke, frying onions, ginger and soya coming from the old courtyard where we lived. It was a scrapyard littered permanently with old chairs, potted plants, bicycles, pans of rice, lines of washing, and songbirds and crickets in bamboo cages. That was when I first decided I wanted to be a chef. But I've been happy in Hong Kong. I didn't want luxury; it destroys spirit and ambition. It makes people idle and fat!'

零 零 零

I got the posting I had hoped for to the Chinese Embassy in London where I was appointed to a senior position in the Secret Service. In this department there were some forty spies and support staff, almost as many as the KGB contingent at the Soviet Embassy! I was still unmarried and my reputation as a dedicated secret intelligence officer was high. My professional commitment had still excluded from my life the possibility of having a wife, although as an entirely heterosexual man I had desires and longings like other men. From time to time I was able to release those natural feelings in a discreet way, often with young secretaries or other members of my staff. They gladly gave themselves to a boss who they admired and respected. If the Party cause demanded them to make a personal sacrifice, they didn't expect any long-term romance to follow. Unfortunately it went wrong for me just before I was posted to Hong Kong. It was perfectly true, a young secretary did become pregnant by me, but it was hushed up. Friendly doctors known by the Service carried out an abortion. It was a necessary course of action for both of us, and as far as I know her life has resumed normality. I know she worked for the Service in Beijing but our paths have never crossed since. She was young at the time and I wasn't prepared to make a commitment to her. I have no regrets and I hope she has none either. I don't think I would have made a good husband, far too keen on my work, neglectful of my family duties, impatient and selfish. My sister always said I was a born bachelor and she was probably right.

Once I had settled into my new job in London, it wasn't long before I contacted Fleur who, as a long-term and established agent, had been passed back to my control from her case officer in America. She came to me with glowing reports of her work with John Poon at Los Alamos. I knew she held the key to the continuing success of our operations to acquire nuclear secrets from the West.

Before she left America, Fleur had been told by our man there to contact me in London. When I made contact, I detected it gave her a break from the monotonous routine of their new lifestyle in England. She later admitted to me how she had missed the raw excitement she had experienced in her dealings with John Poon, the unrestrained interludes of unsentimental passion and the risks they both took together in Los Alamos. From a London telephone box on a special number, she made the call which, on receipt of the prearranged password, was switched directly through to me in my office.

'So how are you?' I asked, hoping to sound unchanged by my promotion, my voice warm with genuine interest in the welfare of my agents and operatives. 'We must meet. I want to hear how you've been since I last saw you. I was wondering about this Monday?'

'I'm free then,' she replied.

'Say we meet at the lobby at the Savoy Hotel at noon? That could be a good place for you, as it's just over Waterloo Bridge and left up the Strand. I'll be there wearing a smart suit like we do here in London! My cover name will be Chan. Your cover name will be Madeleine Wright. I hope you don't mind that name? Hopefully you'll get used to it. Shall we leave our news until then?'

'I'm really looking forward to that. Goodbye, Wu, until Monday,' Fleur replied enthusiastically in a Mandarin dialect.

'Until Monday then. Are you sure you can find your way to the Savoy?'

'Yes, no problem.'

Fleur looked forward to escaping for a while from her mundane house-wifely duties, especially as she and Algie were looking at overpriced properties and listening to estate agents' monotonous and exaggerated claims. So far there had been no hint of pregnancy; such an eventuality was highly unlikely as, unknown to Algie, Fleur had taken every possible contraception precaution. It wasn't her intention to become a mother, a decision she had succeeded in keeping from Algie as the subject had hardly ever been discussed between them. Algie had put no pressure on her to ensure the continuation of the dwindling Stanhope line. Secretly, she intended to hold out for as long as possible, especially as her instincts were decidedly non-maternal. If she had become pregnant, it might have seriously affected her ability to use her vital entrapment techniques and prejudiced her valued role in acquiring weapons secrets for the People's Republic.

She thought about John sometimes, and wondered how much he missed their relationship and whether he had found someone else. She thought it was more likely he would be lazy and had become used to being without her.

The day of her meeting with Wu came soon enough. She purchased a cheap-day-return rail ticket from Weybridge to Waterloo, travelling up after 9.30 am. Crossing over a busy Waterloo Bridge in the bright sunshine of a clear summer day, she paused to take in the magnificent views of London both up and down the River Thames. All along the embankment constant streams of cars glinted in the sharp sunlight that streamed from behind the canopy of shade provided by trees in full leaf. She turned left at the Aldwych into the Strand and by the time she arrived at the horseshoe-shaped entrance to the Savoy Hotel her throat was smarting from the harmful persistence of petrol fumes. She found her way easily to the ladies' cloakroom on the ground floor where she freshened up.

The warm day and her anxiety to arrive at the right place in good time had broken her out in mild perspiration. Her lightweight silk suit in olive green was set off tastefully with a small gilt brooch on her left lapel depicting a teddy bear that Algie had given her for Christmas. Her black leather medium-heeled shoes were ideal for walking the hot, unyielding pavements. Inside her shiny patent-leather handbag she carried her make-up, a spare pair of tights and other feminine accessories.

She left the cloakroom knowing that she looked good, which gave her the necessary self-confidence for the meeting. She went back down to the foyer and it wasn't long before she spotted Wu.

As I approached the hotel I hoped Fleur would see me as the same but rather smarter person she'd known in Hong Kong. I recognised her instantly and went towards her, opening my arms and clasped her in a bear hug to make her feel special to me. She could only respond with one arm; the other one carried her handbag and a fashionable Harrods plastic carrier bag. Even though we hadn't met for over a year, she had lost none of the ability to enchant me.

'Hello, Fleur. You look a million dollars!' I greeted her in a truly Western way, but in Mandarin. I must have sounded unusually rapturous.

'Thank you. You haven't changed much yourself, just a bit more Western, I would say!'
She flushed slightly, possibly because she had expressed her personal opinion to me; normally she would have kowtowed in the appropriate manner.

'That's good. Just how it should be!' I replied. 'We have to sharpen up at the embassy here in London.'

She laughed and the tension between us fell away.

We walked the short distance from the Savoy to Rules, the restaurant in Maiden Lane where I regularly entertained my special contacts and agents. It's a long-established restaurant steeped in a nostalgic Edwardian atmosphere and décor, one of the oldest of its type in London. The menu offers a selection of typically British meat and game dishes, oysters from Belfast and pheasant and venison from Scotland. It was a very special place and entirely appropriate that I should take Fleur there.

We were shown to the table I had booked in my cover name of Chan. As soon as we sat down on the red-velvet-upholstered banquette at the table I had especially chosen, unusually for me I ordered champagne and a glass each of

Perrier water. We progressed slowly through the meal, becoming increasingly relaxed, catching up with what had happened over the last year in Los Alamos. We kept our voices low and avoided using easily recognisable names, taking the precaution of using veiled speech. To eat we both chose the duck and with it I ordered a bottle of non-alcoholic grape juice.

'I'm ravenous, aren't you?' I asked Fleur.

'Yes, rather,' she replied, pushing her chest out to keep her back and posture upright. She smelt fresh, and I imagined she had bathed in lavender water.

We toasted each other and I thanked her for her excellent work, then I started talking more professionally. I have never been good at small talk, but I wanted the enthusiasm for my work to come across. I had often wondered if women found this commitment to my work too intense, making me a boring companion. I was normally a restrained man who was beginning to be taken in by Fleur's attraction.

'As a result of the information gained from Los Alamos, the President of the People's Republic feels confident that in a few years' time, with our scientists working flat out, we will be close to deploying a mobile intercontinental missile equipped with a miniaturised nuclear warhead. It will be based on the W-88 warhead developed in America in the 1970s and recently stolen by us. The potential for miniature design is considerable, and makes it possible to deploy the weapon on lorries rather than on fixed sites. It will be difficult to detect if a missile is in flight, and equally difficult for an enemy to launch an effective counterstroke.'

'Thank you for telling me this. It makes my work come to life and it's gratifying to know that my modest input is a valued part of this huge project,' said Fleur, sitting well forward on the edge of her chair, listening intently to what I had to tell her.

'The weapon will have a range of 5,000 miles, which

means that Britain will be out of range. No doubt in time we could share the technology with our friends closer to Europe who could bring Britain well within their sights.'

We paused in our conversation as the waiter cleared away our main course plates. He presented the dessert menu, suggesting a typical savoury dish of devils-on-horseback for me, an enticing fresh fruit salad from the trolley for Fleur.

While we waited for the next course I leant forward, aware that I needed to whisper. I had taken extra care to choose a table that would be private; usually the babble of a busy lunchtime restaurant was sufficient to counteract eavesdroppers. I had developed a sixth sense over the years and if ever I felt uncomfortable I backed my instincts. That day I felt comfortable.

The closeness of Fleur, however, disturbed me. Her face was near to mine, appearing to be absorbed in what I was saying, her eyes shining. Her hand touched mine and lingered before she moved it away. She smiled mischievously and my pulse quickened. I was put off my stroke and I wondered if she was signalling pleasure in me. It seemed a wild notion and the moment passed.

'We need to know what the British are doing with the information. Our people in America have told us that John Poon is coming over to England to visit the British submarine base in Scotland, where there are four nuclear ballistic missile submarines. I'll tell you as soon as I hear more about the dates and details of his trip and, of course, you should met up with him.'

'Fine.'

'I believe John has a friend who lives here in England – it's a man, actually,' I added hastily, sensing she might be less motivated if I had said it was a woman.

'He's a scientist, half-Chinese and an ardent supporter of our cause. I want you to meet him and recruit him as a useful conduit for passing information, just as you recruited

John Poon. For operations carried out in Britain, when it comes to dealing with submarines and military secrets, it is best to have men rather than women up in the front line, it fits in better with the British way of things. But I have no objection to you controlling them via myself. Instead of having full-time salaried professional staff, the Chinese Secret Service maintains only a small permanent staff cadre. Nevertheless, we've created a huge network of agents and spies deployed all over the world. One regular cadre case officer of ours is able to run several teams of irregular volunteer agents, all at the same time. It will be an added comfort, too, for your man John Poon to have another person working with him.'

'Do you have any more details about this newcomer?' Fleur asked. As she did so she uncrossed her legs under the table and accidentally kicked me, but not enough to make me react. I didn't interpret her action as a secret signal.

'Yes, I certainly do. He is thirty years old and a bachelor, which is rather your speciality, if I may say so. He has an English father and a Chinese mother. Educated at the Hong Kong University, he studied mechanical engineering, which has directed him into weapons technology. He has become an expert in computer technology and after graduating from University he went to the Massachusetts Institute of Technology in America. From there he went to the Lawrence Livermore Laboratory in California. Here in England he is currently at London University lecturing in physics,' I reeled off the background facts which I had learnt by heart.

'So what do you want me to do exactly?'

'There isn't much for the moment. Just introduce yourself to him and say you're a friend of John Poon's. We know he is desperate to work for us and he is happy to have John as a colleague. In due course I want you to co-ordinate their activities, according to instructions you'll receive from me from time to time. You are to keep their morale high, and set up a courier network for any information they might get their hands on. The target for this operation is the British Navy, in particular its nuclear submarine capability.'

We stopped the conversation abruptly as the waiter yet again attentively topped up our glasses. I signalled that I didn't want more by putting my hand over the top of the glass. Fleur, on the other hand, was happy to have her glass filled. I noticed how she had picked up so many Western tastes since the early days in Hong Kong and her marriage to Algie.

'That sounds straightforward enough. The only thing I need is his address.'

'Just a moment,' I said, reaching inside my jacket pocket to find my small diary. I found the page with the new agent's address marked in pencil. 'His name is Vincent Yates, his mother is Chinese. He wears wire-framed spectacles with thick lenses, which gives him a genuine intellectual appearance. He is five feet four inches and speaks with a good English accent. Take this piece of paper, it has his North London address; I suspect it's a flat chosen for being within commuting distance to his work,' I speculated. Fleur took the piece of paper and slid it into her handbag.

'Tell me, what cover story will you give your husband when you start getting involved in clandestine activities here in England? I assume he still doesn't suspect anything?'

'I will tell him I'm seeing some old Chinese friends and connections who have been recommended to me by friends I met in Los Alamos in both the Chinese and Eurasian communities there. I find that the nearer to the truth the cover story is, the more plausible it sounds and the easier it is for me to handle.'

'I know exactly what you mean. My father said something like that to me. "Keep everything as simple as you can. We're in a tricky enough business as it is, without making things any more complicated!"'

After coffee, while Fleur left the table to go to the ladies, I paid the bill in cash. When she came back, we left by the glass front door and soon hailed a cab slowly cruising down Maiden Lane looking for a fare.

'I'll drop you off at Waterloo, then I'll take the cab back to my next destination.' I was careful not to get the taxi driver to take me direct to the Chinese Embassy, so I let myself out somewhere near it.

'Thank you, Wu, that was a delicious lunch and you've spoilt me terribly.'

'Nonsense, you deserve it. I think you'll be rewarded more after this next mission. The Party Chairman knows who you are and he has asked me to thank you personally. I'd be surprised if he does not make you a heroine of the Chinese Republic. The Party will always look after you if you ever return to live in China.'

The taxi drew up on the vehicular section of the station arrival concourse, where it joined the fleet dropping off their customers before patrolling to collect fresh fares.

Having hugged Wu goodbye and held him a little longer, Fleur made her way into the heart of the station amid the press of anonymous passengers. She caught the next train home to Weybridge. Algie had suggested she should aim to leave Waterloo well before five o'clock to avoid the unnecessary discomfort and overcrowding of rush hour commuters.

21

'Butterflies should not talk of snow nor worms of heaven.'

Between operations in London I had time to think back to another part of my father's early career in the service that he had told me about before he died, and how it contrasted with my own experiences. It was at the time of the determined fight back by the Secret Service against the Kuomintang, which was only partially successful.

The Kuomintang had been lucky and the success they enjoyed was mainly with the many frightened defectors, who under interrogation carelessly gave away valuable information. The strengthening co-operation between the Kuomintang and the Foreign Settlement Police surveillance units, combined with the effective deployment of agents provocateurs, had cut down many fledgling Chinese Communist Party units well before they became effective operators. After the mob demonstrations, hundreds of left-wing sympathisers were detained, so that by 1933 the Communist Party's organisation was falling apart and the membership rapidly evaporated. In Shanghai, the Kuomintang had successfully rounded up hundreds of Communists and senior Chinese Communist Party officials. The time had come to preserve what was left of the organisation by the timely withdrawal of all senior Communist Party leaders, who were still in the city and had not yet been caught.

My father had avoided arrest by using a selection of disguises and aliases, using different routes, constantly alert to being followed. Employing the tradecraft he was taught early on, he used to stop outside shop windows; by looking into them he would have seen the reflection of a suspicious tail. The family remained unharmed, but as the danger grew my father knew that if he was captured he would have been a juicy prize for the Kuomintang who would spare no effort, however extreme, to extract information from him. My mother knew nothing of this as my father had chosen to keep the more grisly possibilities from her. But he did fear for his family's safety. He had seriously contemplated that should he ever be captured, whether his family or the Party would come first. A prospect as chilling as that had often kept him awake in the silent hours of the night.

零 零 零

'Fu-fang, how's our baby daughter? Has she recovered from that terrible bout of chicken pox? I'm sorry you've had to look after her alone while I've been away these last few weeks on Party business. I've neglected you both. Just because I've been away so much, it doesn't mean I don't care about you and worry about you both. You do understand that, don't you?' Yong asked comfortingly, and placed both his arms round Fu-fang's slim waist as she stood over the kitchen stove preparing the evening meal with its delicious smells. She never wavered in her view that her husband was a caring family man in spite of his ruthless professional reputation.

'I know your work for the Party is vital to us all. One day the Chinese people will be proud of you. I just hope you're not in danger. I can easily manage here alone, but it's only natural that I should miss you, especially at night. I know you have a duty to the Party and I won't stand in your way.'

Fu-fang turned to Yong and hugged him reassuringly, kissing him tenderly, signalling that she still loved and desired him.

'Thanks for your understanding. There is so much I'd like to tell you about my work. It's intensely interesting but it's secret and I'm not allowed to. If you had valuable information and the Kuomintang ever caught you it would be too dreadful: the less you know the better. It's for your protection too.'

'I know that. My mother keeps me company and she helps with Chin-yee too, which gives me a break. Please don't worry about us.'

'Now I have some news, which might surprise you.'

'What can it be? Is it good or bad?'

'I leave that to you to decide,' he paused before continuing, 'We're to leave Shanghai as soon as possible, at least by the end of this week. Some of my comrades are going to Moscow by sea, but the three of us are going to Ruijin. We will go by train and take only our basic belongings. There'll be accommodation for us at the other end in a small farmhouse. I managed to get hold of it through the Party's connections there. For all our sakes, I'm really looking forward to moving out of Shanghai for a while, particularly in view of the recent bout of arrests by the Kuomintang. We're not at all sure if those being detained will be able to stand up to the harsh interrogation. They'll almost certainly be questioned about my whereabouts, which is why we must leave, to avoid arrest ourselves.'

'I'll get everything ready. What shall I tell my mother?' asked Fu-fang, instantly supportive, not even considering to challenge the domestic upheaval she was about to be put through.

'I know it will be difficult. Our leaving Shanghai will be a great loss to her. Tell her we have been posted away to a new job rather urgently, but it will only be for a short time. Perhaps she will come and stay with us in the country. There is no need to alarm her. Of course she will miss you both very much.'

It didn't take long to gather up essential belongings. Two days later the family took taxis to the main railway station in Shanghai and loaded into the goods van the full packing cases and suitcases Yong had especially purchased in the market.

'Chin-yee is so excited, and now we're about to set off the prospect of leaving the city life is something I'm not sure I'm looking forward to. People in the country have a hard life. We've travelled so little outside this great city and now we are to embark on a long steam train journey,' Fu-fang announced with a mixture of excitement and apprehension as they settled into their seats.

'The Party administrators have booked our seats. As they're rather hard wooden benches I've brought some cushions along to make the journey a little more comfortable. They're in that bag over there,' said Yong.

The compartments with their light wood-veneer finish rattled as the train, drawn by an ageing steam locomotive, puffed its way out through the suburbs of the city. Seemingly endless views of the backs of tenement blocks with clusters of bamboo poles poked through the windows, bent under the weight of drying clothes. The unique smell peculiar to the East, a composite odour of sewers, fish, vegetables, rice and noodles, didn't fade away until the train reached the open countryside.

For two long days the family travelled through areas dominated by paddy-fields with coolie women crouched down looking like one-legged birds, tending the young shoots and protected from the sun by their wide-brimmed straw hats. The train lumbered on relentlessly across single-track bridges which spanned rivers and deep ravines, along riverside tracks, up mountainous passes as steep as any train could cope with, stopping at old railway stations to take on fresh supplies of food, water and coal for the engine. Marauding gangs had been known to regularly ambush trains and Yong was alert to this possibility. As they approached their destination at Ruijin, he sensed there was a certain tension in the air; the presence of military vehicles and squads of soldiers was evidence of a major stepping up of security in the area. Even while the family's baggage was being unloaded, soldiers watched and closely supervised the work of the local coolies.

'Where the hell's our greeter?' Yong demanded of the stationmaster, annoyed he hadn't been met. The tiredness from the long journey had made him irritable.

'I saw someone hanging around earlier on, but they soon left. Perhaps it was because your train was late.'

'Possibly. Can I use your phone?'

'Certainly.' The stationmaster was a cheerful man who took things in his stride, unfazed by unmet schedules.

Yong spoke to the representative, who eventually came to collect them in an old broken down truck. The dirt on the outside gave it the appearance of a farm vehicle never cleaned, always in use, not for show, a working vehicle, rusty and poorly kept. Once they had settled in to their cosy farmhouse in a village outside the town, the representative left them with a few instructions and agreed to collect Yong the next day for introductory discussions in the office.

At the office Yong completed forms for the administrators and took delivery of another old battered vehicle for his own use. When the formalities were over, the representative at last briefed Yong. The short and stocky man was typical of the breed born in those parts, happier speaking in his local dialect than in Mandarin. Yong had been too tired from the journey to take in much about him the day before; though he had taken the trouble to look up his details before leaving Shanghai.

'You've arrived just in time for the beginning of the military encircling campaigns that Chiang Kai-shek is directing against the Central Soviet forces. As you know, the Red Army has countered the first attacks, but if this new tactic of surrounding the opposing forces on all sides is to pay off we need many more soldiers on the ground. We're pretty certain that the foreign military advisers helping Chiang have come up with a novel concept: building blockhouses linked by barbed wire placed around Communist-held areas, and ringed in turn by roads, all covered by gun fire and supported by a massive armed force.'

'How many troops are there?'

'We don't know for certain, but I'm told there are about one million Kuomintang troops lined up against the Communists.'

'That's a lot!' replied Yong, having grossly under-estimated the strength of the opposition all along.

'I suppose it is. But this is a big country and there's no shortage of recruits for the army. With this outnumbering, we Communists are being slowly strangled to death. There's very little chance that a direct military confrontation with the Kuomintang will bring us a victory. We need to weaken the Kuomintang military machine by other means, possibly political, by staging a controlled withdrawal to ground not yet controlled by the Kuomintang and drawing them into areas politically hostile to them.'

'I see.'

'May I ask how you see your task here?' asked the representative.

'Certainly. I was offered a choice before I left Shanghai between becoming Director of the Political Department in Peng Dehui's Third Army Group or Director of the Central Committee Propaganda Department. I've chosen the latter mainly because I don't have the necessary military experience.'

'Your predecessor, the former Chief of Secret Service operations in Hong Kong, has already established an awesome reputation for eliminating suspected revolutionaries using ruthless counter-intelligence and assassination techniques. His dedication has led to the brutal torture and execution of purely innocent people. You can imagine how quickly he established a climate of fear and repression.'

Beatings and murders continued well after Yong's arrival there; his experience in Shanghai had hardened him to the necessary and brutal measures required for successful Secret Service operations. He had lost his innocence earlier on in his career when he led the operation to round up Gu Shunxang's wife and family, ordering their grim execution in the back garden.

Fu-fang and Chin-yee were happy enough in their snug little farmhouse. Although in the depth of the countryside, it was well protected in an area secured by friendly forces and close enough to other houses in the village. Fu-fang soon made friends, helping out in the fields and in return she was transported around the countryside and given free food and vegetables. Despite country life being alien to them, they took to it surprisingly well and Chin-yee apparently adapted well to being carried by her mother in a large cotton shawl tied round her neck and waist.

'Hello!' Yong called to Fu-fang cheerfully, arriving back home in his truck after a day's work at the Propaganda Department. It amused him how long-winded some of the Communist Party job titles were, like 'Assistant Commandant of the Chinese Peasant Red Army University'. He sometimes reflected somewhat cynically that the longer the title possibly the more ineffectual the department, but he didn't linger too long on that thought. Going home to his family in the country gave him the chance to relax and already he felt so much healthier, away from the smog and fumes of a congested and restless Shanghai.

'Are you happy here, Fu-fang?' he asked when Chin-yee had been put to bed after an exhausting day with her mother in the fields.

'It's certainly very different to city life, but we're adjusting well.'

'Good.' He spontaneously pulled her to him.

'At least you like my cooking!' she replied dutifully,

trying to get him interested in her domestic duties.

'Don't be silly! That's not all I like! I've neglected you and tonight you look the just way I remember you when we first met.'

He took her in his arms and carried her to a small bedroom, gently laying her down on the bed. Despite being strong he was a gentle and tender man. Fu-fang hoped the country air would bring them together more often.

'You're still an attractive man, Yong. Steady on, you nearly crushed me! I'm only a frail little woman! I love you. Don't ever forget that!'

'I love you too,' he murmured. They lay side by side on top of the horsehair mattress and drifted off to sleep, content and for the moment safe. Now and again Fu-fang looked across at her husband lovingly through half-closed lids, and stroked the fallen lock of black hair out of his eye so gently that he didn't even stir.

22

'Before telling secrets on the road. . . look in the bushes.'

Vincent Yates had a goatee beard and the appetite of a sparrow. He was undistinguished and lived a lonely life in a small bachelor flat in North London within convenient travelling distance to his work at the university. Recently he had visited Eastern Europe during the university vacation as a volunteer worker in a Romanian orphanage, a place he so nearly turned back from as soon as he arrived. Videos he had seen in London had been helpful, but nothing had prepared him for the place. He had nightmares for days afterwards, waking in hot sweats as recurring images came to him of an old guard sullenly opened the creaking wooden door that led into the entrance hall of the building. The stench of human excreta had almost overpowered him. The grimy walls ran with water, forming rancid pools on the pitted surface of the uneven stone floors. An antique loudspeaker crackled, disjointedly, pushing out uninspiring sounds of local music. But the volume wasn't loud enough to mask the cries of the children.

Handicapped children bore marks on their shaven heads where, with their constant rocking motion, they had banged against the unyielding iron bedsteads. Some children had never been out of their cots, all trussed up, deliberately tied with their hands behind their backs and legs pinned to their chests to make it easier for over-stretched staff to control them. With muscles wasted and joints locked through lack of exercise, they lay hairpin-shaped and inert. They stared out from their cots with blank unfocused eyes waiting for the high moment in the unvarying and tedious routine when they would receive milky pudding food through the teats of feeding bottles. Whenever Vincent moved towards the cots they flinched, expecting to be hit and they screamed back at him hysterically.

When his stint at the orphanage ended, Vincent returned to London deeply affected by his experiences. As a loner, he felt frustrated by his inability to form close relationships, especially with the opposite sex. He had no close family alive in England and despite his Oriental ancestry he had grown up in the comfort of a Western, prosperous and secure environment. His Chinese forebears were the ones who had borne the brunt of the suffering in China at the hands of the cruel Japanese invaders followed by the oppression of the Cultural Revolution under Mao.

Vincent was vulnerable and some said it had interfered with his work at the university, but it was a timely approach when he was asked to work for the Chinese Secret Service.

零　零　零

As soon as John Poon came to England, I arranged for Fleur to get him to meet up with my new recruit. I had decided their mission would be to focus on the top secret Anglo-American project of developing a satellite system to track submarines by the changes they left on the surface of the sea. Their task was to get information about the makeup of the nuclear weapons involved, similar to the American-built Trident systems, capable of being launched from Britain's submarines.

After the initial introduction the two worked well together. I knew from my colleagues in America that John's existing connections at the Los Alamos base gave him bona fide access to the British submarine base in Holy Loch in Scotland. Vincent, on the other hand, as an unauthorised person, stayed back outside the base ready to collate any scrap of information John was able to smuggle out over a two-week period. I couldn't give them more time; it was a long enough exposure to potential risk as it was.

Despite John not being searched when he left the dockyard at the end of the day, he had to be careful that papers and documents of a technical nature weren't missed from files in current use. I had warned him to guard against greed and over-confidence, to make sure that the stolen material wasn't in such a quantity as to alert the authorities to cause a security spot check. As it turned out, everyone he saw was helpful and co-operative, more than happy to share information with him. They had taken him for what he was, a fellow scientist working on the West's top-level arms technology. He was simply one of them and they were mildly flattered that a boffin from America had taken the trouble to come and see the Anglo-American system in operation. The question of trust didn't arise.

Since the time when he first stole secret documents at Los Alamos, John had become an increasingly hardened and fearless expert. I hesitate to say he was over-confident.

零 零 零

In Scotland John had an easy daily routine, taking a taxi from his hotel in Dunoon on the Western side of the Firth of Clyde, a short distance to the naval base. The modest hotel he and Vincent stayed at was close to the harbour with a view across the Firth of Gouroch. The tall picture windows overlooking the water were badly in need of paint; the effects of the harsh West winds off the Atlantic had taken their toll, the external woodwork flaking right down to the bare wooden base. The hotel's restaurant served up hefty courses of freshly caught fish and venison.

Vincent passed the time on the afternoon of the first day alone reading newspapers, at the same time thinking intently about John's clandestine operation on the other side of the water. He tried to look casual; a holidaymaker taking tea with locally made cake and scones, a rare treat, which he relished. It was so quintessentially British.

'How was your crossing?' Vincent asked John when they met up later in the evening in the hotel's friendly bar, staffed mainly by Australians and New Zealanders who cheerfully dispensed drinks and alternated with a colleague to strum out popular tunes on the guitar.

'The twenty-minute ferry trip was rough. There was never a dull moment. Passengers hung onto anything they could. I felt sick. It was hard to see out through the rain-streaked windows. This morning, on the way there, only five other passengers boarded, but no one spoke. They were locals, wearing heavy sweaters and waterproof jackets, obviously not expecting fine weather. Probably used to crossing regularly and totally disinterested in strangers.'

John smiled as he spoke and looked surprisingly relaxed. He didn't have the demeanour of a man bent on a major espionage operation, yet his mission was clear and his mind perfectly focused.

Vincent took an unaccustomed gulp from a frothy pint of rather warm draught beer. 'What's it like on the other side?' he asked, wiping the ridiculous tide mark from around his mouth.

'It's open country, trees are permanently bent by the wind. The rain-sodden countryside is wild with hills covered in rough tufts of grass and heather. When I came back over this evening, the sky had darkened; the wind started to howl, then the storm broke. You're much better off over on this side of the water keeping a low profile!'

'One day I would like to come back here and go over to the other side, perhaps when all this is over. Shall we go and eat? I'm starving.'

Inside the restaurant, which smelt of vinegar and chips, they sat close to the window at a circular table for two with a red plastic tablecloth. There were still a few crumbs on it from the previous occupants. By now it was pitch dark, but the rain splashed impudently against the misted-up windows. Across the loch, the pinpricks of light struggled through the mist and gloom. To other patrons, a motley crowd of tourists and hikers from different parts of the world, the sight of two Chinese men caused little interest.

'I hope you've got enough to do on this side of the Loch?' asked John.

'Don't worry about me, I'm fine. I'll be busy enough when the time comes! Tell me more about your day?' Vincent asked eagerly, desperate to live every moment of the operation through John.

'When I got off the ferry, a taxi was waiting for me. As it was the first day, Ministry of Defence police handed me a prepared identity tag and told to wear it at all times, visible and attached to my jacket,' said John.

'Then what happened?'

'Once the security formalities had been completed, a policeman drove me in a Land Rover past the dockyard with cranes and hoists where a couple of sinister looking submarines lurked. It was like nothing I had ever seen before.'

'So you saw the subs?' Vincent asked with boyish enthusiasm.

'Yes. It was rather eerie with mist swirling like low clouds blown off the Loch and not a soul anywhere. The poor visibility stopped me from seeing other subs moored further out in the Loch itself. I had a creepy feeling, thinking of the huge destructive capability that lay in that base, with such highly technical nautical and nuclear engineering, all contained between those compact submersible hulls.'

'Then what?'

'The building I was shown to accommodates the offices of the scientists, engineers and weapon specialists.'

'Have you got any material yet?' asked Vincent

desperately wanting to feel useful and to fulfil his role in the mission.

'Give me a chance, this is only the first day!' replied John deliberately calming Vincent's impatience.

零　零　零

Fleur reported to me about the detailed preparations for the operation.

'I've made sure Vincent's photographic skills are up to the job. He has got extra strong light bulbs and a special film of the right speed to get a high quality document copy.'

'Good. Is that the best way?' I queried. I knew I had a reputation for being a stickler for detail and thoroughness, but I made no apology for that.

'He prefers to put the material on to film.'

'Good luck. Keep me informed won't you?'

'Certainly,' she replied. 'Sometimes I object to your attention to detail. It pisses me off, but I know it's your job! You're a professional and I respect you for that. I hope you don't mind me speaking my mind?'

'Of course not. That's all part of the teamwork.'

I ended the discussion abruptly. I didn't want to spend longer than necessary on the secure line. We spoke in Mandarin, but it wasn't beyond the powers of GCHQ to monitor all communications traffic however secure we might have thought them to be.

零　零　零

In the evening of the second day John returned to meet up with Vincent bringing with him an innocent looking plastic bag containing single sheets of A4 paper, mainly typed briefs and letters. This time Vincent, who had been in an unsettled frame of mind all day, waited until John was more relaxed before going at him with questions; he recognised that it took a little while for the immediate tension of an operation to subside. Vincent had judged the characteristics of his colleague quickly and had learnt to guage just the right moment to approach him.

'So how did you do it?' asked Vincent.

'In some ways it was easier than Los Alamos. Government staff in Britain tend to have more fixed patterns of work times. Trustingly, I was given crucial files to read over, and I was left alone in a small but well equipped office. It belonged to a top scientist who was away on leave. I was able to photocopy sensitive documents and place them flat inside my heavy woollen shirt. Any search of my briefcase by a guard on the way out of the base would have revealed nothing. This time the original files were kept on base, which I put away in a safe. Before I left, I deliberately called up the duty security officer for him to sign the documents back into a register, and to be satisfied nothing was being taken off the base.'

'Were you scared?' asked Vincent, intrigued by the psychological makeup of someone involved in clandestine operations. He wondered if they had sensibilities like other people, or if emotions had been trained out of them deliberately to make them professional, cool headed and fearless, all the more effective from the lack of feelings?

'I was nervous to start with. My knees shook and the tension made me weary, particularly when I put the first piece of paper on the copier, one hundred per cent alert in case someone came in just at that moment. It would have looked so suspicious if they had. What reason could I trump up for making a copy, especially as we all know it's an illegal act to copy secret documents? My heart was in my mouth, my hands shook. I switched the machine on and it seemed to take forever to warm up. I checked that the first copy was a good quality, hoping I wouldn't have to do it all over again. And so I went on, sweating heavily, tense, concentrating intensely on the job in hand and listening out for unusual sounds, hoping the machine wouldn't jam. The whole thing was such an endless process.'

The mole on John's face began to itch as he related the day's tensions.

'I've been really looking forward to relaxing over here, I can tell you! But there are several more days' work to do, and each day will make the risk even greater.'

Vincent worked late into the nights in his hotel room while John, as an official guest of the Naval Base, was often invited out for drinks or dinner with his hosts. As far as they could tell, no one suspected that Vincent was part of John's team. They were booked into the same hotel but on different floors. By day Vincent posed as a tourist: with a Pentax camera slung over his shoulder he took himself off for visits around the area, keeping well away from the submarine base.

Vincent's knowledge in science and technology had enabled him to sift out the most important data. By degrees the two of them had amassed most of the information they were looking for in a form that scientists back in China would understand.

零 零 零

The morning after completing the job, Vincent posted off the film cassettes to a safe house address in London. From there a courier picked them up under arrangements made by Fleur, but with my prior knowledge and approval. She had called Vincent from different telephone boxes every day, at pre-set times, to find out how he was getting on, using both coded and veiled speech. I was pleased to hear that unwittingly the British authorities had been so co-operative. Apparently Vincent had expressed surprise at the security arrangements when Fleur passed on my instructions for leaving the area.

As soon as the mission was over both men were to return to the south, taking separate trains and different routes back to London. Vincent was to stop off for a night en route to make more certain that he and John were unconnected people. Both were warned to be alert to the possibility of being followed and suitable cover stories needed to be thought up.

Fleur received the film from Scotland and immediately arranged to meet one of my couriers in London, using a series of dead letter boxes. I also wanted Vincent to meet me, to brief me in more detail on the precise nature of the secrets. John Poon, on my instructions, left the country for a secret destination as soon as it was possible. I believed it would have been foolhardy for him to remain in England any longer than necessary. His work for us was complete, but the Service created for him a new identity and a new beginning in another country. Before he left he had an intimate lunch with Fleur, and later that afternoon she rewarded him with a few hours of passion in the safe house that I had acquired for the operation. The Service took care of the arrangements for John's disappearance from then on.

I was aware that John might have harboured personal ambitions as far as his affection for Fleur was concerned. I had tried to blot out the professional need for his relationship with her, but at the back of my mind I was forced to admit a nagging, suppressed jealousy.

I agreed to meet Fleur and Vincent together on Hampstead Heath, a place where we could walk unhindered, rarely crowded on weekday mornings. On this mild autumn day the leaves hadn't yet fallen off the trees. Here and there the new season showed in the changing colours as leaves began their natural evolution, turning from green to yellow and rust before their inevitable year-end extinction. The air was moist and the earth smelt of autumn. The forecast was for cloud and drizzle, the temperature average for the time of year. All three of us wore raincoats as we travelled individually in different carriages on the Northern Line to Hampstead. From the station we walked by separate routes through the Victorian, faintly Bohemian, neighbourhood which ran from the centre of the village towards the edge of the Heath. Stopping in our tracks we spun round to check faces. Having continuously checked against being followed, we rendezvoused outside a prominent house belonging to a famous actor. The locals were quite used to foreign tourists waiting aimlessly outside, hoping for the merest glimpse of the star. We walked on across the park towards the Spaniards Inn. On the way we stopped to sit down on a bench, chattering excitedly in Mandarin, hoping to look relaxed and natural. A boss had once told me that a look of seriousness was more suspicious than one of easy jollity.

I was on my guard, looking around me to see if anyone was trailing us. There was a man lurking in the shadow under an oak tree fifty metres from us, but he moved away. The possibility of imminent danger was never far from my mind. I was like a coiled spring, risking an open-air meeting in a public place, never certain if I had done the right thing until the operation was over. Most of the time I was aware of the gamble I was taking and the danger I was imposing on my agents. I was never complacent. I kept myself fit, careful with my diet and rarely drank alcohol. We Chinese are keen on our food, particular about avoiding red meat, shellfish and dairy products, all things Westerners devour unaware how harmful they might be. If I felt ill I took herbs, which my Chinese friend in Soho got for me. I was sure this helped me overcome the stress. I know that some Western spies drank too much; they also ate too much of the wrong food and sought the comfort of different women to ease the pain of heavy responsibility and the constant exposure to danger and risk. Each of us had our own way of dealing with these problems.

'This is such high quality intelligence, Vincent. Thanks for the films. Please describe what you've got for us in your own words, and of course I wanted to thank you personally,' I said, hoping to sound businesslike, caring and professional. During my career I had acquired a lot of experience in handling top agents and in the subtle ways of making them feel special and well supported.

I studied Vincent more closely. It fascinated me that the heavy plastic spectacle frames encompassing thick lenses might have corrected his chronically short sight. The effect of the lenses was to magnify his eyeballs, giving him an altogether unattractive, rather lecherous appearance. I suspected he was of little interest to women. He only needed an old raincoat and he would have been taken for a dirty old man. Inevitably, he sought praise from other quarters to make up for the lack of affection he might have expected from a loving relationship. I sympathised with Vincent's craving for self-esteem, but it was a weakness both Fleur and I played on.

'Shall we deal with the nuclear weapons aspect of the submarines first, then move on to the radar detection technology?' suggested Vincent.

'Please do,' I replied, having checked that no one was within earshot of us.

'Britain has four Trident submarines. They're called that because of the American-made nuclear missiles they carry. I've been told that they cost the British fourteen billion pounds and represent one of the largest Ministry of Defence purchases ever made. These subs patrol the world's oceans every minute of the day and try not to give their position away. During the Cold War, the nuclear weapons were targeted behind the Iron Curtain. Now under a new government and in the post-Cold War era the weapons have been reduced. By sailing really deep it is expected that the subs will be able to avoid the type of radar technology which we have just leaked to you for our scientists in Beijing to evaluate,' described Vincent, very much in his element.

'I'm with you so far, but I'll let you know when you lose me!' I interrupted, but smiled encouragingly. Fleur, a born actress, well wrapped up in her raincoat with a fur collar, was looking adoringly at Vincent and then at me in turns, giving the impression to any passer-by that she was the object of a romantic discussion between her two male friends. From time to time regular dog walkers passed uncomfortably close to us, their pets sniffing and cocking their legs around the base of our seat. Each of us was on guard while we sat huddled so closely together. We smiled vacantly. Anyone could have been a threat to us, however innocent they looked. A dog walker had excellent cover; I knew that from my own experience. It was Fleur's job to keep a look out and to warn of anyone approaching the bench. Whenever a dog typically nosed around the foot of the bench, we stopped talking and smiled. The dog and its walker eventually moved on.

'Please go on, Vincent. The coast is clear.'

'This highly sophisticated technology tracks the smallest change in the surface of the sea and will detect a large pressure wave generated when a submarine with many thousands of tons displacement passes in the depths below. Both American and British scientists have found a way to track these changes, but it still requires a submarine to be moving fairly near to the surface.'

'I thought you said that the Trident subs move deep down close to the ocean bed?' I queried, still trying to get to grips with the technical aspects.

'You're quite right. Those subs sail too deep to provide any surface trace. However, Britain's fleet of smaller hunter-killer subs are vulnerable to this type of tracking as they move nearer the surface and at a higher speed. So you can see that two situations exist: firstly, slow but deep patrols, which are virtually undetectable; and secondly, the older but faster patrols, which are nearer to the surface and are more vulnerable to detection.'

'Do we have any technology yet in China for tracking these subs?' I asked.

'Not that I know of. I spoke to John before he left the country and he didn't think Beijing had been able to develop anything of any consequence. Up until now they haven't had the right information to copy. The films you now have show detailed technical plans sufficient to build a Trident nuclear missile, but there are still considerable technical problems to overcome to get the satellite submarine-tracking system operational. We're some years away, and by that time the West will probably be even further ahead.'

'Can you tell us a little more about the tracking technology information that you've also got for us? Then we'll go to the pub for a drink and some lunch?'

'It's interesting, to me anyway, that most of the scientific work has been done either at Los Alamos or at the Lawrence Livermore Laboratory in America. In the case of the tracking technology, this was done at the Lawrence Livermore Lab. It's so far advanced it can identify a sub by the individual characteristics of its propeller. If only we could develop this technology in China, we would be able to detect any British or American nuclear sub, including Trident. The satellite radar system can detect deep-level subs; it relies on a combination of complex technology using radar while a computer system sifts the different wave movement patterns as they establish a hitherto undetectable wake,' replied Vincent.

'You're a clever man to be able to make all this sound so simple – it's a rare gift you have, especially for a boffin!' I complimented him. Out of immediate hearing, a black labrador and a tan boxer were fighting. The boxer was hanging onto the labrador's neck and their frantic owners had joined in to separate them, but the scuffle was over in seconds.

'Go on, Vincent, please.'

'The low angle of the satellite in the sky enables it to detect the slightest change in sea level.' Vincent was well away now. 'Advanced computer processing is then used to analyse the radar images and filters out the movements in the ocean due to normal wave activity. It takes into account colliding wakes from two different submarines, for example, and comes up with the sub's speed and direction of travel.' When he was excited Vincent's face became greasy and every so often he had to push his heavy spectacles back up to the bridge of his nose, correcting the slippage with the forefinger.

'This is fascinating, but we must stay calm. I have the information I need now and I've arranged for it to be in Beijing tomorrow on the first plane out. A courier will leave this afternoon, taking it in the diplomatic bag. After lunch, we will separate and return to our respective destinations alone. Then we shouldn't make contact with each other again. I'm the only one of us who has the protection of diplomatic immunity. At least we have got John out of the country, so that leaves you, Vincent, as the next most vulnerable. And you, Fleur, you're also at risk. So keep your wits about you, both of you: be on the lookout! Fleur, doesn't your husband show surprise when you come to London so often?'

'No, he thinks I'm involved in fund raising for a Chinese charity.'

'That's such a brilliant cover story! I like it,' I replied. It was so typical of her to have thought through that particular eventuality.

To an outsider we probably looked an incongruous trio as we moved off along the pathways made slushy by sodden, trodden-down leaves. We stamped our feet to remove the mud and leafmould from our shoes before we crossed the narrow neck of Spaniards Road, which funnelled traffic at a snail's pace right alongside Spaniards Inn itself. Inside, it was typically olde worlde, an attraction to tourists. The sharp autumn sun had just broken through, but we chose to sit outside on wooden benches, the high-backed seats giving us better protection against enquiring eyes and eavesdroppers. Not that we would be talking shop any more, nor would those around us have understood our heavily accented Mandarin speech.

Vincent's shabby little converted flat was on the top floor of a Victorian terraced house that lay three metres back from the pavement. He had bought the leasehold with eighty-eight years remaining for £85,000 with the help of a ninety per cent mortgage loan from the Building Society, and his salary as a senior lecturer covered the monthly repayments. He hardly ever saw or heard the owners of the other flats in the same house, except when he passed their front doors on the way up to his own flat. Sounds of rock music, a couple shouting at each other, that sort of thing. Through the thin partitions he thought he heard the urgent sounds of humping, but that might have been more in his imagination; the ceiling light in the entrance hall had crashed down the week before and he thought the bedroom activity above had been a contributory factor. Sometimes he bumped into the neighbours or their overnight visitors while he was sorting out his mail, strewn carelessly across the black-and-white tiled entrance hall.

'Come in, Jerry, and take a seat!' said Allen Spear cheerfully. As head of the Ministry of Defence Police he welcomed his opposite number, Jerry Flood, from the Metropolitan Police Special Branch. Jerry preferred to come to Allen's office, rather than the other way round. It was more spacious and elegant than his own and he liked the atmosphere of easy respect. There was always a possibility that if they met at eleven o'clock, they might get their business over with quickly, then slope off to a suitable hostelry or to Allen's club in St James's for lunch and a few beers. Jerry preferred to play away from his home patch, bored stiff with his own colleagues' company after thirty years in the Met. During that time people had come to fear that one day he might put his hand on their collar.

'Thanks, Allen. So, what do you make of this report from your boys at Holy Loch? What first made them suspect that documents had been tampered with?'

'Philip, our man up there, has been acting on a hunch after a Chinese scientist came to visit from America. He made some enquiries just before he left and put a tail on the unsuspecting visitor. Philip wanted to get evidence without distracting them. Who knows how much had been got out of the base before our people had any suspicion!' Allen shook his head despairingly.

'What made your man take the trouble to tail him?' asked Jerry.

It was taken for granted that members of the Metropolitan Police Special Branch were superior beings to MOD policemen.

'I don't know. I'm new to this job. MOD Police have discretion to put surveillance teams on certain foreign visitors to sensitive government establishments. After the lessons of the Russian spy scandals of the 1960s, security had to be tightened up. But that was a long time ago. These things have to be done discreetly, of course.'

23

'The fishes see the worm not the hook.'

'Has your man in the North found anything yet?' asked Jerry.

'Good question. Investigators have interviewed the heads of the most sensitive departments in the dockyard offices. It has been confirmed that certain documents were incorrectly filed. Three reports stated that the rearrangement was only picked up a few days after the visitor, a certain John Poon, had left. I understand he has left the country, possibly with a changed identity.' replied Allen.

'So what about the second man in the hotel?'

'The hotel has been helping us with our enquiries. Although this man gave a false name and address, he slipped up. Our Ministry of Defence police got access to his hotel room just before he left, and by pure chance found his home details scribbled on a piece of rough paper. It's the sort of luck one needs in this game!'

'It was a silly mistake to make. So what now?' Jerry's senses were sharpening. He preferred the chase to the kill.

'The Home Office minister has been briefed and at an emergency meeting last night it was agreed that we must use all efforts to bring in the second man. He's ordered a publicity clampdown. We don't want the tabloids getting hold of the story at this stage. It will only serve to warn off our enemy.'

'What help can we give you, Allen?' asked Jerry.

'Could you arrange for a tail to be put on this Vincent chap for a few days? We need to establish his *modus operandi* and be absolutely certain he is our man. He will probably be lying low by now. When you're certain, please let me know and we'll bring him in for questioning.'

'I'll be pleased to help. It sounds interesting,' replied Jerry, not wanting to be left out of the action. Instinct told him this case was going to be a bit out of the ordinary. If publicity were forthcoming, so much the better. A favourable mention in the newspapers at a later stage might help him on to the next rung up the promotion ladder and with it a better pension.

'That'll make a change! You boys are usually so fussy about what you take on these days,' replied Allen cheerily.

'What about that beer?' asked Jerry.

'Good idea, I'm parched. Let's go down to the Coach and Horses. It's not too late to get a table before all those Whitehall civil servants crowd the place out.'

'I hope you won't mind, but I won't be able to stay long. I want to get this operation off the ground. I'm sure you'll understand. Perhaps we could have a grand celebration when we've finished this case?' His boredom with the Met., now distant in his mind.

'I'm all for that!' agreed Allen.

零 零 零

The fever, a Far Eastern strain of flu, had plagued Vincent for three days and nights, before he felt able to get about again and the feebleness started to leave him. His voice croaked rather more deeply than usual, noticeable from the normal pitch which was a bit on the high side.

He had started to shave again, scraping off the days of neglected beard growth, and spruced up his degenerate and sickly appearance. Studying the reflection of his face he saw a man with sores on his upper lip, a man associated with a criminal act of sabotage, not yet detected. His weak eyes strained back at him unable to disguise his underlying feeling of insecurity and terror. The high fever and the days in bed had given him shelter from the outside world. He had felt safe. But now that he was feeling better, guilt and terror started to kick at his heels like a demanding terrier.

It took time for Vincent to come out of denial sufficiently for him to seriously consider that the police might discover him and arrest him for the crime he had committed. Incoming telephone calls were infrequent. As a loner, he stoically bore the fever unknown to friends and acquaintances, except for colleagues at the university who covered for him during his absence. Sometimes, over the long black days of the sickness, he lay back in his bed with crumpled unlaundered sheets knowing he must see out the hours alone and uncared for. Nothing and no one filled those dark days, other than the growing obsession that brought on the inescapable feeling of fear.

His working hours were filled normally, with people to talk to, some who asked his advice, and there were student papers to be read and marked. All this distracted him from the mounting panic. He was hardly ever ill and never in the way he felt now, making the days of enforced emptiness alien to him. Instead, the days were devoted to sleep and the feeble struggle to make hot drinks. As soon as recovery to normal health had begun, an appetite for food signalled the end to his loneliness and suffering.

His recovery was looking more certain when he put on his clothing and left his top floor flat, down the steep staircase with its brown threadbare carpet, past the three levels and down to the front door. He bent to pick up his modest post, spread as usual untidily across the dusty mosaic floor. The silence within the building had increased his paranoia. The only sound was his own heavy breathing as he gingerly opened the heavy stained-glass panelled front door, fearful of the world he was about to re-enter; an instinctive feeling of insecurity.

When Jerry was on operations he didn't call his wife to say when he might be home; it never entered his mind because he was too engrossed in his mission. He briefed his team and in no time they pinpointed Vincent's address in North London. That evening, a small round-the-clock surveillance team started to take it in turns to observe the address. They set up in a parked Ford van, especially adapted for surveillance, with high-powered binoculars, night-vision glasses and cameras with telephoto lenses. The concealed portholes at the back gave the appearance that it was unoccupied.

The team analysed Vincent's daily movements, waiting for the perfect moment before moving in to arrest him. To help them, up-to-date eavesdropping equipment was installed in the building by specialist teams disguised as telephone engineers, and monitored by the team in the van. Another unmarked car was parked farther down the street in the direction of the nearest public transport, which the team suspected Vincent regularly used.

'Once you have everything in place and know the suspect's usual routine, just sit it out and wait for the perfect moment to move in on him,' Jerry had reminded everyone at the end of his briefing. To Jerry and his team this was a routine job, but for the Minister it was so much more. His whole political life depended upon the outcome.

The first sighting that same evening was of the target walking up the road and entering the house, possibly after a full day's work. Upstairs the lights were switched on in sequence. From then on, there was no recorded movement during the night other than the routine switching off of lights at bedtime.

At eight o'clock the following morning, the team inside the van was cold from the long night's vigil and had eked out the last drops of warm coffee from their Thermos flasks before being relieved by a fresh team, warm, well fed and rested.

Without warning, the front door to the house opened, revealing the untidy figure of Vincent leaving to start his routine walk to the underground station. The second car took its cue to drop off one man to follow him to his destination. The tube ride was only a few stops to the London University building where Vincent reported each day. Special Branch teams slavishly monitored Vincent's dreary journey between his home and the University, and fresh watchers were brought in to staff the twenty-four-hour surveillance operation.

'We're ready to go in to get him tomorrow morning, just as he's turning the bend in the road on his way to the station. I've changed my mind about a dawn raid. I'm not certain about the layout inside the building and we haven't got time to rig up the latest hi-tech gadgetry. It could give him time to avoid capture if we went through the front door first, and possibly lose valuable seconds looking for him. Out in the street there'll be no hiding place for him, and we'll have the element of surprise on our side,' said Jerry, all fired up and relishing the operation.

'What will be the charge?' Allen asked.

'Suspicion of stealing secret documents from the Holy Loch submarine base. There's no need to be too specific at this stage. There are sufficient provisions in the Official Secrets Act for us to detain him for questioning. Then we'll get him into the back of the car sharpish, and drive him back to our headquarters for interrogation. I'd like a member of the MOD Police to be present at the interrogation.'

'Fine. Good luck, Jerry, I'll await your call,' said Allen calmly.

The exact position of the ambush was established by an unmarked blue squad car with three plain-clothes Special Branch officers inside. They didn't have to wait long for the myopic form of Vincent in a shabby raincoat to leave the house on time.

Vincent was a creature of habit: he usually had a cup of coffee, strong, black and no sugar in the early morning. Like most commuters he dreamt absent-mindedly on his way to the underground station, taking in little of his surroundings. As he turned the corner some fifty yards from his flat, three burly men leapt out from an innocently parked car. Two of the officers positioned themselves in front of him and one behind. It happened so quickly and slickly that it suggested the players were highly experienced.

'Good morning, Sir,' said one of the men, coming from nowhere and producing from an inside pocket his official police identification. 'We're arresting you in connection with recent activities in the area of the Holy Loch Naval Base.'

After cautioning Vincent, he continued, 'We want you to accompany us to the police station.'
Suddenly surrounded, Vincent's heart pounded and his mouth went dry with the feeling of terror sweeping over him. There was no escape.

'What are you talking about?' protested Vincent. An unkempt strand of hair fell across the right lens of his heavy spectacles. One of his eyes was slightly crossed, giving an impression of untrustworthiness. In panic and desperation he lashed out at his captors and kicked like a panic-stricken mule.

'Just come with us, Sir, and you'll soon find out,' ordered the senior police officer, while the other two restrained him, slamming him hard up against the stone wall, legs spreadeagled, arms wide above his head. He coughed, winded by blows to the body in parts hard to bruise. Then his arms were forced down to tie his wrists together. He was dragged roughly by two other men who took an arm each and bundled him into the back of the car, squeezing him tightly into the middle of the back seat between them. The doors slammed shut. The car sped off.

'What about my work at the university?' asked Vincent in a concerned tone.

'Don't you worry about that, we'll take care of it for you.'

The interrogation room in the basement of the Special Branch headquarters was secured by a steel door and ventilated by an efficient—if rather too cool—air-conditioning system. There was no natural light and the room was sparsely furnished with three wooden-topped tables, steel-framed chairs, three glasses and a carafe of plain water. On one of the tables an interview-recording machine was placed, wired-up and plugged in, ready to be switched on.

Vincent was escorted into the room and formally handed over to the interrogation team: two men plus the representative from the Ministry of Defence police. Vincent was tempted to telephone the Chinese Embassy or Fleur, but he remembered the strict instructions he had been given not to implicate anyone if ever he was caught. As a matter of routine, he was offered the services of a solicitor, but he couldn't see how that could help him at this stage.

The police interrogators gave him the necessary formal cautions and explained how the recording machine worked. First one man, then the other, probed Vincent's past and present life long before they got to the crucial question of his part in the stealing of secrets from Holy Loch. If Vincent felt more relaxed than he had expected, it was due to the interrogators' quiet yet persistent techniques. They had little to go on other than suspicion and the name and address found in the hotel room, but they applied to the court for more time whenever they needed to. The plan was to gain Vincent's confidence, from time to time contrasting the atmosphere by leaving him alone in a cold cell for twelve hours, making him feel isolated, disorientated and uncertain what information his interrogators might have come up with in the meantime.

A young police constable was put on duty outside Vincent's flat, a sentry relieved of his duty at regular intervals. A steady stream of plain-clothes men entered the building, all authorised, some carrying briefcases and wooden boxes. Outside, journalists lurked as close as they could to the front doorstep, waiting, ready to pounce, asking questions of anyone leaving the building. Photographers hovered patiently for the perfect shot, a unique record of infamy. Despite the rain they stayed in position, pacing up and down to keep warm, their limbs close to seizing up; one day something might be worth recording, but there wasn't anything much to go on yet. It was more likely the police weren't giving anything away.

Inside the flat the large open-plan room was without trivia; a bare white melamine writing desk, a shabby armchair, one or two obscure modern art prints on the walls. In the corner an unmade single divan bed. Armed with search warrants they examined everything and looked everywhere, stripping the bed, opening drawers and cupboards, lifting carpets and levering up the pine floorboards. They found nothing.

'Here, Sarg. Can you come here a moment?' asked a plain-clothes constable given the laborious but painstaking task of searching the flat for clues. Anything, absolutely anything, would be useful to pin evidence on Vincent.

'What is it, Johnson?' replied the Sergeant. Keen young constables short on experience pissed him off.

'There's a loft space here and I've found a trap door. It's covered up by a rather crude wardrobe, but there aren't any clothes in it. Hang on – there's no top to the wardrobe. I could climb in and then let the loft door down. It's rather well concealed from the outside. Shall I go up, Sarg?'

'Go on, lad, but make it snappy. We haven't got long before our shift finishes,' replied the Sergeant, a north-countryman of few words, not so imaginative, nevertheless highly reliable and he never panicked. He'd seen a lot in his twenty years' of service.

The constable, dressed in blue overalls, climbed into the wardrobe but found he was too short to get a grip on the loft door.

'Sarg?'

'Yes, what is it this time?'

'Could you give us a hand up here?'

'Coming, son. Blimey, the kids I get given these days!'

The constable made it with the Sergeant's help, standing on his superior's shoulders until he pulled himself up into the loft space above them. He fumbled in the dark recess, unknown in size and shape; a black void, silent, mysterious.

'Where's the light, Sarg?'

'I don't bloody know, do I? Try this – here's a torch.'

'Thanks Sarg. That's better.'

The constable found the light switch and turned it on. The loft space was bare, devoid of anything, no suitcases or boxes. It was surprisingly clean and tidy. Nothing at all seemed to be there. He crawled on his hands and knees and at certain spots he stood up, but mostly he had to keep his head down to avoid the low timber beams.

'Sarg?'

'Yes.'

'I can see a bit of wire.'

'OK, lad, just follow it carefully and see where it leads to.'

'Right.'

He crawled and it led him to a loose floorboard. Raising it up he could hardly believe what he saw.

'Christ!' he exclaimed.

'What's up, lad?'

'You'll have to come up here, Sarg.'

'Do I really have to?'

'Yes.'

The Sergeant needed some pulling up through the loft

door, but once he was squatting over the loose floorboard, which the constable had pulled back, he too couldn't believe his eyes.

'Well, well, what have we here?' was the height of the Sergeant's ability to show emotion.

It was a high-powered radio transmitter, from which ran several feet of wire connected to an aerial, sufficiently powerful to send signals to countries well outside Western Europe. Whoever had installed the equipment had been methodical; the wire was suspended on hooks, all neat and tidy. There was no mess, everything in meticulous order.

The two policemen were sweating now. It was hot up there, airless and the adrenalin was coursing through their bodies. Even the Sergeant, the most taciturn of men, was feeling hot under the collar.

'What do you think, Sarg?'

'I think you've found something very important here. Well done lad.'

'Thanks, Sarg.'

'We'll have to get Special Branch onto this. But don't say a word to those press people, whatever you do. They're getting impatient for news and they'd go mad about this.'

'Right, Sarg.'

'Good morning, Vincent, did you have a good night?' enquired one of the interrogators when they returned to the room mid-morning. Their manner was disconcertingly hearty for the time of day.

'Not really, it's freezing in here,' complained Vincent. It was dawn. He had had a bad night awake on a hard bunk. During the night the cold wind pushed through the vents.

'Don't worry, we'll do something about that. We hope you've been thinking hard about why you're here. We've been waiting for more information from our contacts before starting our session today, and now we're in a position to ask you more specific questions.'

All Vincent could muster was a grunt in response.

'We know you were in a hotel with a colleague. Who was he?'

'I don't know.'

'Oh, I think you do. Why was he with you?'

'I don't know,' Vincent spat out angrily, a man fearful of discovery.

'You're not being very co-operative, Vincent, are you?'

Vincent said nothing.

'That's not very sensible, is it? You know very well that we'll find everything out in the end. My colleague here has certain information he wants to ask you about. Over to you, Brian.'

'Good morning, Vincent. We know that certain top-secret information was removed from the Holy Loch base and we know certain documents went missing for a short time because they were put back in the wrong place, slightly crumpled. The irregularity was spotted by a thorough security check only a few days after you and your mate left the area. We know your accomplice was a John Poon and we suspect that you were the person who assisted him. What do you say to that?' asked the new interrogator.

'No comment. How should I know?' replied Vincent evasively, with more than a hint of insolence.

'Don't you take that tone with me!' replied the interrogator beginning to lose his patience. 'That's just what I thought you would say. I'm now bringing the interview to a close.'

He spoke the time and his name, then switched off the recording machine and the team withdrew, leaving Vincent under the eye of a police guard. Their tactic of leaving the room for long periods was deliberately aimed at making Vincent insecure, wondering what might come up next.

Back in his cold, poorly lit cell Vincent's feeling of

isolation were reinforced, interrupted by repetitious interrogation sessions and unappetising meals of watery stew, with over-boiled cabbage and lumpy mashed potato, the tea weak and tepid. It was basic fare, but Vincent had no appetite.

At four o'clock in the afternoon the door of the interrogation room reopened to admit the same team of interrogators.

'Vincent, we've been delayed because we've been in touch with our people in America. They've told us that your colleague, John Poon, has admitted that you helped him copy the documents. What do you say to that?'

Vincent was ashen-faced. Were they playing dirty now? The stress had started to take a debilitating effect on him.

'Is that really what he said? I don't believe you.' His lips were dry and sore, his cheeks shrunk with exhaustion and lack of food. He seemed to be in pain. As he sat he moaned and strained his weak eyes towards the sharp light.

'That's where you're wrong, old son!'

'No. No, no. . . ' Vincent kept saying in desperation, his head in his hands.'

'The answer, unfortunately for you, is yes. Bad luck! Now will you co-operate with us?'

The interrogator opened up a new packet of cigarettes and started to light up, knowing full well that Vincent was a smoker and would no doubt be suffering withdrawal symptoms from the lack of nicotine. In his weariness Vincent had concentrated on preserving his strength, the way Fleur had briefed him.

'Go on, then,' said Vincent languidly, resigned to the fact that his role as an accessory had been discovered. He had been looking for something in his life; having reached his objective, he now realised it wasn't worth anything after all, and his face reflected the torment.

'Good. Now let's just go over your part in this affair, shall we? We need more time, so we will have to apply to the courts to keep you in custody. Don't worry, it's only a formality!'

'Excuse me, Sir, can I have a word with you?' interrupted an officer who knocked on the door and had walked into the room without waiting for the answer, signalling that they should talk outside the room.

'Yes, what is it?' They stepped into the corridor.

'Are you having difficulty in breaking him?' he whispered.

'It's not easy, why?'

'Our boys have found a high-powered transmitter in the loft of his flat.'

'Excellent! We'll get him going on that. Well done. Just in the nick of time, too.'

By degrees and over a few days, the chief interrogator extracted the information he needed from Vincent. He was a deceptively mild man, but his calm ways enabled him to hold out during an interrogation for hours on end, waiting for the crack to appear, conserving his energy by remaining impassive.

Vincent raised his sullen eyes towards the steady well-fed face before him, a face whose energy highlighted his own feeling of immense weakness. If he had been lulled into thinking his interrogator was soft, he was quite wrong. He was certain now that the cycle of betrayal of the secrets was complete, with the vital copies now firmly in the hands of Beijing scientists. By confining himself to answering questions solely about his own part in the operation, he hoped it would have diverted attention away from his accomplices. Nevertheless, it was a high-grade Chinese Secret Service clandestine operation which had been authorised at the highest level of the Communist Party in Beijing with such serious international political and media implications that he could hardly have imagined in his present state.

It occurred to me that the British government was likely to protest to the Chinese authorities, demanding that a number of our embassy staff in London be sent home on the suspicion of spying. Beijing, in retaliation, would expel two or three from the British Embassy there, on some pretext. That was the most likely tit-for-tat punishment for members of the respective diplomatic staff.

Such protection, though, wasn't available to Vincent. Charged formally with contravening the Official Secrets Act, it took lawyers on both sides three months of hard work to bring the case to the Old Bailey: the Central Criminal Court, a court well used to trying rapists, terrorists, murderers and spies.

零　零　零

Throughout this time Fleur had remained undetected, and Algie saw more of her than he had done for a very long time. He had wondered if she was getting broody and wanted babies. Only a few people really knew what a web of duplicity she had woven around her loving and unsuspecting British husband.

24

'If you stand straight, do not fear a crooked shadow.'

In the prison block doors were slammed shut. They didn't close like other doors: they were metal and heavy and made too much of a din. The daytime was filled with sounds of jailers clanking their keys, locking prisoners up. Officers escorting the prisoners everywhere; they were closely guarded at all times, even when the minimal regulated exercise was taken.

Meals for Vincent were delivered into the cell through a hatch in the door. At night sounds on walls or doors tapped out like Morse code, echoing eerily throughout the block. Was it a signal? What was the message? Who was it for? Was it a cry of distress? There was sobbing, too, and demented crying out.

Pimps, murderers, paedophiles: all were there, filled to bursting point. The atmosphere never still, reeking of distrust, plotting and danger. Danger for the insiders, danger for those outside, and danger for the prison officers. Those who went in depraved mixed with others of similar persuasion, ending up an even greater threat to each other and to society in general.

Less high-risk prisoners took meals together and exercised together. The older, more experienced ones tended to dominate the younger prisoners. Unfortunate younger men were impelled to have sexual relations with older men just to secure their own protection. Men fought over food and each other. Violent threats were made to fellow prisoners who, in the judgement of their peers, had committed unacceptable crimes. There was never a day when ingenious attempts weren't made to smuggle in cigarettes, drugs and knives. Vincent fought two things:

the monotony and the threat of victimisation.

零　零　零

While Vincent languished at a high security prison in Greater London, the Party hierarchy in Beijing was busy seeking out agents with links to the Triads, the Chinese Mafia. On many occasions, going back years, the Party or the Chinese Secret Service had deliberately used the Triads to do its dirty work, successfully diverting suspicion away from themselves. In return for favours, the Secret Service turned a blind eye to most of the Triad's activities.

Wong, a Triad boss in Beijing, had been sent to London to meet up with me to discuss a certain deal. We met at an Italian restaurant called Marco's in the Brompton Road, which I knew to be quiet at lunchtime. We had met before on more than one occasion in Shanghai, particularly when I had needed some special favours. Wong was the older of the two of us by about ten years. Although he was in his late sixties, he was fit and his small compact body complemented a sharp and agile mind. His hair was thinning but the receding served to accentuate his high, wide and shiny forehead.

At the restaurant we studied the menu and ordered a bottle of imported Italian mineral water and a pasta dish.

'How are things with you, Wong?' I asked confidentially.

Wong's eyes were preoccupied as if he was hatching an idea; so different to the last time we had met, when he found things which had previously been of immense interest, suddenly became boring to him.

'Not bad. We have had endless pressure from the British, who are constantly trying to intercept our drug supplies into Hong Kong. In spite of that we've got a really good scam going using credit cards!' Wong seemed full of energy.

'How does that work?' I asked.

'It's like this.' Wong's enthusiasm had suddenly become

infectious, but his normally dull dark-brown eyes had been trained over the years to hide his feelings in life's constant game of poker. He possessed a charm that had won him followers, and a lifetime's experience showed in the lines on his face and in his shrewd eyes. With a good scheme on the front burner he became excited, much like a schoolboy.

'A customer uses a credit card to pay for goods at a Triad-controlled shop in Hong Kong. The assistant takes the card to the back of the shop on the usual pretext of checking the credit limit, and then passes the card through a machine which records the information on an electronic strip. Blank cards are produced in China then smuggled into the Colony, where they are authentically embossed with the stolen card's customer details and electronically programmed. Do you like it?'

'It sounds so simple,' I replied.

There was an unwritten understanding between the Triads and the Secret Service that the secrets of each would be safe in the hands of the other. Each needed the other's co-operation to function effectively. Besides, a fraud of that magnitude could have brought much needed foreign money into mainland China, which confirmed the importance of the Triads as contributors to Communist Party funds.

'The great advantage of this plan is that the customer still has his card. They won't suspect anything wrong until the credit-card company and the customer see the bills some weeks later. Until then a lot of money has been spent!' Wong chuckled aloud, revealing a mouth full of gold fillings.

'What about your other activities?' I was keen to see if there was any overlap with operations we were involved in. I was concerned that Wong might have lost his edge to initiate daring and ingenious scams.

'The British are using very sophisticated signals equipment to interrupt our drug smuggling operations in the Colony. Top communications experts from the British Communications Headquarters in England have been taken on board Royal Navy patrol vessels when they head out of Hong Kong harbour and into the East Lama Strait on an anti-smuggling run. Apparently, they have scanning devices which flick through the frequencies known to be used by our Triad drug-runners operating out of the remote fishing villages along the Pearl River delta on the mainland of China.'

'Do they have much success?' I asked.

'Sometimes!' Wong smiled, which crinkled up the crow's feet lines around his eyes. 'They're looking for a sixty-foot glass-fibre hull, powered by five 225-horsepower Mercury outboard motors, which propel the hull forcing it literally to jump across the water at speeds of over seventy miles an hour. You can see how suitable this hull is for smuggling, and it can out-manoeuvre anything on the water. It's a real cat and mouse game. The British pick us up on the scanner as we move out into the delta loaded up with heroin on our way from the Golden Triangle to the West via China and Hong Kong. There the goods are unloaded at a quiet quayside and replaced in the ship's hold by a stolen Mercedes or BMW. You know that a new wealth class has been developing in China ever since our Chairman has flirted with the concept of a free-market economy as a cure for our financial problems? Anyone among the new moneyed class wanting a smart modern car has to face a 150 per cent import tariff, so you can see how the smugglers are able to make a profit both ways!'

'Do they ever get caught?' I asked.

'I'm afraid so. The British communications technology is so good that they can pick up conversations by radio, then lie in wait at the drop-off point. Recently by intercepting radio traffic, the British and Hong Kong authorities caught one of our smugglers with a pure heroin consignment worth over US $5 million. They also got the brand new

BMW, which had been stolen and was ready to load onto the ship for the return trip!'

'What about your activities here in England?' I enquired. 'Frankly, there are many world-class Mafia-type gangs operating here. More and more are getting footholds in London. The Triads' main interests are in drug trafficking, prostitution, illegal immigration from China and Hong Kong, illegal gambling, extortion and fraud. I think you'll agree it's a pretty extensive list!'

'How does the immigration scam work? There is always news about illegals coming into Britain.'

'Firstly, there are enormous profits to be made out of the immigrants. I have people all over the mainland, but mainly in the south, who act as agents. Immigrants pay over US $10,000. This will get them a flight from China to Australia then a long tortuous journey to France. For more money they get false documents enabling the immigrants to fly directly to Paris. Once in Europe they can either stay in Paris being supported illegally with a place to stay in the numerous Chinese restaurants, or they move on to other parts of Europe such as to London in container lorries with little air to breathe in. Each leg of the journey costs more money and goodness knows how many illegals are living in England. In eighteen months in France alone, couriers from the Chinese criminal network there paid US $500,000 each day to the gang at the centre. That money was then laundered and the funds transferred to bank accounts in Hong Kong and the mainland. Sometimes people in containers die of air starvation and never make it alive, but those are the risks they have to take.'

'It's a huge organisation,' I replied. Just at that moment the Italian waiter removed the empty plates of the pasta course.

'Do you want anything else to eat, Wong?'

'No, that's fine, thank you. Just coffee, please.' replied Wong.

I ordered coffees and checked that no one was in earshot of our table as I leant across to talk to Wong rather more conspiratorially. Wong's eyes had reverted to their flat and glazed-over look. As he studied me, I wondered what was in his poker-player's mind. He knew I was leading up to something; he had known me long enough, going back to old Shanghai days, to realise something was up. When I first joined the Secret Service, Wong was one of the first contacts the Service handed over to me to run. At first, being so new and inexperienced, I was uncertain how to deal with such a knowledgeable operator. He wasn't easy to handle, often bullying me, failing to make a rendezvous, contacting me only when it suited him and for his own gain. It took a long time to develop a mutual trust, but he eventually became useful to the Service and to me. He was an unorthodox character, brilliant but unpredictable.

He had spilt a forkful of pasta onto the front of his dark grey suit and began rubbing it off with his linen napkin when I interrupted his concentration.

'We've known each other now for many years, and I hope we've developed a degree of trust between us. It's vital that what I say to you goes no further. I need to know if you can help me, not personally, it's strictly Secret Service and Party business and it will be a great service to the People's Republic of China.'

'This sounds interesting!' Wong perked up.

'One of our agents, a half-Chinese lecturer at London University, has been caught smuggling top-secret weapons technology information out of Holy Loch the Royal Navy's nuclear submarine base in Scotland. I can tell this to you quite freely because it's public knowledge, no doubt you already know about it. To get to the point, this man has been arrested. He doesn't have diplomatic immunity, and he is now in custody in a prison awaiting trial at the Old Bailey in a couple of months' time.'

'I'm with you so far,' replied Wong, inclining his left ear

towards me. He was going deaf on the other side.

'We're concerned that our man will almost certainly be found guilty. It will be a high-profile trial, and the Western press will give it a lot of attention, especially as it looks bad for the British government – lax security and so forth. If he is found guilty, we anticipate he will be sentenced to jail for twelve years or more. During those years he will be pursued by determined newspaper reporters offering him a fortune to spill the beans, to reveal the names of other agents and much, much more. Basically, we need to get him out of custody before the sentencing. Do you have any ideas?' I asked and paused. 'I don't want any violence. We can get false documents, passports and private access to Vincent in the prison. We can help with impersonation too, if you choose that route.'

'This is a very ambitious request! I understand what you want, but I'll need to visit your man soon. I'll do a detailed reconnaissance to see exactly how these guards operate. What do you want to us to do with your man when we've got him out?' asked Wong.

'Deliver him to meet me at an old warehouse building. I'll give you more details nearer the time. We'll pay any fee you ask; it's vitally important to us to get him out.'

'When I'm more certain I can do the job for you, I suggest we meet again. We've got some time yet, haven't we?'

'Yes, I expect we've got two to three months,' I replied.

25

'If the ox won't drink, don't bend its neck.'

While Vincent's case waited to be heard at the Old Bailey an associate of Wong's visited him at the prison, a frail young man with an active mind. He asked Vincent many questions, and stared at him with melancholy eyes for long stretches without saying a word. Vincent found it disconcerting. The man particularly asked about the administration of the prison, and seemed to focus on security and the temperament of the guards. Vincent was tired and feeling depressed at having surrendered to the authorities. In his present situation he wasn't called on to make decisions, they were made for him and his mind had sunk into numbness.

'Who are you?' Vincent asked.

'You don't need to know my name. I'm a friend, who has been asked to help you. Several years ago I was sent to England on a grant by the Chinese Communist Party to study chemistry at London University, and now I am working with some associates in Chinatown practising herbal medicine. I know I should go back home to repay the Party for their investment in me, but we've come to an agreement that I'll be of more use here in London.'

'I see,' said Vincent, grateful for the visit.

'What's the food like?' the visitor asked, feigning concern but more eager to get on with the main reason for the visit.

'It's OK. Just enough to keep one alive!' Vincent replied sarcastically.

'How do you think the trial will go?'

'Lawyers acting for my defence visit me at all hours with files and papers. They ask me questions, and then go over the same ground again and again, looking desperately for loopholes and a way to frame a decent case; a plausible one that might convince a jury. They try hard, but I'm afraid they may not produce a strong enough one. It's very frustrating here, with my liberty being so severely restricted. It's cold and very weird at night, but boredom is my greatest enemy.'

'What about your loyalty to the Party? How do you feel about that now?'

'During the dull periods I've gone through everything repeatedly in my mind. I admit it's almost an obsession with me. I try to look at everything that has happened from every angle. Sometimes I resent having been sucked in to collaborate in the way I have. One minute it was exciting, the next I'm locked up in here with a huge loss of face. I convince myself it was all for a good cause, but I really wonder if my personal sacrifice is worth it. Would you be more certain if you were in my shoes?' Vincent asked.

'It's hard to say. The Party knows it has a debt to you, and is doing all it can to help you. Tell me, Vincent, is there any chance these guards can be bribed?'

'Certainly! I've been in here long enough to know that every sort of scam goes on. Some jailers are involved in conspiracies, amenable to bribes, and they've been known to act as couriers in two-way drug deals. I've been told that some guards have even been bribed to allow inmates to have sexual intercourse with their visitors. Nothing inside here is what it appears to be on the outside. The high walls and stout security gates at the entrance to these prisons are just symbols of the restricted territory we inmates are forced to occupy. They don't stop unauthorised activity from going on inside, believe me!'

'Would you say you could get virtually anything if the bribe was big enough?' asked the visitor.

'Yes, I would say so,' replied Vincent.

'One more question, if I may? It's annoying talking to you through this plate glass security partition.' The anonymous visitor was clicking the joints of his fingers menacingly, as if preparing himself for a fight. 'Are there any circumstances under which we could talk privately together in a room, possibly without a guard being present or perhaps with a guard agreeing to wait outside the room?'

'I think so. The other day a fellow inmate arranged a favour through the head warder – a "screw", they call them. Perhaps he had to refer to the Governor, I don't know, but he got a private room to himself where the guard stayed outside the door. It was a very private and emotional matter. His mother had recently died and he needed comforting by his family, which they could hardly do satisfactorily with a sheet of glass between them!' replied Vincent.

'I see. Surely the point is that you're being held in custody pending the outcome of your trial. You are not guilty yet until found so by the jury. Perhaps the authorities may take a more lenient view of you having more private visits while you are still on remand?'

'Who knows.'

'I must go now. Thanks for answering the questions. I hope to see you again soon. Good luck with the trial.'

Vincent stood up behind the glass panel out of respect for his visitor, and waved with his right hand until he was gone from view. Then he returned to the cell he shared with another prisoner, Bill Field, convicted for his part in an armed robbery on a building society branch in Stoke Newington. Bill was a cheerful companion and popular among his fellow inmates, who welcomed his cheeky, cockney ways and scant respect for authority. He had brought his East London shrewdness to every situation in the prison, and his advice on various scams was always sought. At first, Vincent was confused by Bill's way of speaking; using unfamiliar sentences liberally spiced with rhyming cockney slang. He used the word 'sussing' something out or giving something or someone the 'elbow'.

He was a gang boss, whose fertile mind never stopped thinking up newer and more amazing scams. Being such a creative man, Bill felt the restriction of being hemmed in by the confines of the small cell, with the two bunk beds, slop out buckets, a table and two chairs between the two of them.

Vincent had fallen into the prison culture reluctantly but calmly. His fellow prisoners had spared him the internal judgement of a kangaroo court directed mainly at paedophiles. He had feared his alleged offence of stealing defence secrets might have provoked both mental and physical abuse from xenophobic inmates. But the main targets for punishment were those whose crimes were deeply resented by their peers and judged to be unacceptable. He had seen proof of this when inmates appeared with cuts and bruises and were generally ostracised. A lonely, unpopular prisoner could quickly become suicidal in the dog-eat-dog environment of one of Her Majesty's prisons.

During several weeks the defence lawyers went over statements and recorded more interviews with Vincent. The defence's case was still thin, and their only hope of winning was to see if the prosecution could come up with the necessary evidence to prove Vincent's guilt beyond all reasonable doubt. The burden was at the door of the prosecution to prove him guilty, and until they did so to the satisfaction of the jury, Vincent was innocent. The defence intended to undermine the prosecution's case by doubting the veracity of witnesses' statements, by cross-examining them under oath and by challenging the conclusions of prosecuting counsel. Vincent's team needed to rely on clever courtroom tricks, but more than that good luck was needed.

I felt guilty having left Vincent in the lurch. He was alone when once he had been part of our team, and now his predicament weighed on my mind. I sent one of my officials from the Secret Service at the Embassy in London to attend the court and report back to me. He posed as a member of the public, and I told him to get to the court early each day to get near the front of the queue. He called me from a telephone box during the breaks to keep me up to date with the trial.

The Central Criminal Court is in a street called Old Bailey in the City of London. Opposite the imposing court buildings on the other side of the street there is an assortment of Irish bars, restaurants, sandwich bars, a travel agency and offices housing financial institutions. Pubs and bars here cater for a variety of tastes. Small groups huddle together around their legal advisers listening to points of law or tactical moves. There are the vindicated, and other groups may be relatives of a defendant whose case had been lost, commiserating with each other. The scene hardly changes from day to day.

Among those were the loved ones, families and friends, all trying desperately to prepare themselves for the pending result. An air of grim courage and dignity attached to them as they crowded close together, seeking physical and emotional comfort, stunned, a miserable acceptance of the inevitable, their worlds dramatically torn apart. Lives shattered by disloyalty, lies and crime. Shattered dreams, liaisons, love affairs, a climate in which the meaning of love itself was tested to the limit. For the convict it was a bleak moment, emotions raw, time suspended, unseen friends and supporters with their own private reasons to mourn.

Securicor vans transported the defendants each morning, escorted by police squad cars, one in front, one behind. The flow of traffic was held up for only a few seconds as the convoy passed and disappeared into the grim basement world of the Old Bailey. Escorted from the vans to temporary cells by prison officers, defendants awaited the summons into the courtroom. Inside, the formidable and tense atmosphere dominated the routine. Defendants sat in their allocated area listening to the long drawn-out evidence and cross-examination of both the prosecution and the defence counsel. Each side pitted their wits against the other, pulled tricks, made theatrical gestures, aiming to sway the jury to their way of thinking. A court is a forbidding place, awesome in its effect on defendants and witnesses alike, a stage on which advocates play out serious adversarial drama.

26

*'Of a dead leopard we keep the skin. . . of a
man his reputation.'*

The court was full. So full it was hard to see how so many
members of the court, the jury, the press and public could
be squeezed into the single courtroom. Despite its size it
still wasn't large enough to cope with the turnout.
Doorkeepers and ushers of either sex dressed in uniform
black academic gowns had an authoritative presence about
them. They manoeuvred quietly and purposefully, waiting
patiently for instructions; unflappable servants, obedient
and reliable. The presiding judge entered eventually by a
side door shortly after an usher had brought the court to
silence and ordered everyone to stand.

The trial had begun. Vincent sat in court studying the
faces of the jurors, as they were sworn-in. He had no
objection to any of them. There were rather more women
jurors than men, and three jurors of either sex were of
mixed race, more Afro-Caribbean and Indian subcontinent
than Chinese or Eurasian. He would have preferred more of
the latter.

The presiding judge addressed the court.

'I warn the court that this trial could go on for several
weeks. You should all be prepared for that, particularly
you, ladies and gentlemen, members of the jury. It will be a
challenge to keep alert over the whole period; because of
that I intend that the court will sit for short periods
followed by a break before a further session. I warn
members of the press that severe action will be taken on
anyone who writes an article that in any way attempts to
influence the course of the trial and prejudices either the
defence or prosecution cases. The jury will decide on the
verdict, and I will direct the proceedings of this court. As

far as court discipline is concerned, I will not tolerate misbehaviour or unwarranted outbursts. Should I feel it necessary, I will not hesitate to instruct miscreants to be detained in custody. For those members of the public who may not be aware of court practice, photography is forbidden. I have agreed with the press to allow the services of a court artist whose sketches will be displayed outside the court each day. That is all I have to say for the moment. Are you opening the case for the prosecution, Mr Fortescue?'

'Yes, M'lud.'

Charles Fortescue, QC was a distinguished gentleman in his mid-fifties. The silk's wig clamped to his head highlighted a florid face perched solidly on a thick bull-like neck. His gimlet eyes shone like a terrier's chasing a fox and he viewed the world contemptuously over the top of half-frame reading spectacles. He had a fearsome reputation for winning cases, earned a fortune and was ruthless in his ability to shape a case. Many a witness had been cowered under his cross-examination. He was charismatic, ferocious to his juniors who, despite being the butt of his bullying ways, hoped one day to be like him. As head of chambers he was master of all he surveyed, arrogant and persuasive. His wife, the glamorous Hanna, had left him a few years back for a younger man. Charles had taken the separation badly but tried desperately not to show it, finding solace in his liking for good food and fine wines. But the excesses of good living, evident by his increased weight, hadn't dimmed his agile mind. His tone was rough and aggravating.

'Members of the jury, I will outline the case before you. To begin with I will familiarise you with the political situation, geography and publicly stated strategic aims of Britain, of the United States and of China. Members of the jury, I think you will find this helpful background information. Then I propose to outline how the accused was apprehended and held on suspicion of spying. You will be shown what part the accused played in the serious charge of acquiring Western nuclear weapons secrets and submarine tracking technology. I will call witnesses to support our case, who will be available to be cross-examined by my learned friend Mr Jeremy Mossop, QC for the defence.'

Jeremy Mossop was in total contrast to Charles Fortescue. Where the latter was short, round and overweight, Jeremy Mossop was tall and thin, a sensitive man, happily married as far as anyone knew. He was known for his left-wing sympathies and had a successful record defending ethnic and minority cases. He was the younger man, cerebral, incisive and ambitious. Where Charles Fortescue was flamboyant in his use of language, Jeremy Mossop was economical, short on style; cold, persistent, soft voiced, able to penetrate the uncertain evidence of evasive witnesses.

Day after day, the witnesses appeared and statements by police interrogators were examined and challenged. Jeremy Mossop made little effort to hide his distrust of the police, suspecting their evidence, looking out for flaws. Each time either counsel thought he had scored a favourable point, they glanced towards the jury showily; the audience they sought to impress. On several occasions, Vincent wanted desperately to shout out that the witness was lying but he had been told to restrain himself and any communication he made to the court should be made through his lawyer. But most of the time Vincent's head was lowered through inertia.

The atmosphere was formal; the public galleries were quiet, awaiting the drama to begin. Sometimes the waiting was worth it; during long, dull days time dragged. Members of the press filled the gallery; sometimes they laughed at the judge's dry humour as he cast out rare witticisms quite deliberately, expecting the nuances to be picked by an audience tuned to his idiosyncrasies. This particular judge delighted in amusing his court, but within limits; it took the monotony out of the proceedings.

The hot humid weather hadn't stopped bewigged members of the court from wearing their full uniform. Despite the conditions, no concessions to climate were made. The only visible sign of discomfort was the occasional pushing back of the wig off the forehead, which gave the wearer a faintly ludicrous appearance.

Barristers and juniors filled their sectors of the court room, sitting in a tight group, much like a crew of a rowing boat, close and expected to pull in the same direction, passing notes to each other, alert to the tide running in the court. Every contradiction was noted as they eagerly supported their senior counsel. One junior staggered into court each day, arms laden with the mountainous piles of assorted files and papers. One day he was so overloaded that his vision was severely impaired; the young man tripped, scattering papers everywhere causing an undignified commotion while the rest of his team scrambled on the floor in a frantic attempt to scrape together the strewn documents. Once sorted, the good order of the court was restored.

Witnesses came and went; mostly they were for the prosecution. Police officers in uniform or civilian clothes stood erect in the witness box, took the appropriate oaths, and waited to be led through their evidence by a series of questions from counsel. The ponderous terminology delivered in police-speak language sounded solid, but a skilful defence counsel, able to marshal words, ambushed and tested the boundaries of credibility ahead of the final assault. Did you really do this? But you said that! Are you not mistaken in your opinion? Why this? Why that? Dazzled by the silver-tongued erudition, witnesses became confused however hard they struggled in the face of brilliant advocacy. Years spent in examining witnesses had given counsel an instinct for truth, able to tell from the eyes and voice if something was being held back.

Jerry Flood read his evidence from his police notebook, audibly and measured before being questioned rather aggressively by the defence counsel with suggestions of bullying during arrest and interrogation. It was enough to put ideas into the minds of the jurors. Jerry had expected that. Nevertheless it irked him; he wished that one day his experience in the force would be respected. 'Fucking bastards,' he thought to himself, his knuckles whitening as he gripped the sides of the witness box. Then he consoled himself by thinking of the apple crumble his wife would be making for him – but without custard.

Doubts might start to form in the minds of the jury. Inconsistencies by witnesses under intense cross-examination were exposed. This was the very essence of the drama that members of the public and press had been looking for. If an adversarial punch had been landed, titters would run through the court, not quite disruptions. But if ever disorder threatened, the judge intervened with 'Silence in court!' and hush would descend once more, onlookers settling back and wondering optimistically when the next bit of entertainment might come.

The slightest distraction in court was noticed. An angry wasp had furiously buzzed around the clerk's papers, a man normally unflappable but who was trying hard to ignore the tiny creature. He flicked at it casually, but it escaped. The audience had spotted everything; all eyes focused on his very personal battle. The whole court followed the scene with increased intensity. Then it landed right in front of him. One sharp, well-aimed swipe with a ruler cut the wasp in two, the parts swept to the floor unceremoniously by the elbow of his gowned sleeve. A restrained cheer went up from the area of the press, which rippled through the court. The judge nodded, ack-nowledged the applause and smiled, his normally tight lips curled upwards at the sides. It had taken his mind back to when he made his first fifty runs in a cricket match as a schoolboy.

Meanwhile, the jury, colourful in their variety of dress, sat day in, day out, patiently taking notes, attentive to the influences of counsel, assimilating different versions of evidence, forming opinions, exasperated by legal prevarication and tactical delays. Some days the heat was too much, and the temperature had an effect inside the court. One member of the jury was spotted falling steadily into a deep sleep. His eyes closed slowly, the head fell forward then sprang up several times, trying to fight off the inevitable, but the battle became lost; at first mild, then heavy snoring finally overcame him.

'Would that member of the jury who has lost concentration please rejoin us?' asked the judge, tactfully halting proceedings.

The colleague sitting next to the offending juryman went red and dug him in the ribs. 'Wake up for god sake!' he whispered.

'What?' he jumped, 'Where am I? Oh, Jesus!'

'Thank you,' said the judge. 'Proceed, Mr Fortescue.'

'Thank you, M'lud, I am obliged,' replied Fortescue, ingratiatingly.

Three weeks passed in this way, interspersed with long lunch breaks during which Vincent ate basic prison rations in his cell, always under escort. The judge and his cronies enjoyed a three-course luncheon in the Old Bailey court building served by waiters and accompanied by fine wines. Counsel grabbed a bite at a nearby restaurant. The trial moved inexorably into the fourth and hoped for final week.

零　零　零

Back in his prison cell, there was too much on Vincent's mind for early sleep. He had no room for other thoughts than the verdict, but he would accept the decision calmly. He was short of rest, having woken before dawn, and well before a mysterious older Chinese man visited him.

Although they met either side of the glass panel, the visitor slipped through the aperture a letter, which he told Vincent to read asking him to be quick.

'Have you any questions?' the anonymous visitor whispered, pushing the letter back into his inside pocket.

'What about the guards?'

'Don't worry, we'll take care of that.'

27

'One dog barks at a shadow. . . a hundred
bark at his sound.'

'That is the conclusion of my submission for the defence M'lud,' said Jeremy Mossop having summed up, but in his heart he knew it had little chance of being accepted by the jury.

He had tried hard to undermine the evidence of witnesses in his cross-examination, but to little effect. Twice the foreman of the jury had passed a note to the judge, asking that the case proceed more quickly. The jury didn't think there was any merit in Mossop going on, trying to break down a witness unnecessarily, just for the hell of it. He had been getting nowhere, wasting time, and the jury had seen through his tactics.

The judge had kept the trial moving over the three weeks, admonishing in turn both defence and prosecution counsel. He had kept tight discipline in his court and reprimanded without the slightest hesitation if he thought counsel had overstepped the mark.

'For weeks you have been giving your full attention to the facts of this case. Members of the jury, I thank you for your attention. Now you are faced with deciding on the verdict. Take your time to weigh the facts. The prosecution's case hinges largely on the finding of the accused's personal details in an hotel room near Holy Loch and the subsequent surveillance and detention of the accused for questioning. The accused has admitted his part in a spying operation possibly, you may think, once the radio transmitter was discovered. The defence case is that the accused was an unwilling participant in the operation, forced into playing a minor part. Defence counsel may also have put the suggestion into your minds that the defendant was bullied into making a confession by his interrogators. Furthermore, it is alleged that he played only a minor part and that the major participant is out of the country. Members of the jury, you need to decide if there has been sufficient proof to find the accused guilty. If you are not satisfied that there is sufficient proof, then you must acquit. On the second count, you must decide if the defendant's part in the operation was undertaken as a willing participant, which makes the question of the degree of his involvement insignificant. Again, you must be certain that the prosecution case is proven to your satisfaction beyond doubt. Members of the jury, please retire now for your deliberations.'

'The court will rise,' ordered the clerk.

The judge bowed and retired. The jury followed into a windowless, air-conditioned room especially set aside for their deliberations and where an usher attended to their needs, offering liquid refreshment and sandwiches. The foreman, an unemployed meat porter from Smithfield market, called the disparate group to order. Before him sat people of such a variety of experience and viewpoints that he knew it wouldn't be easy getting a consensus.

'Ladies and gents, I've never done this sort of thing. Have any of you been on jury service before?' asked the foreman nervously. At fifty-five his ruddy, chubby face glowed as the flaps of excess skin around his jowls wobbled whenever he spoke.

'No,' they replied self-consciously, mumbling, needing a lead.

'Fine. Shall we just start off then by showing hands: first, those who think he's guilty?'

Six hands went up.

'OK. I could of course cast my vote, but we aren't unanimous by any means. Can we hear please from those who don't think him guilty, and why they think that?'

Not one member of the jury had failed to follow virtually every aspect of the case. Pages of handwritten notes were referred to, quotes noted from evidence and cross-examinations. Jurors fought their corners fiercely. They had almost become advocates themselves, fluent and convincing in arguing their viewpoint. The group had divided into those for guilty and those for acquittal. It soon became a trial within a trial, invariably going over old ground, the women members tending to be more sympathetic to the not-guilty verdict. Backwards and forwards went the arguments. More sandwiches. More bottled water. Overnight, the members adjourned to a specially designated hotel at a secret address, returning the next morning with clearer heads ready for a fresh start.

'Good-morning everyone! Now can we have please a show of hands this time to see if we're any nearer to a unanimous verdict. Raise your hand, please, for those who think he is not guilty.' The foreman said, trying again to get a consensus.

Members were more hesitant this time before raising hands, looking around self-consciously for someone else to make the first move. Two hands went up.

'We're getting closer to a verdict. Now can I take the second charge relating to the degree of the defendant's involvement, and ask for a show of hands? Please show those who think he was fully implicated, regardless of others involved in the mission.'

Ten hands went up. There were still two undecided members, one woman and one man, both Afro-Caribbean.

'The judge has directed that he'll accept a majority decision rather than a unanimous decision. Ladies and gentlemen, I think we have at last arrived at a guilty verdict on both charges.'

'This is not right at all!' exploded one of the Afro-Caribbeans, 'I don't think he is definitely guilty.'

'I'm sorry, you're entitled to your opinion but the

majority vote stands.'

'I'll raise a complaint.'

'You're entitled to do that too, but not here. I suggest you raise it with the court administrators and clerks after the case.'

'I certainly will!' he replied, still belligerent.

The others were relieved they had finished and could go back to their normal lives. They had been together for a long time, and no good would come from arguing the case any further.

As the trial came to its conclusion, the press stepped up their interest, filling the public galleries to capacity with reporters. Cameramen were directed to wait outside from the early hours for that crucial shot of key players in the drama. Elsewhere in the street, crowds of special-interest groups generated a carnival-type atmosphere, undeterred by the level of security the police normally reserved for IRA terrorist trials.

On the final morning the accused man appeared before the judge. His head bowed, he looked vulnerable and thin, a young Chinese man in an ill-fitting lightweight grey suit, dispirited, powerless to change the course of events in which he found himself.

'The court will rise!'

'Has the foreman of the jury reached a verdict?' asked the judge formally. He had come to the court especially for the result and sentencing. Then he hoped to go home and have a round of golf, thinking the fresh air would do him good before he presided over a fresh murder trial involving suspected IRA terrorists.

'Yes, M'lud,' said the foreman nervously. It had occurred to him that the Chinese might seek him out and take revenge in a most unpleasant way, but he tried to dismiss that thought. As he rose to his feet he spotted a gathering of Chinese huddled together in the public gallery, eagerly awaiting his answer, sitting well forward in their seats.

'Can you speak up please, so that the court can hear?' asked the judge.

'Sorry, Sir – I mean M'lud.' The foreman for all his size and weight was unsteady.

'How do you find on the first charge, guilty or not guilty?'

'Guilty, M'lud.' The foreman had taken a deep breath before making his announcement, then he felt his face flush and the pit of his stomach ached.

'And on the second charge, guilty or not guilty?'

'Guilty, M'lud.'

The court was hushed. As the guilty verdict was announced, the Chinese group muttered amongst themselves, much like birds on a telephone wire. But they were too noisy for the judge's liking.

'Quiet, please, in the gallery. I will adjourn the court for one hour before resuming for sentencing.'

'The court will rise,' announced the clerk for the umpteenth time.

The defence team spoke briefly to their client to console him, more as a matter of formality and to demonstrate a duty of care. He was surprisingly unemotional and it was impossible to read his thoughts.

As the court rose to resume the sentencing, the judge entered, solemn and majestic.

'The accused will stand.'

Vincent did so obediently, looking ahead of him sightlessly and flanked by two uniformed policemen.

'You have been found guilty of the two charges. They are both serious offences, particularly as they involve clandestine operations against the defence of this country. We have to protect ourselves against the acts of which you have been a part. It is in your favour that you have no previous convictions and that you were a secondary player in the theft. Having weighed all these factors, I now

271

sentence you to ten years' imprisonment on each charge, making a total of twenty years.'

'The court will rise!'

The court quickly dispersed, counsel's papers were gathered up. Informal chats by groups in hushed tones went on at the same time as the steady exiting from the public gallery, similar to the end of a theatre performance. The jury returned to their normal world, no hint of being recent participants in a major trial. To some the return was welcomed; to others the trial had brought an importance to their lives that they might miss now that it was all over.

The convicted man was led down to the basement and bundled into a Securicor van. As it passed under the heavy electronically operated security doors, which had been raised especially for the van, a mob of photographers surged forward with their cameras raised high, aiming in the direction of the darkened windows. The armoured van, under escort, sped off back to a different high-security prison, the prisoner hidden from view behind the bulletproof tinted glass.

The *Evening Standard* printed an eye-catching headline, just in time for sales to the waves of commuters returning home at the end of the day.

CHINA SPY FOUND GUILTY

28

'For a swift arrow, pull hard on the string.'

The night before the verdict he had sat in his cell wondering if it was the last time he would hear those weird tapping noises through the night. His last strong sensation had been of cold. Full of foreboding, he felt lonely, and uncertain of his fate.

He tried to read a book – a thriller – but his eyes couldn't focus on the pages sufficiently to absorb anything much. He felt more like a man going for an operation, drugged before the thrust of the anaesthetist's needle, numb and fuzzy-headed. He wondered if the prison warders had put something in his tea.

He thought about the note he had received. Could it have been serious? Why did someone want to take his place? Was that really likely? Was it possible to find someone who was sufficiently identical to him? Would a near perfect look-alike exist outside China? If he didn't, would the replacement have needed some minor facial cosmetic surgery to match his features?

The night was long and he dozed off from time to time. The long trial with endless days in the courtroom had weakened him physically, yet he wasn't tired from physical exercise, more from the lack of it. Soon the ordeal would be over; soon he would fall into the deep sleep he longed for.

At dawn, the cell door opened and a warder escorted him out along the corridor, the clanking echo of his studded shoes reverberating through the block.

'Come this way, sunshine!' A screw barked.

Vincent followed a little behind the others, his bladder full, the overnight contents ready to be discharged. Hunger gripped him too. It was an hour before breakfast and the

273

usual dispensing of a mug of lukewarm tea. He was unwashed, smelly. Feeble and dazed he was led into the visitors' room, normally made available to relatives for private discussions with a guard outside.

'Go in there, sunshine, and don't take too long. I'll be outside here and I'll be back for you in a few minutes.'

Three Chinese men in raincoats stood before him, one coat worn much longer, almost down to his ankles. Vincent noticed the man was the same height as himself.

'You got the note, Vincent? We've been lucky to get this meeting with you to wish you well before the verdict and sentencing. The prison authorities gave us special permission to see you because you have no other relatives alive in this country.'

The man kept talking, and deliberately kept up the chat in Mandarin. In the flick of an eye, without a pause in the conversation and no further instruction, the man in the long raincoat took it off and passed it to Vincent. He put it on and exchanged shoes with the stranger, who now stood on the very spot Vincent had just moved away from. But he was too clean as he was. He realised the contrast with Vincent's unkempt condition, which he quickly remedied by tussling his hair and applying spittle to his face to make him feel dirty.

'Must go now!' said the leading man, satisfied the switch-over had been accomplished. He opened the door to the room much earlier than the guard had expected.

'Thank you. We have had brief words, but we can't stay any longer,' the lead man said formally.

The guard must have thought this strange; relatives in this situation usually took longer. Perhaps, thought the guard, the Chinese were less sentimental on these occasions.

'Just wait a moment, please. I'll get you an escort out of the building.' The guard signalled to his colleague, who was pacing up and down the passage to keep the circulation going in his legs. As an ex-infantry soldier, he missed the more strenuous demands on his feet. Soon he would take a break with a cup of tea in the canteen.

'Alf, these visitors here are ready to leave now. Can you escort them out?'

'Yea. Come with me, please gents. Everything all right? It won't be too bad for your chap,' he said, attempting words of comfort.

'Thank you,' replied one of the group.

Vincent followed, not letting his eye meet the guard's, hoping the comb he had passed through his hair and the wipe of his face with a saliva-dampened handkerchief would avoid close scrutiny. His heart was pumping fast. He felt vulnerable, so close to being found out. He would be in even deeper water on a charge of impersonating a prisoner while attempting escape. Would the daring, high-risk plan come off? He must stay cool. Avoid eye contact at all costs. Keep walking. Look natural. His visitors chatted to him non-stop to make him look a normal part of the group. He was terribly aware he might stand out, but mostly it was in his imagination. Now he had a personal problem; his bladder was full to bursting. He was experiencing the intense swollen sensation, the pressure and the virtual inability to think of anything else apart from the challenge of walking without wetting himself.

'I want a piss, badly,' he said between clenched teeth.

'You wait, you idiot. Tie knot in it!' replied one of the others firmly.

Vincent used all his powers of concentration to get through the gates and out into freedom. The very first thing he did was to unzip his trousers and slash along the side of a rubbish bin. The relief was fierce, intense; the strong flow seemed never to stop.

'Come on! Get it over with. Now we go to my car.' It was the voice of the older man he had seen before, the one who passed him the message under the glass panel.

零 零 零

On the south bank of the Thames in an old disused wharf and warehouse complex in Docklands, I waited. The cold east wind was blowing down the river and despite my heavy coat I felt chilled to the bone. The sky over the city was dark and a gentle mist swirled up from the river. Persistent dampness pervaded everything; streets were shiny, warehouse doors dripped and wooden planks slippery with mildew. All around me were signs of decay; old doors swinging in the wind, dragging clanking and rusty chains behind them, no longer serving any purpose in the wilderness of eerie dereliction.

I knew I had a difficult task ahead of me, and I wasn't looking forward to it. It had occupied my mind almost obsessively for the previous two days and nights. Throughout the days there was occasional sunlight and a light wind. There was a strange feeling in the air. Something had gone out of the atmosphere: a feeling of a future without a point, the elements somehow forecasting anger.

A black Jaguar drove up and parked outside the warehouse complex. Out of it stepped Wong and Vincent, leaving the driver and another man inside. The older man had found his way to the disused office where I was waiting. I learnt later that Vincent had talked non-stop from the moment he was in the car, pouring out the trauma he felt.

'Well done, Wong,' I said, greeting him through chattering teeth.

'It all went off quite smoothly. Before I hand over Vincent here, you give me the 100,000 dollars in notes? You have the stuff with you?' asked Wong, screwing up his hard, shrewd eyes.

'No problem, here you are. You can count it out if you

like!' I replied sarcastically. I unzipped an envelope from inside my coat pocket. I was peeved that Wong didn't trust me, but then no one trusted anyone in our business.

Wong glanced at the wads secured by rubber bands, fingered them and appeared satisfied. He left Vincent alone with me, returned to his car to drive away from the scene along the dreary streets and back into the flow of London life. I looked at Vincent and noticed how he had become harder through the recent trials and bouts of loneliness.

'Vincent, come and see a special view up the river. There is something I want to show you,' I ordered benignly, despite the cold wind driving down the back of my neck. I didn't feel strong, despite having eaten well with noodles and chopped pork before coming out, hoping it would fortify me for the events ahead. I didn't hate Vincent. I had nothing personal against him, other than doing my duty to the Service and to the Party.

'Why do you want me to do that?' Vincent asked. He was hungry and alert. So far the operation had gone like clockwork. Vincent's bedraggled, unwashed and under-nourished frame looked pathetic, like a rag-doll. I felt compassion for him, but I had to put my feelings aside.

'I don't like water! I might fall in. I get dizzy.'

'I'll come with you,' I replied, fearing the whole operation was in jeopardy. Vincent wasn't reacting according to the plan and surprisingly I had known nothing of his fear of water and heights. Even our meticulous research hadn't uncovered this weakness.

'Why? Surely there's no need?' Vincent asked.

'I want you to see something,' I said.

'Why?' he questioned again.

'You'll see soon enough.'

As I came up alongside him, I placed my hand on his arm to lead him, but he flinched. He sensed that something wasn't quite right. Backing his judgement he hit me viciously, in panic and fear, trying to free himself from my grip. I wondered if he had learnt to fight his corner during his time in prison. He caught me in the solar plexus and nearly winded me, but I managed to struggle with him. I lashed out in desperation and caught the sleeve of his raincoat. I wanted to get him nearer to the edge of the jetty. I picked my way across rotten planks, hoping he wouldn't fall through, and out of control myself. I desperately hung on to him. At first with one hand, and just as my arm weakened he wrenched free, but I twisted and got a fresh hold on him with my right hand. This time it was firmer, and I managed to pull him towards me, still struggling, and put my foot behind his heels as I jerked him backwards. He tripped and stumbled. His head hit a jagged plank and a rusty nail grazed his right ear. He lay prostrate and dazed, his strength weakening. I was determined to finish the job.

I had only a few seconds. I thrust my left hand deep inside my coat pocket and pulled out the Browning automatic nine-millimetre pistol with its silencer in place. My other hand was free, but Vincent regained his senses and lunged towards me menacingly, shouting expletives. He was wild with rage and charged at me defiantly, despite seeing that I was armed. He seemed to disregard the advantage I had.

He lurched towards me like a boxer in the final round. I took aim and fired. The first shot hit him in the neck. I followed it up with another, this time straight to the head, blowing part of his forehead away. For a few seconds his startled, now gentle eyes met mine questioningly. It is a look that will haunt me forever. 'Why me, why betray me?' they asked. The thin body twitched as air left the lungs and blood oozed from the grotesquely shattered skull. Vincent was already dead. All that remained was the breaking of the physical cord. It was even more certain when my foot toppled him into the grey-brown swirling river below.

Except for the swinging doors with their trailing chains and the screeching of the circling gulls, there was little other noise. I walked off to my car alone and drove through the deserted streets of old Docklands. I threaded my way through the urban wasteland until I rejoined the busy world on the Jamaica Road, found a gap and edged into the slow traffic lane behind the tailback of buses, heavy-goods vehicles and cars making their slow, polluted progress round the southern boundary of the city. My hands were shaking and I felt sick, but I had to drive on, trying hard to be unaffected; but I was, more deeply than I had ever expected.

While I drove, I reminded myself of the long history of service that my family had given to the Chinese Secret Service, and how much we had all learnt from my father. I wondered how he would have felt in the same situation. I remembered a particular saying of my father's: 'Never tell anyone anything more than they really need to know.' I drove on, aware of people looking at me. Was it accusingly? Was it was because of my Oriental features, or did they see me as an executioner? What sort of life could I return to now? Could I carry on my work as a spy? I had no family other than my sister, no wife to go back to in China. For how long would I be able to suppress my feeling of guilt and remorse in favour of the higher justification of acting for the benefit of the People's Republic? As a trained spy, my mind tried hard not to wrestle with these sensitivities, but as a human being it wasn't easy.

While I negotiated the car back into the stream of life, the executed body of Vincent floated up river, swept this way and that by the tide. Soon it would become better concealed in the darkness of night as heavy clouds spilt sheets of rain on the already swollen tide. He would be washed up soon enough, but not before the body became decomposed: fish would feed off its flesh and greedily strip the once warm bones.

Vincent's body carried no messages and his extinction, for a time unknown to the world, had been recognised by only a select few as being the supreme sacrifice for the People's Republic of China. Thanks to Vincent, the Party's ruthless appetite for stealing secrets had been sated. Finally satisfied, the authorities intended to wash their hands of his existence forever. Both East and West denied knowledge of the identity of the body when it was eventually washed ashore. Was there a conspiracy to hush it up? Could the British have agreed with the Chinese to a policy of silence?

John Poon had disappeared for good, having successfully changed his identity. Algie and Fleur pursued their married life in England. Algie's career took him to the top of the company where he headed the international sales division. Fleur reluctantly – and partly to take attention away from her espionage involvement – produced a baby son for Algie, who was thrilled, remaining as ever blissfully unaware of the dramatic events his wife had taken part in.

The West continued to be soft and unguarded in matters of security while China, using the cunning tradecraft developed over many years, and ruthlessly hardened in the profession of espionage, seized every opportunity to acquire more secrets.

However hard I tried to forget the incident, I suffered terribly from guilt and depression. Vincent was a decent man and I had betrayed his trust. Some days I couldn't face the world, but I knew I had somehow to come to terms with the part I had played in the incident. I wrestled with my conscience. My doctors prescribed herbs, which I brewed up each day, but they didn't cure my troubled mind or blot out the deeds I had witnessed.

I returned to Beijing a broken man, no more use to the Service but they continued to support me. My sister, Chin-yee, finally separated from her husband, came back from Hong Kong to look after me in a modest farmhouse well out of the way in the deep countryside some miles distant of Shanghai. Occasionally I occupied myself by taking the local train into the big city to marvel at the new developments, but I wasn't a happy man. I always wondered if what I did was right. I felt a loathing for the world and for myself. I couldn't see any future, but my doctor believed I would in time recover.

My sister had quite unexpectedly been very patient with me, our estrangement mended. She told me she was making up for the difficult years we had together, and she hoped things would be better between us, less acrimonious.

But I never did avenge my father's honour in the way that I would have liked.

29

'No needle is sharp at both ends.'

I was a complex person and had been plagued by bad memories and fear. The more I tried to confront those two impostors, the worse it became. I was waiting for my own death, and I didn't care when it might be. I slowly got better and as part of my psychological recovery, under an alias, I was sent back to London to face the scene that had been the cause of my breakdown.

Impetuously, I telephoned Fleur, quite on the off-chance she might be at home and still at the old address. She was and we met up. She kindly agreed to accompany me down to the river to the old Docklands site, even more battered now than before, and difficult to reach the water's edge through lack of a solid footing. Curiously, at that very spot, no development had taken place. Yet all around, new flats, the tower blocks of Canary Wharf and office blocks had been built, and were now occupied right along the water's edge, the Dome in the distance. But right there was nothing. It was as if it had been deliberately left untouched, a shrine.

'Come here, Wu.' Fleur said to me, opening her arms wide then placing her hands gently on my neck, sensing the emotions going on inside me. 'You're a good man,' she smiled to reassure us both. 'You mustn't suffer this burden alone any longer. I've missed you and secretly I have admired you all these years. I left Algie last year; we'll be divorced soon. My life had no purpose in continuing to live a lie. Algie has custody of our son and has come to terms with our divorce. Our marriage can't be rescued; we come from such different backgrounds. His father was right after all.'

'Why are you telling me all this?' I asked.

'Seeing you again now, I realise that I love you and have done for years. Now I'm free and I can give you the love and affection you've denied yourself for too long.'

'Fleur, you astound me! You always have done!' I said, taken totally off guard. I held her head in my hands and looked deeply, passionately and sincerely into her eyes. 'It's all too much for me. I never even suspected you might have feelings for me.'

'There you are! Now I'm going to take care of you. Will you let me do that?' She spoke gently, hesitatingly.

'You might be disappointed in me,' I said. I didn't know if I was in love with her; I had never been in love before, so I didn't know. She certainly appealed to me, and I couldn't let her out of my sight.

'I won't be. I know everything will be fine. We'll take things slowly.'

She seemed to understand what was going on in my mind. I took her in my arms, feeling strong again, and pressed my body against hers; she yielded to me softly. I had never experienced such a show of surrender and I wasn't going to let her go.

'Aren't I rather old for this sort of thing?'

'Nonsense, Wu! We'll be lovers forever, I'll make sure of that!'

'One day we must tell our story,' I said.

'Yes, but there are other things on my mind at the moment!'

'Mine too! Let's start afresh.'

Epilogue

Fifty years on from Mao Tse-tung's victorious Communist Revolution in China, an exhibition of waxwork figures depicting the ten greatest Chinese political heroes of the century is exhibited in Tienanmen Square in central Beijing. The figures include Mao himself, complete with the special suit he had made for him by his tailor, and the original Red Flag. Among the others are Deng Xiaoping, who is credited with bringing free-market reforms to China; Chou En-lai, the Prime Minister of Communist China; Sun Yat-sen, founder of the National People's Party; and the current Communist Party leader, Jiang Zemin, who undertook a landmark state visit to Britain. A visit punctuated by open protest against the undemocratic Communist regime, but the demonstrations were glossed over by Western heads of state for fear of upsetting the leaders of such a vast economically important country with a population of over one billion. The West sees it as a huge potential for business, stretching for many years ahead and signposted by Jiang Zemin's declared pursuit and acknowledgement of the free-market economy.

But as the West rushes in to sign up juicy contracts, human-rights questions remain. Where are China's 50 million missing women? Apparently aborted or drowned at birth, the preference being for boys under China's one-child policy. How many people are unofficially executed each year? Apparently more than in the rest of the world put together.

Behind the majestic buildings and the inescapable fascination of its Eastern culture, much of the state-run businesses are foundering. Corruption and old-fashioned Communist bureaucracy routinely misappropriate foreign investment funds. Taiwan, the comparatively tiny breakaway republic of China – as poor as Communist China in 1949 when they separated from the Communist mainland – now has a per-capita income twenty times that of its giant neighbour. The Communist regime has attracted universal condemnation for its policy of reprisal in the massacring of tens of thousands of Tibetans loyal to the Dalai Lama in his refusal to agree that Tibet is part of China. Celibate monks and nuns have been compelled to commit gross sexual acts in front of terrified crowds of devout Buddhists. The brutal putting down by force of the Beijing student rebellion in Tienanmen Square in 1989 was watched on television by millions around the world as hundreds of dissident Chinese were slaughtered by the military and crushed by their tanks.

What of Shanghai, that thriving cosmopolitan city of the 1920s and 1930s? Shanghai is busy recreating itself, aiming within a decade to be one of the great cities of the world. It is an aim many believe to be achievable. Back in the 1920s, cranes dominated the skyline as the distinctive art-deco buildings which lined the Bund along Shanghai's famous waterfront were in the course of construction. Some of those European-financed structures remain, including the Peninsular & Oriental Building and the Hong Kong Shanghai Bank Building, which now houses the Pudong Development Bank. Today, it is estimated that 25 per cent of the world's cranes are at work in Shanghai, towering over armies of sinuous Chinese workmen employed on over 20,000 building sites, labouring flat out, night and day.

On the city's east bank, the Pudong district is reputed to be the biggest economic development in Asia, with over 140 skyscrapers rising out of the rubble and mud. The new skyline mixes uneasily with the hitherto familiar sight of crumbling old colonial mansions and ruined shacks with washing hanging out to dry, the more traditional face of China. Old men still wear their baggy Y-fronts as

286

they pore over their newspapers, and their women still prefer old-fashioned pyjama-style suits. But not far away a modern tower block stands glittering as its massive plate-glass windows reflect the sunshine, and the goods in its ground-floor shops bearing famous Western designer names like Versace and Ralph Lauren are on sale. Shanghai was as if it had been suspended in a time warp during those barren Maoist years. The Bund with its old buildings, many of which have been preserved. The Old Peace Hotel built in the 1920s is a little faded now. The old Shanghai Club, the exclusive watering hole of the British expatriate, still stands but is now home to a Kentucky Fried Chicken outlet!

The Chinese Army is the largest in the world and the Chinese Secret Service under its masters the Chinese Communist Party, remains skilful and ruthless, deploying the sort of techniques which all Secret Services deploy with varying degrees of success. If Western Secret Services are to be active in what remains of the Communist sphere of influence, then they must be equally imaginative, intrepid, brave and risk-taking.

There is fall-out from the April 2001 US spy plane and Chinese fighter aircraft collision which resulted in the loss of life of the Chinese pilot and the grounding, capture and stripping of the US plane on the island of Hainan. In the minds of both the US and China it has brought home the possibility of military confrontation. The People's Liberation Army is more determined than ever – despite the largest budget increase for a decade of eighteen per cent to modernise its weapons – to gain a greater slice of the financial cake and more political influence. The spy plane incident has brought a greater sense of nationalism to the Chinese people, prompting them to support the PLA in their quest to combat the US. Shanghai street television screens increasingly push out pro-PLA propaganda. But the problem for China is that it is not yet ready to confront the US; however, soon it will be, particularly if China continues to succeed in stealing Western weapons secrets. In the meantime economic curbs will be threatened and could be implemented, despite the prospect of forgoing the tempting access by the West to the 1.3 billion people market. The US could have blocked China's membership of the World Trade Organisation, but that would have been a toothless sanction. There is a growing feeling in China that they are not yet ready to open up for such a wide involvement. Elements at the top would prefer to get on with its own privatisation programme with the potential to copy the Eastern European experience of lining the pockets of greedy and corrupt Communist Party officials. Many quarters have been surprised too by Beijing's successful but controversial bid to host the 2008 Olympic Games.

The world stands as spectators watching the US, the superpower wanting to stay that way, slug it out with China: the emerging superpower willing to gain military strength by any means.